THE
MOCHE
WARRIOR

Berkley Prime Crime Books
by Lyn Hamilton

THE XIBALBA MURDERS
THE MALTESE GODDESS
THE MOCHE WARRIOR

THE
MOCHE
WARRIOR

An Archaeological Mystery

Lyn Hamilton

BERKLEY PRIME CRIME, NEW YORK

HAMILTON, ⌐

THE MOCHE WARRIOR

A Berkley Prime Crime Book
Published by the Berkley Publishing Group
A Member of Penguin Putnam Inc.,
375 Hudson Street, New York, New York 10014

The Penguin Putnam Inc. World Wide Web site address is
http://www.penguinputnam.com

First Edition: April 1999

Library of Congress Cataloging-in-Publication Data

Hamilton, Lyn.
    The Moche warrior / Lyn Hamilton.
      p. cm.
    ISBN 0-425-16809-3
    I. Title.
    PS3558.A44336M63   1999
    813' .54—dc21   98-41519
                                                 CIP

Printed in the United States of America

10 9 8 7 6 5 4 3 2 1

Acknowledgments

In the writing of this book, I am indebted to many people for their assistance with the research and their support, particularly Dr. Andrew Nelson, Chris Nelson, Neal Ferris, Manina Jones, Susie Wilson, Celia Fairclough, Jim Polk, and, as always, my sister, Cheryl.

Those readers interested in seeing and learning more about the real Moche warrior should seek out the book *Royal Tombs of Sipan* by Walter Alva and Christopher B. Donnan.

For the '97 Complejo de Moro

THE
MOCHE
WARRIOR

Prologue

The great warrior *is dead. For a time, the fighting will cease, the hand-to-hand combat still. For a time, the priests will halt the processions in the great court at the foot of the huaca, the incantations, the sacred flow of blood into the cup. So too will cease the parade of prisoners, ropes around their necks, hands tied behind them, their weapons wrenched from them, naked, humiliated in defeat. There will be other ceremonies, others will bow now before the Decapitator.*

The Great Warrior is dead. Already the priests prepare the royal tomb, digging deep down into the huaca. The beams, the vigas, to roof it are chosen; the adobe bricks to line it, each with the mark of its maker, have come in from the countryside. All is in readiness. Now it is time for us to prepare the great one for his journey.

The Great Warrior is dead. We are vulnerable without him, without the incantations and rituals that pro-

tect us. Without him, the waters from the mountains may alter their course, the crops shrivel to dust, the fish from the sea disappear. We must send him on his way with great ceremony. We must choose the new Warrior soon.

Lizard

1

"WOE TO THE inhabiters of the earth and of the sea, for the devil is come down unto you," the man thundered, arms uplifted, eyes fixed on some distant vision.

"Revelation 12:12," I muttered to myself. I should know: I'd heard it many times in the three days since the neighborhood's resident lunatic had staked out a small square of pavement right in front of my store, Greenhalgh and McClintoch by name, to proclaim the end of the world. When he wasn't quoting the scriptures, he recited Shelley's poem *Ozymandias* over and over, attacking with gusto the part where Ozymandias tells the mighty to look on his works and despair. I wasn't sure which was worse, Shelley or Revelation.

"Revelation 12:12," he boomed, and at least I had the satisfaction of knowing that my education in the apocalyptic texts was proceeding apace.

"First, a terrible fire," he said, his voice dropping to a conversational tone as he tried to draw a small group of tourists into his circle. The besieged four-some edged their way cautiously past him. One could hardly blame them. He was dirty and unkempt, with the eyes of a true fanatic. ''And I saw as it were a sea of glass mingled with fire,'' he went on.

Revelation again, I thought.

''Revelation 15: verse 2,'' he intoned. ''Then men will die. The wages of sin is death,'' he added.

''Romans 6:23,'' I said. I couldn't stop myself. The man was getting to me, however much I blamed society for its inability to deal compassionately with the mentally ill. He was, after all, driving away my customers. Tourist season, and people were avoiding that section of the street like the plague. And no wonder. Here I was hovering across the road, hoping for a distraction so that I could dash across the street and into the shop before he caught sight of me. If he saw me, I knew what would follow: Ecclesiasticus.

''All wickedness is but little to the wickedness of a woman,'' he yelled, spotting me at last. ''Ecclesiasticus 25:19.''

I winced and quickly rushed past him, beginning to mount the steps to the shop door.

''The fault is yours,'' he screamed, his finger pointing directly at me, his eyes fixed on mine as I backed up the last two steps and hurled myself through the door. The scales tilted in favor of Percy Bysshe Shelley.

''Are you all right, Lara? What is the matter with that dreadful man?'' Sarah Greenhalgh sighed as I hurtled through the door.

''Off his meds, I'd say,'' opined Alex Stewart, a retired sailor who is my neighbor and our indispensable help in the shop. ''Or maybe it's just the millennium," he added. "Brings out some kind of primitive fear in us, I think. You've seen the papers. People all over the world worrying about signs in the heavens and everything. All the portents for a cataclysmic finale to life as we know it are there, apparently."

"I just wish he'd find another piece of pavement to harangue everyone from," I sighed. "He is so bad for business! I hate to call the police, though. He is kind of pathetic."

In a way, though, as I think back on it, the man, although undoubtedly deranged, was right. Not in the strict chronological sense, perhaps. The man in our storage room was dead, murdered, before, not after, the fire. But for a time, the devil, or at least his earthly henchman, did walk among us, and, while it still hurts to admit it, I do have to assume some responsibility, some guilt, because in a way everything that happened stemmed from my inability to deal with a touchy personal situation.

The messy saga begins, in the police files at least, with the incident in which my shop got trashed and almost burned to the ground. But in my mind the story goes back a few months further than that, when Maud McKenzie up and died.

Maud was the resident eccentric in Yorkville, where Greenhalgh and McClintoch is located. She and her husband Franklin were proprietors of a strange little place from which they sold bits of everything, some antiques, some junk, called—God bless them—the Old Curiosity Shop. They lived above the store. Maud and Frank had been there forever, as far as I was concerned. The house in which the store was located had originally belonged to Maud's family, and long after her family had sold and moved away, Maud and Frank were able to buy the old building back. They'd been there when Yorkville was a run-down city neighborhood, had watched it become the focus of the sixties culture when all the best coffeehouses and folksingers were there, and had weathered the times when the sixties turned ugly and the drug scene moved in. Then when Yorkville had its renaissance as a posh shopping area, they carried on much as before.

They were founders of a rather informal merchants' association, more social club than anything, that several of us shopkeepers belonged to, getting together once a week at the Coffee Mill for what we called a street meeting. We coordinated our Christmas decorations, put together a fund for advertising the area, dealt with vandalism, the usual thing. But mainly we liked to gossip: who was renovating, who was going out of business, who was moving in. At one time, a few years earlier, when my husband Clive and I were splitting up and I had to sell the shop to pay him off, I'm sure I too was much the subject of discussion. We monitored the street as if our livelihood depended on it, which of course it did.

We were a tight little group, all friends, partly because none of us were in exactly the same business, and therefore not direct competitors. We had a fashion designer, a bookseller, a hairdresser, a craft shop owner, my antique furniture and design shop, and a linens shop. Newcomers were not excluded exactly. It just took a unanimous vote to get someone new in, and we didn't choose to vote that often.

When Frank died, Maud carried right on. We could never figure out how she managed. Perhaps the shop did better than any of us guessed. There's no question if you rooted around enough, there were treasures to be found there. But there didn't seem to be much in the way of new merchandise moving into the shop after Frank died.

When Maud became a little, as she put it, unsteady on her pins, the coffee meeting moved to her place, each of us taking a turn bringing a carafe of coffee and some cookies. But then one day, my friend Moira and I went over to check on her because the shop didn't open on time. Maud, who'd been prone to what she referred to as "spells," was lying at the bottom of the stairs leading to her apartment on the second floor. A bad fall, the coroner concluded. A broken neck and fractured skull.

I think Moira and I both thought, as we discovered Maud lying there, that the neighborhood would not be the same again, ever.

Much to our surprise, Maud and Frank had had rather more money than we would have guessed. A very tidy sum, actually, just over a million dollars, not including the sale of the building and contents. The bulk of the money went to a couple of charities, the old building and its contents to a nephew in Australia we never knew they had, and there was a nice little fund set up with the stipulation that our coffee group— we were all individually named—should get together once a year for dinner in the restaurant of our choice for as long as we were able.

Conversation for the next little while focused almost exclusively on Frank and Maud.

"Where do you think all the money came from?" I wondered out loud, Moira having dropped in for a coffee before our respective enterprises opened for the day.

"Investments," Moira, owner of the local beauty salon, ventured. "Once when I went over," she went on, tapping the table lightly with her perfectly manicured nails, "Maud was working at her desk upstairs. Looked like bonds to me."

"But you have to have money to invest!" I replied. "If personal experience is anything to go by, these places don't make anyone rich."

"Maybe they were just better at it than we are," Moira said, including herself in this rather generously, since she is a very successful businesswoman.

I remember that day very clearly for some reason, looking around my shop, which was looking particularly nice, in my estimation, and thinking how content I was with my life for the first time in a while, how my universe was unfolding entirely satisfactorily. Business, if not brisk exactly, was steady. Sarah and I worked well together. She left the buying decisions up to me and so I got to take four extended buying trips a year to parts of the world I loved, while she, the born accountant, managed the shop very efficiently. We'd built up a nice roster of repeat customers who kept us going through the lean times.

On the personal side I had, I thought, a pleasant life. Partnerless for a year or so, I found that, despite thinking about the former love of my life—a Mexican archaeologist by the name of Lucas May—more than I would like to, and still occasionally having to resist the temptation to call him and beg him to come back to me, I enjoyed being single.

I got together with friends like Moira as often as I could, and one evening a week I took a course at the University of Toronto, usually about some aspect of ancient history or languages, partly because it was related to my business, but mainly because I was interested in it. I'd long since realized I'd never be a scholar, but I enjoyed knowing a little about a lot of things, and in particular learning about the history of the places where I went to do my buying.

I had some not very onerous surrogate parenting responsibilities for a young Maltese couple who were living in Canada while the young man, Anthony Farrugia, studied architecture. These duties I shared with a friend of mine, Rob Luczka, a sergeant in the Royal Canadian Mounted Police, whom I'd met in Malta a year or two earlier and with whom I'd stayed in touch. The young Farrugias lived in a basement apartment in the house Rob shared with his daughter Jennifer and his partner Barbara. I looked in on the Farrugias from time to time, called Anthony's mother about once a month to report, and, when I was in town, had Sunday dinner at the house with Anthony, his wife Sophia, and Rob and his clan. Life, if not overly exciting, was extremely comfortable.

"So what's going to happen to Maud's junk, do you think?" Moira said, interrupting my thoughts.

"The nephew in Australia has no interest in any of it," Alex interjected. "The house is to be sold, and the contents auctioned off. Molesworth & Cox," he added, naming a swank auction house.

"Well, if you say so, Alex, then it must be true." Moira laughed. "I don't know how you do it, but you seem to know everything."

Not quite everything, as it turned out. A "FOR SALE" sign went up on the property soon enough, and the building was snapped up almost immediately by a man who was one of the larger property owners and landlords in the area. Shortly after that it was being renovated for a new tenant. For whom, exactly, the landlord wasn't saying. He would only allow as how this tenant was upscale, exclusive and exciting, which didn't tell us much. We all liked to think we were all of those things. Large hoardings hid the renovations from our view, try as much as we might to peer in. Even Alex Stewart couldn't find out who the new tenant would be.

Then, with great fanfare, the hoardings came down and the shop was shown in all its glory. CLIVE SWAIN, DESIGNER, ANTIQUARIAN, the sign said. My ex-husband, the rat, right across the street in competition with me!

From that moment on, my comfortable little world began to unravel.

"My goodness, some men are hard to get rid of! Hang around like dirty shirts!" Moira exclaimed.

"This is so awful," I moaned. "I started the business in the first place," I said, quite unnecessarily, since Moira knew this only too well. But I had to say it anyway. "The only reason he got into this business is because I was dumb enough to give him half when I married him. And he was such a jerk, insisting I sell the store to give him the money when we split. It was sheer luck I was able to buy back in again with Sarah. Now what does he up and do? Right across the street!"

Moira made sympathetic noises. "He certainly seems to be able to get women to take care of him, doesn't he? First you, who figured him out and booted him out the door. So he takes up with this new woman—what's her name, Celeste—who, let's face it, buys him a store.

"I don't think he'll be much of a threat to you,

darling,'' she went on. Moira called everybody darling. "After all, he never did an honest day's work in his life, now did he?''

That much, I thought, was true. Clive was a brilliant designer, and we'd been a good combination for a while. However, it didn't take a genius to notice that soon after we were married and I'd given him a half interest in the shop as a wedding present, he'd taken to lying about hotel pools ogling young women in bikinis while I pressed a rented Jeep up steep mountain roads to get to the perfect wood carvers, or argued with customs agents in some hot, sweaty warehouse.

Technically Moira was right. Clive didn't like to work. But he'd remarried, a wealthy woman by the name of Celeste, and she had more than enough money to hire people to do the work for him. I tried to make light of it, assuring Sarah, who must have wondered what she'd done in a previous life to deserve finding herself involved in this battle, that Clive would not be a problem.

The truth was, however, he could work hard when he chose to, and he'd been a ferocious adversary in our divorce proceedings. I considered him very much a threat, but more than that. I'd loved him once, we'd been married for twelve years, and seeing his name in elegant gold letters on the sign across the street was a constant reminder of something I considered a personal shortcoming, as if the failure of the marriage, and Clive's behavior, was somehow due entirely to inadequacy on my part. I dreaded the inevitable first meeting, and my anxiety made me furious, both at Clive and at myself.

I tried to put as good a face on as I could, and made a point of carrying on much as usual, concentrating on the details and the routine of my life. There were the plans for my next trip to Indonesia and Thailand, and the handling of the latest shipment from Mexico. On the more social side, there was dinner at Rob's house on Sundays, where as usual this time of year, Sophia, Jennifer, and I would sit on the back deck and watch Rob and Anthony barbecue, while Barbara, a perky blonde with a ponytail and gorgeous physique, and a shoo-in for the Martha Stewart award for perfect housekeeping should there ever be such a thing, passed exquisite little hors d'oeuvres and tossed salads of leaves and other ingredients I couldn't even identify.

There was also the auction of Maud's possessions at Molesworth & Cox. I thought I'd attend to see if I could purchase some of Maud's things, some stuff I could sell in the store, and a personal memento or two of Maud and Frank. I'd asked Alex to watch out for the auction notice for me.

Alex did one better and got me a copy of the catalogue, which he was perusing one day while I arranged a new window display, assiduously avoiding glancing across the street at Clive's shop.

"Well, what have we here?" I heard him mutter. "Here, have a look, Lara. Is this what I think it is?"

I glanced at the catalogue and smiled. "Cape Cod," I said. "Good work, Alex. I might not have noticed that."

"Won't Jean Yves be pleased?" he replied. "You'd better get there in lots of time for this one."

"This one" was a set of six pressed glass water goblets, dating to the 1880's, in the Cape Cod pattern, to be auctioned off the same day as Maud's possessions. The Jean Yves in question was Jean Yves Lassonde, a French actor who'd come to Hollywood ten years earlier to make a movie, and had stayed in America, buying a farm in upper New York state and settling in. I'd met him a number of years earlier, back when Clive and I had been in business together, when Jean Yves had been in town making a movie.

He'd wandered into the shop, called McClintoch and Swain back then, and had loved the place. That first visit, he'd purchased a beautiful old mirror and an antique teak armoire which I'd arranged to have shipped to his farm. After that he dropped in whenever he was in town, and almost always bought something. On one visit, I'd sold him a very large carved oak refectory table from Mexico, complete with sixteen matching chairs with beautifully carved backs and nicely worn leather seats.

He'd joked at the time that he didn't know what he'd do with such a large table when he'd only been able to find five antique goblets in a pattern he'd begun to collect: Cape Cod. Even though North American pressed glass was not my specialty, because he was such a good customer, and a really lovely person, I'd done some research on the subject and discovered that the molds for pressed glass were regularly passed across the U.S./Canadian border, and for a period of time the pattern might have been manufactured at the Burlington Glass Works on the Canadian side.

Armed with this knowledge, I'd been able to find a goblet at an estate sale outside Toronto, and I'd sent it to him with one of his shipments as a little gift from the shop. He'd been thrilled, as I knew he would be. He accepted the goblet as a gift, but insisted that, if I found any more, he wanted to pay for them. I'd come across two more after that, and he'd been able to find one himself, so now he had nine. Seven to go. And here in the Molesworth & Cox catalogue were six of them. Jean Yves would be pleased indeed.

The day of the auction was hot and muggy, and I entered the august and cool premises with a sense of both relief and anticipation. I don't buy much at auctions: Most of my buying is done direct from the craftsperson, or from my agents and pickers in various parts of the world. But there is nothing like an auction to get the adrenaline flowing and to bring out the competitive spirit in most of us.

Molesworth & Cox brought a veneer of old-world class and sophistication to that competitive flame. An old British company, founded almost 150 years ago, when treasure from the far reaches of the Empire poured into London, it proudly displayed the escutcheons that heralded it as a purveyor of goods to Her Majesty the Queen and one or two of the lesser Royals. The company had expanded to North America several years earlier and had established auction houses in New York, Dallas, and Toronto. The Toronto establishment was located on King Street just a block or two from the towering bank edifices where a considerable amount of Molesworth & Cox merchandise could be found gracing the boardrooms of these modern-day cathedrals where mammon reigns supreme.

The outside of the establishment was so discreet that you'd be inclined to miss it unless given explicit directions, just a subdued bronze plaque beside a quietly elegant door hinting at what was within.

The place still had an air of British Empire, carefully maintained, and it always reminded me of what I imagined a British club in India during the days of the Raj to be: lots of palm fronds; large windows shuttered against the sun and the heat; highly polished brass; dark wood; worn leather chairs; and strong, dark tea—Assam, perhaps—served in translucent china cups from an etched brass tray, the quiet smell of expensive cigar lingering in the air.

Visitors rang the doorbell to gain entry, and once inside found themselves in the viewing rooms, two on either side of a center hall. The rooms were painted in a dark, dark green, and Oriental carpets covered the floors. As I always do at an auction, I quickly surveyed the room, checking to see if there was anything of interest beyond the specific objects I was looking for. I found Maud's things right away, and mentally settled on a couple of sterling silver frames for myself, and three pairs of old brass candlesticks for the shop.

The water goblets were in the second room, and as quickly as I could, I checked them out. Pressed glass is highly collectible these days, and the prices have reached the point where there are inevitably fakes around. They looked okay to me, and of course they had a Molesworth & Cox certificate of authentication to back them up. There was a reserve bid of $175 on them, which was fine. Jean Yves was prepared to pay about $50 per goblet, and this left some maneuvering room.

Following my usual auction strategy, I spent as little time as possible on the objects I really wanted, feigning indifference, and then spent time looking at what I didn't want, in this case a set of Royal Doulton china with an impeccable pedigree, having belonged at one time to the Duke of something or other, and purportedly commissioned especially for a visit to the Duke's castle by none other than Queen Victoria. I don't know what I think I accomplish with this mild subterfuge; I can't imagine anyone bids high on objects because they saw me looking at them. Superstition, perhaps.

At Molesworth & Cox, purchasers are required to register and establish credit, and once they have proved themselves worthy, are given a number and a paddle with that number on it. No unseemly yelling at M & C. To make a bid, one merely raises one's paddle with a hand sign for the amount if necessary, in as refined and dignified a way as possible.

I took my seat early, sitting as I usually do in the middle of the row toward the back and watched others take their seats in front of me. The usual suspects were there—about a dozen dealers, one or two of whom I knew by name, the others only by sight. I was a little disappointed to see Sharon Steele. She's a dealer with an antique store on Queen Street West specializing in old glass, and I expected she too would be interested in the water goblets. There were also a few yuppie couples, an Arab businessman or two, and a few obviously wealthy Chinese. There was also Ernie, an older gentleman who had been at every auction I'd ever attended in this place, and someone I'd never seen buy anything whatsoever.

One person seemed rather out of the ordinary, and I'd never seen him here before, not that that meant anything. I noticed him only, I think, because he seemed rather out of his element. He was medium height and build, dark, his collar and cuffs were a little worn, his shoes a little scuffed, his greyish-green suit a little shiny, nothing that would look out of place anywhere but here, perhaps. He was nervous, and if anything, rather furtive. He kept his hands in his pockets, his eyes kept darting about the room, and from time to time his tongue would flick quickly out of his mouth and back. In the very bad habit I have of giving strangers nicknames, I mentally named him Lizard.

I half expected Lizard to leave when the time for the auction came, but he didn't. In fact, he had obviously passed muster because he had a paddle, number nine, and he took a seat several rows ahead of me and off to the right.

Maud's mirrors and candlesticks were to be the third and fourth items up for sale, and the goblets, the tenth. Bidding was brisk for the first few items, but I had little competition for Maud's possessions and got both the frames and the candlesticks for what I considered a satisfactory price. I then sat back to wait for the goblets. Sharon Steele had not yet bid on anything, so I figured she was waiting for the goblets too. I knew her to be a conservative bidder, so I thought I stood a reasonable chance of getting what I wanted.

Sharon was number eighteen, I was twenty-three. When the goblets came up, opening with the reserve bid, a number of people put in bids, but by the time the bidding reached $230, only Sharon and I were in. The auctioneer seesawed between the two of us until we got to $300, Sharon's bid. This was Jean Yves's limit, but I raised her to $310 hoping that would be the end of it. It wasn't. Sharon, it seemed, wanted these pretty badly too. By this time I was mentally calculating how much of a loss I was prepared to take. Jean Yves was a good, no, a great customer, and business wasn't bad these days. But Sarah and I would never get rich, and as the saying goes, on a good month we could almost pay the rent.

As another saying goes, he who hesitates is lost.

The bidding hit $400, and for a few seconds I lost my nerve. Much to Sharon's surprise and mine, someone farther back raised the bid to $450, and the gavel came down. "Sold to thirty-one," the auctioneer said.

I was sitting dealing with my disappointment when a voice I knew only too well came from behind. "I think Jean Yves will be pleased with the goblets, don't you?" the voice asked amiably.

Clive. I turned around to find my ex-husband, a smug expression on his face, sitting directly behind me. He was very elegantly attired, maybe Armani, I remember thinking—Moira would know—with very trendy little wire glasses and an expensive-looking haircut.

"Why are you doing this?" I hissed at him. He was stroking his moustache as I spoke, a gesture that at one time, I seemed to recall, I had found profoundly attractive, but which now just incensed me.

"Doing what?" he asked innocently. "I just thought I'd pick these up for Jean Yves. I was afraid Sharon would get them, so I leapt in."

"You didn't do it for Jean Yves. You did it for the same reason you opened up across the street from me," I whispered, acutely conscious that people nearby were watching us, but too angry to care.

"You did it to spite me," I went on. "Why? I gave you half the money for the store, and surely Celeste has enough money to keep you in style," I hissed.

"But it was never the money, my darling. I just need a chance to express my creativity," he said.

Yeah, right, I thought. "I'm not your darling," I sputtered, getting up from my seat and heading for the door.

By the time I'd climbed over the legs of several

people sitting between me and the aisle, the tears of rage I was determined not to show pricking at the back of my eyes, the bidding on the next item had already begun. As I was about to stumble out the door at the back of the room, I saw someone lurking—there is no other word for it—behind a potted palm. I could not imagine what he was doing there. He didn't appear to have a number, and he looked, if anything, even more out of place than Lizard. He was dressed completely in black, and he was concentrating very hard on the bidding that was going on. As I went by his hiding place, he turned, his concentration broken by my passing, and for a moment he stared right at me. It was all I could do not to gasp out loud. His eyes were very dark and hooded, and the backs of his hands were covered in dark hair. For some reason I cannot explain, something about the way he held his arms out from his body, almost like pincers, reminded me of a crab, or perhaps an enormous black spider, and a poisonous one at that. His eyes held mine for a second or two, and then he turned back to the bidding.

Intrigued, I turned back as well. The bidding was getting really competitive, and two parties were battling it out for something, number nine and number thirty-one: Clive and the Lizard.

The item that was being auctioned was a box of small objects that had not been claimed in customs and was therefore on the block. I'd seen it on my quick survey before the auction began. I really hadn't taken much notice of it, and in my haste to get out of the place, I hadn't heard the description of it from the auctioneer. My vague recollection was that there was a fair amount of junk in the box, and maybe a couple of things that looked interesting, although nothing I cared about.

But I knew which object held Clive's attention: a small carved jade snuff bottle. Collecting was one of Clive's passions, and on a scale of one to ten, snuff bottles would score a nine point five with him. He had an impressive collection which at one time we'd displayed on the shelf beneath a glass coffee table in our living room. I'd managed to find a few nice ones as Christmas and birthday presents, and he'd invariably been pleased with them.

The bidding was getting quite hot and moving up fast. Lizard, when he wasn't holding up his paddle, was casting desperate glances back toward Clive. The price continued to rise. Clive was leaning forward in his chair, and Lizard was mopping the sweat from his brow; he wanted the box that badly. But it was clear that Clive had the resources, Lizard did not.

As the gavel was about to come down on his bid, smelling victory and convinced he had won, Clive leaned toward a pretty young woman sitting next to him and whispered something to her.

And then, on impulse, I did to Clive what he had done to me. I held my paddle up, and before he knew what was happening, I found myself the proud owner of a box of junk that was suddenly worth, by my own action, $990. It was a malicious thing to do, to say nothing of infantile, reckless, and even foolhardy.

It was also one of the worst mistakes I have ever made.

2

"CLIVE GOT THEM!" Moira shrieked. "How awful!"

We were sitting in the little office at the back of the store, just after closing, contemplating the wretched box of junk I'd purchased. As we did so, Diesel, an orange cat who holds the title of Official Shop Cat, leapt up on the table and stuck his nose in the box. After a moment or two of poking about, he looked up and, giving me a look of pure disdain, stalked off to more interesting and rewarding activities. "Dumb, I know," I said to the little beast's retreating back.

My moment of triumph at having wrenched the snuff bottle away from Clive was very short-lived. In fact, I didn't make it out of the building. The feeling lasted only until I used my personal credit card (how could I charge this moment of madness to the shop?) to pay for it. The $1000 tab, $990, to be precise, put my credit card perilously close to the limit, and I skulked back to the store in despair.

An hour or so later, Moira appeared, her dark hair in a sleek and sophisticated new hairdo, dressed in a long grey cotton sweater with matching leggings. She looked spectacular, as usual, and I had the feeling she had a date, but she said she'd just been passing by and decided to drop in. I had my suspicions that Alex, sensing my gloom, had called her, but neither of them said anything.

"I think what you really have to do," Moira said, after a few minutes of quiet contemplation on both our parts, "is to get someone to make this jade thingy into a pendant of some sort which you'll wear every day. Every single day," she added, "while you parade up and down in front of Clive's store."

I had to laugh. "That's better," she said. "Now let's see what else you've got here. Maybe there'll be a treasure and you'll get to recoup your losses."

"I doubt it," I said. "If there'd been something of value here, Molesworth & Cox would have found it and pulled it out for a separate sale, wouldn't they?"

"You never know," Moira insisted. "Let's look. What do you figure you could get for the snuff bottle?"

"Four, maybe five hundred, tops," I said.

"See, we're halfway there," she said. "Only five hundred or so to go."

We began to delve into the box, the contents of which were not, in my opinion, worth anything near what I'd paid, even allowing for a generous $500 for the jade bottle. Undeterred, Moira rummaged around.

"Isn't this cute?" she said, pulling a small object out of the box. We both stared at it. Moira often used words like cute and thingy, and some people made the mistake of assuming she wasn't too smart. In fact, she'd enjoyed a private school education, finishing school in Switzerland, and a couple of years at Cornell before she thumbed her nose at her snotty family and went off to become a hairdresser. Now she owns one of the smartest and most successful salons in the city. Over the past year or two, since I'd been back in the shop, she'd become a really good friend.

"What is it?" I asked.

"It looks like . . . a peanut. A silver peanut," Moira said. I rolled my eyes, and we both collapsed laughing. It did, indeed, look exactly like a peanut, and it was approximately life-size. I felt the weight of it in the palm of my hand.

"Actually," I said, after a moment or two, "I think it's real silver, and possibly old. The workmanship is excellent. It's so real-looking, you can almost imagine breaking it apart and finding the two little nuts inside. And look, here," I said, pointing to a tiny hole in each end, "I think it must be a bead."

"See, what did I tell you?" Moira said. "A treasure. Hard to say if there's a market for a single silver peanut, though," she added, and we both laughed again. I was happy to find I was beginning to see the humor in all this.

"At least it's not plastic like these," Moira said, pulling out a string of beads that would have made someone in the sixties proud. I sighed. "Or ugly like this," she added, displaying a particularly awful brooch.

"No wonder this wasn't claimed in customs," I moaned. "It wouldn't be worth the trip to pick it up!" I said, opening a wooden box. Inside, carefully packaged in straw, was a flared bowl or vase, about six or seven inches high. On the inside of the flare was drawn, in beautiful detail, a serpentlike creature, which undulated around the rim. On the outside, below the flare, another fine line drawing had a quite fantastic scene in which elaborately clothed figures, some of them quite human looking, others with the heads of birds and animals, wrapped around the stem.

"Wow. That's beautiful!" Moira exclaimed as I carefully lifted it out of the protective packaging. "What is it? It looks very old."

"It does," I agreed. "However . . ." I turned the bottom of the pot toward her, so that she could see where the words *hecho en Peru*—made in Peru—had been etched into the clay.

"And then there's this," I said, holding up a small card which I translated for her. "Replica of a pre-Columbian flared vase," I read. "Made in Campina Vieja, Peru, which, if my Spanish serves me well, means old small farm. A small town, I expect."

She laughed. "It's a good thing I'm not in your business," she said. "This might have fooled me."

"Well, it might fool just about anybody," I said. "The thing about replicas, you see, is that unlike re-productions, which are essentially copies, replicas are made to exactly match whatever is being copied: same materials, same method of manufacture, everything. In fact, sometimes when a replica is made, a mistake is deliberately put in it somewhere, so that it will not be taken for the original, should the documentation that identifies it as a replica get separated from the work. It's possible here, for example, that one of the lines of the drawing is different from the original. Rep-licas are very costly to make, by and large, but pre-

Columbian works are so valuable that I would think it might pay to make one. And at least in this case, it is clearly marked as such, and not the work of the unscrupulous among us who have a short lapse of memory, shall we say, and forget to put the *hecho en Peru* on the bottom.''

"That's when tourists pay way too much for what they think is an authentic pre-Columbian piece, and then try to smuggle it back home wrapped in their dirty underwear, I suppose," Moira said. "What is it a replica of, do you think? It says Peru, so Incan perhaps?''

"I'm not sure. As you well know, I studied Mesoamerican history for a while, the Maya in particular, but I can't say this is like anything I've seen. The fact that it's made in Peru might make it Incan, but I really don't know. Maybe I'll do a little research, just for fun, when I've got a minute.''

"Could you ask Lucas about it? He should know about Peruvian stuff, shouldn't he?'' Moira asked, rather coyly I thought. She'd always liked my former partner, Lucas, and thought he and I should get together again. In her mind, I'd broken off the relationship, when in fact, he was the one who'd ended it a year earlier. He couldn't do his patriotic duty for Mexico and maintain our relationship, he'd said. In Moira's world, this was a mere technicality, however.

"He's an expert on the Maya, Moira, not Peru. And it's over, okay?''

"Whatever," Moira said. Nothing short of a total reconciliation would satisfy her, I concluded. As irritating as this occasionally was, it was also sort of endearing. "Well, whatever it is, could you sell it in the shop?" she went on, turning the vase in her hands. "I

think it would look good with the type of stuff you
sell. You carry pre-Columbian reproductions from
time to time, don't you?''

"I do and it would," I conceded. "It would fit in
very well, in fact. But what would I charge for it? Do
you think I could get five hundred by any chance?''

"Probably not," Moira replied. I made a face at
her. "Gotta go," she said, rising from her chair.
"Date. A new man. Do you think he'll be The One?''

"Probably not," I said, mimicking her.

She laughed. "Come on over to the salon. I'll treat
you to a free haircut next time you're in. And it should
be soon," she said, reaching over and pulling a long
piece of hair down in front of my eyes.

"Thanks," I said. "That's very nice of you."

"What are friends for?" she replied. "And you can
do something for me when I bomb out, as usual, with
this guy."

"You don't bomb out, Moira, you dump them," I
said. "But I'll be here."

After she left, I took a closer look at the contents
of the box. Right at the bottom there was a smaller
version of the wooden box that had contained the vase.
This one too had a card declaring the contents to be a
pre-Columbian replica. The object was round, about
two to two and a half inches in diameter, made of what
looked to be gold and a turquoise stone of some kind.
In the center was the tiny figure of a man with an
elaborate headdress, carrying a scepter or something,
and what appeared to be a shield. The scepter could
actually be removed from his little gold hand, and a
string of beads around his neck were each individually
made. The rim of the circle was surrounded by the
smallest gold beads. On the back of it was a rather

hefty post. This time I thought I knew what it was. It would be one of a pair of ear ornaments—ear flares they are sometimes called—used by pre-Columbian peoples of Mexico, Central America, and presumably South America too. The workmanship, even for a replica, was really quite extraordinary, and promising myself I would take some time to look into it, I rewrapped it in tissue and set it carefully in the desk drawer.

The vase, I decided, would sell. I thought I'd try a price of $150—the drawing was exquisite, and it would make a very unusual decorative item for someone. I found a good place for it on a coffee table, where it could be seen all round for maximum effect, and propped the card, with my handwritten translation, against it. The peanut I decided to keep, to clean it up and thread it onto a very fine silver chain I had, to wear around my neck as a reminder of my impulsiveness. Perhaps next time I went to an auction, I should wear it, I thought. On a more positive note, it would make a very interesting piece of jewelry, a bit of a conversation piece.

The snuff bottle? I would have to decide what to do with that.

As I put the box away, I caught a glimpse of a piece of paper wedged between the packing material and the side of the box. I carefully extracted it and found a letter, written by an Edmund Edwards, proprietor of something called Ancient Ways in New York, to a gallery in Toronto I'd not heard of, although that didn't mean anything. Toronto is a big place. It was called the Smythson Gallery, and the proprietor according to this letter was someone called, appropriately enough, A. J. Smythson. The letter was all very formal, befitting a gallery that had affiliates in London,

Tokyo, Bonn, and Paris, as the letterhead discreetly informed you. Mr. Edwards sent his regards to Mr. Smythson, said that he hoped the merchandise had arrived in good order, and that, since many other objects were available, he also hoped to be of service in the future. The letter was dated just over two years earlier. On a whim, I looked up the Smythson Gallery in the phone book, but it wasn't listed, nor was there an A. J. Smythson, although there was something familiar about the name, and the rather unusual spelling. Perhaps the gallery had closed, which would explain why the box was never picked up in customs. In any event, I decided, it was really no affair of mine, so I tossed the letter into the wastebasket.

The next few days more or less went back to normal, except for two things. One was that the security alarm took to going off in the middle of the night for no apparent reason. On two separate nights, and twice on one of them, I had to pull on jeans and a sweatshirt, and drive to the shop to meet the police. Neither time was there any indication of anything unusual. The following night, the alarm went off only once, but this time the policeman told me I'd be sent a bill for his services because there'd been one too many false alarms. I had the security company come to check out the system, but they told me it was operating just fine.

The other aspect of the week that made it a bit different from the norm was that I spent every spare minute dreaming up horrible things to do to Clive. These ranged from taking a hammer and smashing his beloved little jade bottle to powder right before his eyes, heaving a rock or two through his sophisticated front window display, or spray-painting his Armani suit. I did none of the things I imagined, of course.

Well, one: I called the police and had his spanking new BMW, which he persisted in parking illegally, towed. It was particularly satisfying to watch him sprinting down the street in a futile attempt to catch up to his car. It's amazing, really, the depths to which we sink in dealing with an ex-spouse.

The trouble with this small victory, of course, was that while at the time it struck me as a masterful stroke, it merely escalated the conflict. He'd taken the goblets, I'd taken his snuff bottle. At that point we were more or less even. But I couldn't let it alone, I was still so angry. In my heart I knew, of course, that there must still be something unresolved in that relationship, even though a few years and another love had gone by. It didn't take a psychiatrist to figure that one out. But I kept going anyway, as petty as I knew it to be. And knowing only too well just how immature Clive was, I knew he'd figure out who had the car towed and would find a way to retaliate.

I didn't have long to wait.

A few days after the car incident, Clive swept into the store. "Just coming to say hello to my neighbors," he said. "The place looks very nice, Lara. And this must be your new partner. Sarah, is it?" he said in his most charming voice.

Sarah murmured something polite, then disappeared in the back, wisely not wishing to be part of this little scene. I smiled weakly, then went to assist a customer in the second showroom. I heard Clive wandering around in the front room. In a few moments I heard him talking to an old customer of ours. "George!" he exclaimed. "How nice to see you again. Still collecting New World santos?" he asked. I heard George murmur a reply. "I have one you really must see, quite exceptional,'' Clive went on. There was a pause. ''Right across the road, George.'' I could picture Clive pointing across the road, and I excused myself for a moment from my customer. But it was too late. Clive, his arm on the shoulder of one of our oldest clients, was steering him over to his shop. He'd stolen a good customer right from under my nose.

It was not until the next day that I noticed that the silver peanut was missing. I'd been working on it a bit in the shop, and I thought I'd left it either on the desk in the little office or in the small drawer behind the front counter. But it was in neither place and a search of the whole shop turned up nothing. There was, in my mind, only one possible explanation. I marched across the street.

''I didn't think you'd stoop so low as to steal something, Clive,'' I huffed. ''An auction is one thing, but this petty theft—''

''What are you talking about, Lara?'' Clive replied. ''Surely taking a customer away is not theft. Why don't we call it healthy competition?''

''I'm not talking about George. I'm talking about the peanut,'' I replied, knowing as the words came out of my mouth that I sounded like an idiot.

''The peanut,'' Clive sighed. ''My God, Lara, you really are losing it. Take a vacation or a Valium or something. There's nothing wrong with my setting up shop across the street. Why do you think the big shopping malls have competitors at either end? Why are whole streets lined with stores selling the same kind of merchandise? Because it's good business, that's why. With you and I both here, this could end up being the antiques center of the city. There's business enough for both of us. So please stop this nonsense about peanuts!''

I just looked at him. ''Come on,'' he wheedled. ''Let's kiss and make up. Or shake hands at least. We were a good team once, weren't we? We're even on the auction, and I'll forgive what you did to my car, if you'll forgive the abduction of George.'' He held out his hand. After a second or two, somewhat reluctantly, I took it.

''Welcome back to the neighborhood, Clive,'' I said.

''That's better,'' he said. I mentally pictured myself spray-painting his lovely beige suit purple. It helped a lot.

There didn't seem to be any more to be said, and so I turned to go. ''I don't suppose you'd sell me the snuff bottle?'' he said.

''Sure,'' I replied. ''Eleven hundred dollars.''

He laughed. ''Three,'' he said to my retreating back. I kept going.

''Okay, okay,'' he called after me as I crossed the street. ''Four hundred, make that four fifty if you'll throw in the rest of the stuff in the box.''

I ignored him.

The next few days were quiet, if you don't count the arrival at our front door of the resident nutbar with his news of impending doom. In fact, his presence made the store so quiet that Sarah decided to take a few days vacation, right in the middle of tourist season, leaving the shop to the care of Alex and me. I heard nothing more from Clive. I still didn't trust him, in fact I never would, but so far the cease-fire seemed to be holding. There was no sign of the peanut. Alex and I both looked for it, and I still was not entirely convinced Clive hadn't taken it, holding it hostage for the snuff bottle or something. But Clive said no more on that subject, and finally I had to conclude it had been stolen. Shoplifting is a disagreeable fact of life when you own a store, and the peanut would be very easy to snatch, particularly if I had been careless enough to leave it out on the counter, which I supposed I must have done. Just in case, though, I took the little gold and turquoise ear ornament home with me while I decided what to do with it.

One evening, my little group of friends decided to get together for a drink. We went to the bar in the Four Seasons, just down the street from our shops. Moira, who changes her hairdos and her men the way the rest of us change socks, brought her new man, whose name was Brian. Brian was subjected to a baptism of fire, if ever there was one. Elena, the craft store owner who rather fancies herself as an amateur therapist, did a snap psychological profile of him to his face; Dan, tall, thin, scholarly, the perfect bookseller, interrogated him about his reading habits; and Moira and I talked shop most of the time. Brian seemed very nice, but had he asked me, I wouldn't have held out much hope for him.

It was a pleasant outing for me, until Clive arrived and pulled up a chair, leaving me wondering if this was coincidence, or if one of the group, a traitor, had invited him. After a few minutes of watching him being charming, ingratiating himself with my friends, most particularly Moira, I decided it was time to go, and headed for my car. Only then did I realize I'd left my keys—car, home, shop, all of them—at the store. I was damned if I was going back into the bar to ask for help with Clive there.

I looked at my watch. The store was open until eight, and it was now about eight-thirty. With any luck, if it had been a bit busy, Alex would still be there, doing the paperwork, putting the cash in the safe, and generally straightening up the place.

I went first to the main door. The shop was dark, and since it was just twilight it was difficult for me to see in, particularly since we had a metal gate that we pulled in front of the glass doors when we closed as an extra security precaution. Disappointed, I turned to leave. Perhaps, I hoped, Alex had found the keys and, not knowing where I'd gone for a drink, had taken them home with him. He lived just three doors from me, so I would be all set. I'd cab it to Alex's and leave my car in the parking lot overnight.

Just then, I heard a clunk against the door behind me. I turned back in time to see Diesel pawing at the glass in some agitation. I went back to the door and tried to peer in. Diesel turned and disappeared into the gloom, but I could see him framed against the light from the small window in the back door opposite me, circling and circling in the middle of the room.

Gradually my eyes adjusted, and I saw what had upset Diesel. Someone—it could only be Alex—was wandering erratically around the store. I rattled the gate as hard as I could, but it wouldn't budge, and Alex, if that was who it was, did not appear to notice me. There had to be something seriously the matter with him. I ran down the alleyway beside the shop and around to the back door. It too was locked.

There was a wrought iron chair and table out on a tiny patio where we occasionally take a coffee or lunch break. I picked up the chair and heaved it at the back door. The glass in the little panel in the door shattered, and I was able to reach through the small opening and unlock the door. Instantly the alarm went off, but I didn't stop. I figured that would bring help faster than a phone call. I raced up the four steps to the main floor.

It was, as I had feared, Alex. He was wobbling a little, almost staggering, and muttering to himself. A stroke, I thought. He's had a stroke or something. But then I noticed there was blood in his hair, and a bruise was forming on the side of his head above one ear. He's fallen, I concluded, and hit his head.

I went over to him, being careful not to startle him. "What happened, Alex?" I said, taking his arm as gently as I could. He looked toward me, but his eyes were not focusing properly. "Let's go," I said gently. "I'm going to take you to the doctor, okay?"

"Can't," he said finally, the first intelligible words I'd heard him say. "Not finished. Something I have to do." He mumbled incoherently for a moment, then said, "I have an account to settle with . . ." He looked confused. "With someone," he said vaguely.

"I'm sure it can wait until later," I said soothingly. "Now you just come along with me." It was hopeless though. He wasn't going to leave. I knew I would have to get help. I gently eased him into a chair and headed for the desk.

Throughout our conversation, if you can call it that, the alarm was making a terrible racket, which struck me as a bit odd. I didn't think Alex would have set the security system until he was ready to leave the shop. The reason for the alarm would soon become clear.

As I reached for the phone, there was a roar, then a crash, and I was thrown backward as the storage room door just a few feet away from me was blasted off its hinges. Dense, black smoke filled the air. The sprinkler system activated. There was smoke, there was water, Diesel was circling my legs, howling in terror, the alarm rang on and on. Fire, I thought, it's the fire alarm.

But it was even worse than that. Crumpled just inside the storage room was a man. He lay on his side, his back to me, knees drawn up a little, not quite in a fetal position, and his hands had been tied behind his back. I couldn't see his face, and I couldn't bring myself to look. He did not move at all. I thought I could see blood, though, on the side of his neck and his hands. For a second, I had this vision of a man on his knees, begging his executioner to spare him, then falling over into the position in which he now lay.

I had a decision to make, and I made it. I couldn't get all of us out. I left the man in the storage room, who was, I reasoned, almost certainly dead, and grabbing Alex, who was now unconscious, heaved him up into my arms like a child. Yelling at Diesel to come with me, I tried to make my way to the back door. I couldn't see where I was going, and I started to choke and gag. I hit my shins on some furniture, ran into the side of something, and, still holding Alex, fell to my knees. Down low, the air wasn't quite so thick, and I could see a tiny shadow just ahead of me. It was Diesel. I pulled Alex up on my back, his arms draped over my shoulders, and, following the cat, crawled to the back steps, then to safety, the sound of a distant siren moving toward us.

"Help's coming, help's coming," I said over and over to Alex's unconscious figure until the police and firemen arrived.

3

WHAT WOULD FOLLOW were some of the blackest days of my life.

I spent the night in the hospital, under observation, it was explained to me, because of all the smoke I'd inhaled. Being under observation extended beyond the medical, I quickly ascertained, to the presence of a policewoman by the name of Constable Margo Chu, who, having little if anything to say for herself, sat in the only chair in the room, leafing through fashion magazines by the hour.

I was a mess, as even the most cursory exploration and a mere glance in the bathroom mirror made clear. My knees looked like raw meat, a gash on my left hand had required several stitches, and with a severe muscle spasm in my back, and ribs sore from coughing, I could barely stand up straight.

Nevertheless, I was still much better off than Alex, who drifted in and out of consciousness, the result of a bad concussion. His condition was described as "guarded," whatever that means. I knew what they were worried about. I'd overheard the nurses talking about him: swelling of the brain.

I kept seeing him in the ambulance, the mask over his face, and tubes running from his arms. He was so still, his face the color of chalk: the man who'd befriended me after my divorce, a kind of second father to me, who'd made me feel at home in a new neighborhood, looked after my house while I traveled, who was indispensable now, in the shop, and who, more than anything else, was my friend, in such distress.

And that other fellow, who was he? What was he doing there? Was this a robbery gone wrong? Who had done what to whom? Had the man in the storage room hit Alex? It could not possibly, knowing Alex, have been the other way around. And if he had hit Alex, what then had happened to him? He hadn't tied his own hands behind his back. My head hurt thinking about it, and none of it made any sense.

I was allowed to leave the hospital late the next morning. I asked to see Alex before I left, but they wouldn't let me. He was in intensive care, and only relatives were allowed in. I pointed out that I was the closest thing to a relative he had, but even then they suggested I come back the following day and they'd consider my request. PC Chu drove me home, where Moira was waiting for me. She bustled around very efficiently, getting me settled in my favorite armchair, bringing me lunch, and trying to make me laugh.

"In case you're too traumatized to figure it out," she said, "the tempura shrimp, the California rolls, and the yellow fin tuna sushi are for you. The yuppie deluxe, organic, gourmet cat food in this lovely jar with the darling little hat on it is for Diesel. You may share the single malt scotch.''

I tried to smile to please her, I really did, but gave it up. I felt close to tears most of the time, and anyway my face, like every other part of my body, hurt. And there was much to be done.

"I've got to get up," I said. "I have to clean up the shop: I can't leave it all to Sarah, and we've got to get back in business. We can't afford to be closed for long." I tried to stand up.

"No. Listen," Moira said, pushing me back. "Your friends are on this. You can't get into the building, anyway. The police won't let you. As soon as they do, we'll get a group together and do whatever needs doing. Sarah will be back soon. Until she gets here, the rest of us will pitch in."

I thought about that. "What do you mean, the police won't let me in? Why not?" I demanded. "It's my shop!"

"I don't know," she said vaguely. "I expect they have to investigate things, and don't want a lot of people getting in the way. I'm sure that's it."

Moira tried very hard to get me to rest, but I couldn't. I decided that I would call my insurance adjuster and arrange to have him meet me at the store the next morning, by which time, I was sure, I'd be up and around. I'd been dealing with the same insurance company for years, had never had a claim, and did not expect any problems.

The person I usually dealt with was not in, but I was referred to an agent by the name of Rod McGarrigle. Rod and I did not hit it off. In the first place, he had a rather distracted air about him. I had the impression that he was doing something else while talking on the phone to me, because from time to time I could tell that he put his hand over the mouthpiece while I was talking to him. His answers to my questions about coverage, the possibility of payment for lost business, and so on were discouragingly vague.

Finally, in exasperation, I asked him bluntly, ''Am I or am I not covered for this?''

''You are covered for this, Ms. McClintoch,'' he replied, ''unless, of course, you, your partner, or anyone in your employ is found to be guilty of a felony.''

A felony. How nice. ''Then I will expect payment promptly,'' I said tartly before hanging up in his ear.

I told Moira what he'd said, and she made sympathetic noises, but she changed the subject immediately and began to tell me droll little stories about how Brian had been traumatized by meeting her friends the previous day. I gathered the relationship had not survived drinks with her friends, but she didn't seem perturbed about it. Even in my painkiller-induced grogginess, I was beginning to wonder what exactly was going on that I was missing. It did not take long to find out.

PC Chu went off duty soon after that but was immediately replaced by PC Mancino, a fresh-faced young man who insisted upon calling me ma'am, and who told me several times how proud he was to have worn blue, to use his expression, for seven years now. I took this to be his way of telling me that he was older and more experienced than he looked.

Shortly thereafter he was joined by his sergeant, Lewis he said his name was, and if he had a first name, he didn't reveal it. He struck me as a man who had no perceptible imagination or sense of humor, and who was on top of that a stickler for detail. He began by asking Moira to leave, which she did, reluctantly, telling him she would return in forty-five minutes, implying by her tone and her glance that he should be gone by the time she got back. Moira is not to be messed with, I've learned, and as Sergeant Lewis seemed in imminent danger of finding out for himself.

Lewis talked in phrases punctuated by emphasis rather than sentences, almost as if he thought he was restricted to a finite number of words in his lifetime and didn't want to run out before his final exit. He also had a disconcerting habit, whether by design or just because his mind worked that way, of asking questions in what appeared to be an entirely random order. He asked, in my opinion, an inordinate number of questions about where I'd been from 7:35 on, and with whom, and what I had done from the time I'd left the bar in the Four Seasons until the police and fire truck had arrived at the shop. None of my answers seemed precise enough to satisfy him. PC Mancino took laborious notes.

I told him in great detail about drinks in the bar, who had been there, when people had arrived, and then added, "I'm sure my friends can confirm all of this for you."

"Taken *their* statements already," he replied non-committally.

"All right, then," I said. Why exactly would he need to do that? I wondered. Only minutes into the interview and I was beginning to realize that Lewis and I were not going to get along. Here one of my dearest friends has been badly hurt, I said to myself, some stranger has ended up dead in my store, which just happens to be in flames at the time, and this fellow wants to know how many drops of vermouth there were in my martini and where I parked my car.

"Southwest corner Yorkville and Avenue Road. *Then* what?"

"I realized I'd forgotten my keys, left them at the shop, so I went back hoping to catch Alex before he left. As I've already told you," I added. This was the third time he'd asked for some clarification on a matter I considered perfectly straightforward.

"These your *keys*?" Lewis asked, oblivious to my dislike, pulling a black-and-white photo of a key ring from his briefcase.

I nodded.

"Sure?"

"I can't imagine they would be anyone else's. The key ring's a gift from a friend in Mexico. It's silver, and an unusual design—the Chac Mool from Chichén Itzá."

I looked over at the puzzled PC Mancino. In seven years of wearing blue, he had not encountered the Maya/Toltec city of Chichén Itzá, nor the angry god that guards one of the temples. I spelled both for him. He blushed.

"Keys all there?"

"I think so: house, Alex's place, Moira's, car, shop door—same key opens the back and the front doors—warehouse, storage room. That's it. Yes, all there."

"Partner out of town, is she?" he asked, taking one of those little mental leaps I found so hard to follow.

"Yes. She's gone on a wilderness camping trip in Algonquin Park with her friend and his two sons. She'll be back tomorrow or the day after." There I was being imprecise again. He scowled.

"Business been good lately, has it?"

"Fine. Yes."

"Don't owe a bit of *money* or anything, do you?"

"No, as a matter of fact, we've actually turned a small profit the last few months." I could predict the next question, and sure enough, out it came.

"*Insured*, are you?"

"Yes, of course."

It didn't take a genius to figure out where he was going with this one: insurance fraud. Maybe that explained why Rod McGarrigle had been so evasive. But it was much worse than that.

"*Then* what?"

"Then what, what?" I asked, baffled by all the mental hopping around Lewis was doing.

He looked at me as if I were of subnormal intelligence and said, "What did you do after you realized you'd left your keys behind?" He clearly resented having to use all those words to get me back on track.

I told him how I'd gone to the shop, peered in the front door, realized something was wrong and gone round to the back to try to get in.

"Door *locked*, was it?"

"Yes. I used a chair to smash the window. Come to think of it, the chair was lying on its side close to the door. It had been knocked over."

"Wind?"

"I don't think so. It's wrought iron and pretty heavy."

"And *then*?"

"I reached through the broken window, pushed the bar, and got the door open, and went over to Alex."

"Who was where, *exactly*?" Lewis went on. Clearly my answers were not yet precise enough.

"Wandering around in a daze," I replied.

"His *precise* position?"

"Near the tan sofa."

"Near?"

"In front of it. A couple of feet, more or less, in front of it."

"His appearance, *in detail*?"

"Dazed, as I said. He had a cut over his left ear, and he was sort of staggering around."

Lewis winced. He didn't like expressions like more or less and sort of, I could tell, but at this moment I was too tired and sore to care.

"Say anything?"

"I think I asked him what happened, and then suggested he leave with me," I replied, misunderstanding the question.

"*He* say anything?" Lewis asked, impatient at my inability to answer the question he was asking.

"He was babbling really. The only coherent thing he said was something about not being able to go because he had some unfinished work, an account he had to settle."

For a second or two both policemen sat motionless, Mancino with his pen poised over his notebook, Lewis looking like the proverbial cat that had swallowed the canary. I looked from one to the other. Knowing Alex, it had simply never occurred to me that there was more than one way of interpreting what he'd said. Lewis, I knew right away, also thought there was only one interpretation, and it was not the same as mine.

"You can't think Alex is to blame for this," I gasped. "He would never do such a thing."

"*Exact* words?" Lewis said finally.

"He was worried he hadn't got all his work at the shop done!" I exclaimed. "That's all."

"*Exact* words?" Lewis repeated.

"He said, 'Not finished. Something I have to do. I have an account to settle with someone,' " I replied reluctantly. "It's an old-fashioned expression, settle an account," I added, horrified at the direction this conversation was taking, and upset that my report would reflect so badly on him. "Alex is getting on a little, and he's lived all over the world, and he uses some rather quaint expressions. It means pay a bill. He's been looking after the finances while my partner is away."

"Known Mr. Stewart *long*, have you?" Lewis said, this time very quietly.

"Long enough," I retorted. "About four years, long enough to know that he would never hurt a flea."

Lewis said nothing. Mancino scribbled furiously.

"Have you figured out *precisely* what that other person was doing in my store?" I asked, anxiety making me belligerent as I desperately tried to get the investigation back on what I saw to be a more reasonable track. "Did he break in, not realizing Alex was still there? We don't keep much cash in the shop, just a small float in the safe in the tiny office behind the front desk. Most people pay by credit card these days, so there's rarely a large amount of money in the shop, but a thief wouldn't necessarily know that," I rattled on.

How had the thief got in? I wondered as I spoke. While the shop was open, perhaps, hiding in the storage room and then surprising Alex? Once the store was closed, both the front and back doors were locked. The back door was always locked: It had a panic bar for ease of exit but locked automatically behind you. It had been locked when I got there, that I knew for certain.

And the fire? We didn't keep all that much in the storage room. We had a warehouse several blocks away where we kept the bigger pieces of furniture until there was room on the floor. The storage room contained some of our records, a place for our coats, and some of the smaller decorative items which we kept there to replace objects as they were sold. We didn't keep anything flammable, and I couldn't imagine how a fire could have started. Did that mean the fire had been deliberately set? Was the thief trying to cover his tracks? Was he even trying to make sure Alex could never identify him? It was a horrible thought.

My thoughts turned back to the present, and I found Sergeant Lewis watching me carefully. "So," I said, "was it a robbery?"

"*One* possibility," Lewis said.

I told him about the security alarm going off three times in the previous week. "I thought they were false alarms, but now I'm not so sure," I said, pressing on despite his refusal to tell me anything. "Do you think someone was trying to break in then? Was the fire deliberately set?"

Lewis ignored me. Suddenly he leaned forward.

"*Know* this person?" Lewis asked, taking an eight by ten black-and-white photo out of his briefcase and setting it before me. If he'd wanted to shock me, he was very successful. It was the dead man in the store, photographed in such a way that I could see his face, his hair singed and one cheek burned, a dark ugly line on his neck. I gasped. Lewis waited.

"No!" I finally blurted out. Technically that was true, but I wouldn't have wanted to be hooked up to a polygraph at that very moment.

"*Certain?*"

I nodded. There was no question I was being a trifle too literal here. I really didn't know who the victim was. But I had seen him before. The problem was, every time I opened my mouth, I seemed to implicate Alex: Surely Lewis would never have suspected Alex if I hadn't said what I had. I determined I would have to be very careful what I said from now on. Volunteering more than was asked for was not a good idea, it seemed.

"*You* know who he is?" I asked, adopting Lewis's particular style of speech as my own.

It was his turn to nod. "Then why ask me?" I responded.

"Turned up in *your* storage room for starters. A little *crispy* have to say, but recognizable. Ever been to Peru?" he asked without missing a beat.

Now why did that question not surprise me? "No," I replied.

"Ever done business with anyone in Peru?"

"Again, no."

"Any reason to be dealing with someone in Peru, in an official capacity or otherwise?"

"Not that I can think of."

"Your friend Stewart has, I expect," he countered.

I didn't reply, cautiously deciding to take this as a question, not a statement.

"*Been* there, has he?"

"He may have," I replied. "I don't know. He was in the merchant marine for twenty years. He went a lot of places."

"Merchant marine, was it? Down on the docks, I expect. Lots of things go down around the docks. Went to Peru. Not so long ago, either," he replied evenly. "Purser too. Dealt with customs officials very likely."

What was I supposed to infer from that? Lewis's elliptical references were definitely getting on my nerves. "What do you think happened that evening?" I said, forgetting my determination to keep quiet. "Alex tied this guy up, killed him, set fire to the place and then bopped himself on the head? So badly he has a concussion, I might add?"

"Strange, I grant you. But more likely than the other way around, wouldn't you say? No sign of anybody else there," he said, raising his head and looking right at me. Mercifully I heard the door open, and Moira came in.

"So you've *never* seen him?" Lewis persisted, pointing once more to the photo of Lizard.

There didn't seem to be any way around this very direct question. To say yes now, however, after I'd said I didn't know him, would make me look as if I was hiding something, maybe covering for Alex. "No," I lied.

Lewis looked at me for several seconds, then turned to Mancino. "That's it, then. We'll be off. We'd like you to come to the store with us tomorrow morning to see if there's anything missing. We will be pursuing various lines of enquiry."

"You do that," I said in as authoritative a manner as I could muster. Then I just hung in until the two had left before bursting into tears. Moira was horrified, of course. She thought they'd been badgering me, and maybe they had. I couldn't tell her though.

Lizard. It was the man I'd rather facetiously called Lizard, the man who had dueled it out with my ex-husband for a jade snuff bottle at Molesworth & Cox.

Dead, burned, in my store. Was it another of Clive's little pranks that had gone very wrong? Had he sent someone to steal the snuff bottle? He'd been prepared to pay enough for it. Top price, actually, and I'd refused. Lizard had wanted the box too, very, very badly. But if he'd broken into the shop, how had he been killed? Not by Alex. Even leaving aside the fact that he would never do such a thing, Alex was barely conscious. So who else was there?

More to the point, what had I done? Rather than helping the police with their investigation, I'd actually lied about knowing Lizard. Now what?

I called my lawyer. She was vacationing on Maui for a week.

I called Rob Luczka. "Answer the phone," I ordered, as it rang and rang. I knew he and Barbara had been in Montreal visiting her sister, but I was praying they'd returned.

"Hello," he said at last.

"You're home," I said, relieved.

"Just got in," he said. "What's up?"

"I really need your help. The most awful thing has happened." I started to tell him about Alex, the body, and the fire.

"I'll be right there," he said, interrupting me. I heaved a sigh of relief. While Rob and I occasionally seem to inhabit different planets, I consider him to be a friend, and despite the occasional round of bickering from time to time, usually over what I see to be his rather black-and-white view of events, I hope he feels the same about me. It made me feel better knowing he was on his way over.

Less than half an hour later we were ensconced on my back deck with a pitcher of iced lemon tea. It was a beautiful warm summer evening, and more than anything else I just wanted to sit there and enjoy it and not think about what had happened. After discussions about the weather, Montreal, and the Blue Jays, Rob gently turned the conversation around to the subject at hand. He was very sympathetic until I got to the part about the photo of Lizard.

"I told Lewis that I didn't know the person in the photo, but in fact, while I don't know exactly who he was, I have seen him before, at an auction at Molesworth & Cox." I hesitated, hearing his sharp intake of breath. "I thought they were accusing Alex of something awful, and me of arson, insurance fraud, and my hand hurt and I had a headache," I rattled on. Even to my own ears, I sounded like a whiny brat.

"This is murder we're talking about here, Lara. How do you think it will look for you and Alex if— make that when, not if—the police find out you had seen the victim, that you lied?"

"I was thinking maybe I could say I'd had a brain wave or something, a sudden return of memory. I was in shock, you know, after the event . . ."

Rob looked at me as if I'd just crawled out from under a rock. He was absolutely furious. His jaw was clenched so tightly I thought his teeth would crumble. "So you're planning to pile lies on top of lies, are you? You think this is quite all right to do?"

"Spare me the lecture, Rob," I shot right back. "I made a mistake, okay? Most people do that from time to time. Maybe not you, of course. Maybe not that Ms. Perfect you live with. But most of us do. I don't want a speech about ends never, ever justifying means, or on the duties and responsibilities of a citizen or whatever. I'm asking you for advice on what to do about this situation, how to help Alex and get out of this mess."

After what seemed an eternity, he spoke very quietly. "I will have to tell them what you have told me." I felt a sudden wave of sympathy for his daughter Jennifer, who I knew was subjected to this particular strain of morality a lot, and who suffered from it.

"Even if it looks bad for Alex too? Rob," I pleaded, "I thought you were my friend. I asked you for help as a friend."

He stood up. "I am a policeman, first and foremost," he said. "If you didn't want me to report it, then you shouldn't have told me." He started to walk away.

"Well, maybe you don't have your priorities straight," I said to his rigid back. He kept walking. "Maybe life is not quite as neat as you think it is," I continued.

"Ask Jennifer what she thinks," I called as he reached the gate. It was a low blow. I heard the gate latch firmly behind him.

4

IT TOOK ME a while to figure out what was missing, in part because the shop was such a mess, but also because it was not what I expected.

Constable Chu was back on duty the next morning and drove me to the shop. I was grateful for the lift, because I hurt even worse that day than I had the day before. I felt as if it would take a shoehorn to get me behind the wheel of my own car.

I had been dreading this moment, not just because I was frightened at what I would find, but also because I was worried about what to say to Sergeant Lewis. The question was, had Rob told him about Lizard or not? If he hadn't, then perhaps I could try my memory-coming-back-to-me story, but if he had, then saying that would only make it worse.

I was feeling terrible about Rob. I knew that I had done to a friend something that one should never do: put him in an unconscionable position. I wanted to call and apologize, but he had been so angry I was afraid to. I had thought a lot in the wee small hours of the morning about why I had been acting so childish of late. I am no spring chicken after all. In fact I am old enough to have grown children of my own instead of behaving like an infant. I could operate a business reasonably efficiently, travel all over the world without a qualm, but when my ex-husband moves in across the road, I go slightly nuts. Clive was right. It was time for me to get a grip.

But how, exactly?

A mixture of smells greeted my nostrils as I stepped in the door: part doused campfire, part wet dog, and partly, to my hyperactive imagination, the odor of death. I pointed out the spot where I'd found Alex to Constable Chu, then looked around as she made notes.

The fire itself had done surprisingly little damage. The storage room door had blown out, and it and the frame were badly singed, the walls in that area marked by smoke stains. The sprinkler system had done what it should and put out the blaze very quickly.

The water damage was something else, however. Already the paint on some of the antique wood pieces was beginning to peel away, and watermarks were showing up on everything. The sofas were absolutely sodden, and the carpets on the floor, some really lovely old kilims I'd picked up on a hair-raising trip through Pakistan a few months earlier, squelched as I walked over them. I desperately wanted to get an industrial cleaner in, but the doors were still barred by yellow police tape. If we weren't allowed in soon, nothing would be salvageable. I could have cried.

Lewis arrived. "Anything *missing*?" he said in his usual succinct manner.

I looked around. The store is a bit of a barn really,

just one large room with a teeny office behind the front desk, the storage room at the back, and another small showroom off to the right. In order to make the merchandise look more inviting, we had room arrangements in several areas of the shop: a dining table and chairs with places set, a candelabra hanging from the ceiling above; a living room arrangement against one wall, with a sofa, side chairs, end tables, coffee table with accent pieces on it, and perhaps a wall hanging or a carved mirror behind the sofa.

When someone bought an item, we rearranged the setting so that it wouldn't look bare. In other words, our merchandise was constantly in motion. Alex would have known exactly where everything was, but it would take me days to make a complete inventory. In any event, I did my best to have a careful look around.

I started with the office where I had left the jade snuff bottle. Much to my relief, and somewhat to my surprise, it was still there. It had been tossed into a corner along with the contents of the three drawers in the desk, but it was not damaged in any way that I could see. The safe was still locked. The place was a mess, but I couldn't see anything missing.

I forced myself to go and look in the storage room. That room was pretty well a write-off. I could see the chalk outline on the floor where Lizard had been found.

''There's nothing missing in the office that I can find,'' I said to Lewis, giving him a progress report. I looked toward the storage room. ''Did he burn to death?'' I asked, my voice shaking, and thinking what a really horrible way that was to die.

''Garroted. Wire pulled so tight, it cut into his neck.

Burned too, and locked in just to make sure. Some-
body wanted him dead.'' Lewis paused. "*Your* keys
too. In the storeroom door. Locking him in. Not necessary. Wasn't going anywhere.'' Before I could re-
spond to that implied accusation, he concluded, ''Keep
looking.''

Horrified, I carried on as instructed. A jewelry case
at the front desk had been opened and the contents
jumbled up. There were a few nice pieces in there, but
as far as I could tell, nothing was missing there either.

I was perplexed. I'd thought that Lizard was interested in the snuff bottle: It was the only thing of any
value in the box from the auction. But it was still there.
So what else could it be? On the assumption that it
was no coincidence that I'd taken the objects he'd
wanted at Molesworth & Cox, I thought about the contents of the box.

I turned back to the main room. The vase, the reproduction pre-Columbian piece with the lovely serpents on the rim, was missing. I spent almost an hour
going over the place, in case Alex had moved it while
I was out, but it was the only thing I could find that
was gone.

I was afraid to tell Lewis that only a strange-
looking vase from Peru was missing. If it wasn't robbery, then he'd go immediately to some other theory,
one I was certain I wouldn't like, and one that would
not be good for Alex. Remembering my commitment
to myself of the night before, I decided I had to tell
him regardless. It occurred to me that if I did it right,
I might be able to set him on the right track in his
investigation.

''There's only one object that I can see that is missing,'' I told him. ''It is a vase, about six and a half

inches high, and it is a reproduction pre-Columbian ceramic made in Peru. It was quite lovely, actually. I got it in a job lot at Molesworth & Cox, the auction house, a couple of weeks ago." There, I'd told him about the auction. Maybe he could take it from there.

But no. "*Fake,* is it? Look again," he said. "Can't imagine someone taking a fake Peruvian pot and leaving the jewelry and money, can you? Unless, of course, there was a reason other than robbery." It was the longest sentence I'd heard him utter, and I didn't like what he was implying any more than when he'd hinted at it the first time.

After another hour of looking about, Lewis let me leave. PC Chu drove me home. She told me I'd be asked to come in to headquarters to sign a copy of my statement.

My house seemed very quiet and very lonely. I checked my answering machine to hear Moira telling me in a motherly way not to forget to take my pills and to be sure to have something to eat. Sarah had called from a phone booth on the edge of Algonquin Park to say she'd been delayed and wouldn't be back for another day. She apologized for calling me at home rather than the shop, but she said she hadn't been able to get through to the store. "Maybe there's a problem with the phone, or maybe I dialed incorrectly," she said. There's a problem with the phone, all right, I thought. It's been trashed, burned, and doused. I was not looking forward to telling her about what had happened. There was a message from a friend and colleague, Sam Feldman, telling me how sorry he was to hear about the store, but no message from Rob.

It occurred to me that I hadn't heard from many of

my colleagues and friends, but perhaps I couldn't blame them under the circumstances. It was possible, of course, that people were giving me time to recover. But I was more than a little concerned that people, people I considered friends, were out there wondering if indeed I had arranged for the fire at Greenhalgh and McClintoch. The newspaper reports seemed a little ambiguous on the subject, I would have to say.

I began having rather morose thoughts about the future, along the lines of maybe if this doesn't get cleared up soon everybody will be crossing the street to avoid having to talk to me. I knew if I stayed at home by myself I would get really depressed, so I decided to pull myself together and go out. I'd imposed on Moira too much already, but Sam Feldman had been nice enough to call, so I thought I'd pay him a visit.

Sam and I had met years before when I'd taken a conservation course he'd given at the University of Toronto. At the time he was a museum director, but later he decided to go commercial, as he described it, and opened a gallery on Queen Street West. His museum had specialized in eastern antiquities, and he'd been very helpful in sharing his contacts in that part of the world when I branched out and started buying there. In return, I'd given him advice on setting up shop, and we'd stayed in touch. I liked Sam: I always found him funny and articulate, and I thought a visit with him would cheer me up.

I carefully eased myself behind the wheel of my car and headed down for Queen Street. Sam was there, along with his young assistant. "Hi," I said. "Thanks for your message. I'm a bit at loose ends, so I thought

I'd see if you had time for a coffee. Do you think you could drag yourself away?''

''From what?'' he asked wryly, gesturing around the room. ''Do you see customers? Do you see a *single* customer? For this I left a low-paying but steady job in a museum? Where shall we go?''

We left his assistant—Janie, he called her—and headed for Starbucks. ''I guess you were implying business is not exactly great,'' I said.

He laughed. ''Oh, it's okay. No fame and fortune, though. But I always thought I'd like working for myself, and I do. Sorry about your place. Dreadful thing. Insured?'' I nodded. ''Good,'' he said. ''You'll let me know if there is anything I can do.'' I smiled my thanks.

We chatted awhile, and then it struck me that Sam might indeed be able to help with something, by way of information. ''Would the name A. J. Smythson and the Smythson Gallery mean anything to you?''

''Oh, yes,'' he replied. ''Surely you remember too.''

''The name sounds familiar, but I can't really recall why,'' I said. ''So tell me. I can tell from the expression on your face that there's a good story here.''

''It's quite a tale, all right, but good isn't exactly the word,'' he replied. ''In fact it is precisely the wrong word. Smythson, Anton James Smythson—his friends, I wasn't one of them, called him A. J.—was an art dealer on King Street West. He had his gallery in one of those industrial buildings that are being converted in that old part of town. He lived in a fabulous loft over the store.

''He was very successful, in a way I am coming to realize I never will be. He threw the most extravagant openings for his artists, and I attended several. A little collegial schmoozing, you could say. His gallery was only a few blocks from mine. Champagne, caviar, oysters. Only the best. But the parties in the gallery were nothing compared to the private parties he threw in his loft. These were unbelievable. I only got invited to one, but it was spectacular: flowers everywhere, fabulous food, witty entertaining guests, movie stars, politicians, all the glitterati.

"Really, he had it all. Lovely stone cottage in the country, winter residence in San Miguel de Allende. He also had good taste. Make that exceptional taste. The paintings he owned personally in his loft were to die for." He paused. "Actually that is an entirely inappropriate expression considering what happened, forgive me. But he had a couple of Rothkos in the dining area of the loft that I would have given my eyeteeth for.

"Unfortunately he also had a few weaknesses. One in my mind was that he was just a little too successful. This may sound like sour grapes; I mean no one is ever likely to call my gallery a huge success, but when you're in the business we are, you have to be careful not to accept stolen goods. It's easy enough to do, and it is done. You and I both know that. You know that when you're buying antiques in the East, for example, you have to make sure that they are not national treasures, that they have an export permit." I nodded.

"It's easy enough to be fooled, of course. I recall when I was collecting for the museum, someone brought me some very exceptional silver pieces. Very old, Persian, about thirteenth century. I was desperate to add them to the collection. You know the rules as well as I do. Canada is a signatory to various UNESCO conventions on trade in art and artifacts, and particular agreements with various countries, and it was therefore necessary for me to ensure that these objects had left Persia, or Iran, before Canada signed the agreement with that country.

"I asked the person who had brought the objects for that proof. The person was not asking for money, incidentally, which is just as well because the museum, in fact most museums, have no acquisitions budgets anymore, and they rely on donations. The person merely wanted a tax receipt for them. Easy enough to do. This person—who shall remain nameless—showed me some documents that indicated that the pieces had been in New York in the late 1950s, which technically meant that we could accept them. But you and I both know that all kinds of stuff came out of Iran when the Shah was deposed, and a lot of the old, wealthy families hightailed it out of the country with the family treasures. I decided in all conscience I had to do some more checking. I did, and in a way I'll forever regret it, because I found that the objects had been in Iran until after the Shah left in 1979, and that the New York documentation was false. I could have accepted the counterfeit proof. If it ever came out, which it probably wouldn't, anyone would have thought I'd just been fooled. But I didn't. I know I did the right thing, but it was not an easy thing to do.

"I tell you all this only by way of saying that I always had the impression that Smythson wouldn't have gone that extra mile to check. That's all I'm saying. Maybe it went further than that, and he knowingly handled illegal goods, but I have absolutely no first-hand knowledge that this was the case. When I went to his apartment for that party, some of the objects I saw there—really, really exquisite—were things I wasn't sure he should have had. I couldn't prove anything, of course, and I didn't even try. Live and let live, you know. But after that evening, whenever I shook his hand, I had the feeling I'd been slimed.

"This is getting to be a long story. And now the part I'm sure you will remember. Smythson had at least two other weaknesses: cocaine and beautiful young men."

He hesitated for a second or two. "We've never discussed it, but I assume you may have noticed I'm gay," he said.

"Sure," I said.

"Well, Smythson had a bit of a reputation in the gay community. How do I put this delicately? He liked the rough stuff. He did the whole bathhouse thing. In the end he was found with his pants down, literally. The police were not too forthcoming on the details, but I gather it was pretty gory. The theory was that he'd taken the wrong beautiful young man home. There was lots of cocaine in his blood too, so the other theory was that it was a drug deal gone bad."

"I do recall now," I exclaimed. "It was much in the news for a couple of days, but I don't recall hearing they caught whoever did the deed."

"They never did. I have a theory, of course, of my own. I think it could have been either the drugs or the sex. But I also think it could have been the art, and, being a member of the gay community myself, I think the police leapt to the conclusion they preferred. Not that they didn't have reason to reach that conclusion. He'd been in trouble before, possession of drugs, not selling, and he got off on a technicality, but the record was there. But I've always felt that the bias was there too. In other words, it was a prominent gay man, so it had to be sex and drugs, if you see what I'm saying, so they didn't look at anything else. And maybe the hint of an idea that he'd gotten what he deserved.''

"I don't suppose one of the investigating officers was named Lewis,'' I said sarcastically.

"I don't know,'' Sam said. "Why do you ask?''

I told him about my conversations with Sergeant Lewis, and about his elliptical way of speaking and his insinuations. "It's not so much what he says as how he says it that bothers me,'' I said. "He thinks Alex is guilty of something, but he never comes out with it.''

"I can imagine your Lewis fellow doing the investigation into Smythson's murder.'' Sam paused, then leaned forward in the way I'd described Lewis and said, "Bit of a *poufter*, was he?''

"Which bathhouse *exactly*?'' I countered.

"*Precisely* how much cocaine?'' Sam said.

I smiled at him. "You've cheered me up, Sam, as you always do, even though you were making a serious point here. Thanks for your help.''

He looked at me. "I don't suppose you can tell me why you were asking about Smythson.''

"I'm not sure exactly. Smythson was supposed to be the recipient of something that ended up in my shop and now has gone missing. I'm sure it's a coincidence, but I was just wondering. The stuff wasn't picked up in customs, which could have been because he was dead by the time it arrived. It was sent a little over two years ago if I recall.''

"He died around that time, I'd think,'' Sam said. "Was it something old? An antiquity? I always thought he might be in the illegal antiquities market.''

I described the vase to him. "It was a replica," I added.

"Are you sure?" he said.

"I think so. It had *hecho en Peru* etched in the clay on the bottom, and there was a card with it that clearly identified it as such."

"Sounds fairly definitive," he said. He looked at his watch. "My goodness, I have to run. I actually have a customer who made an appointment to come in. Can you imagine? A real customer." He laughed and shook my hand, and we went our separate ways. He'd given me a lot to think about.

On my way back home I stopped in at the hospital to try to see Alex. This time I persuaded the nurse that I was Alex's stepniece and should be allowed in to see him. They told me his condition was now considered stable, and while he had suffered some memory loss, he was reasonably alert. I edged past the policeman at the door and tiptoed into the room.

He was asleep, I thought, and for a minute or two I stood just watching him. He looked so pale, and frail, and small. Alex is not a large man, but he has always seemed larger than life to me. He's not young; he retired a few years ago, but he has such energy and he is interested in absolutely everything. In the early days of my divorce, when I first moved into the neighborhood, he took me under his wing. He specializes in lost souls, I believe, and at the time I was clearly one of them. I hated to see him looking so frail and so old.

He stirred. "Lara," he exclaimed. "How good of you to come!"

"I would have come sooner," I said. "They wouldn't let me in. I've told them I'm your stepniece," I added.

He grinned. It was wonderful to see it. "I've always felt we were related in some way."

"Alex," I said. "What happened?"

"I'm not doing all that well at remembering," he said slowly. "The police have been here. They asked me a lot of questions. I can recall locking the front door at eight, and then going into the office to close things up." He paused for a moment, and I was afraid he was dozing off again.

"Your keys," he said finally. "I can remember seeing your keys on the desk, and realizing you'd forgotten them. Then . . . what did I do then?" he asked softly, almost to himself.

"I phoned. I phoned Moira's salon to see if they knew where you had gone, but it was closed. I thought you'd discover the keys soon enough, so I propped the back door open with the chair, so you could get in. I was afraid that I wouldn't hear you in the office, and I thought it would be okay to leave the back door open.

"I was wrong," he said. "I vaguely recall thinking I had heard something in the showroom, and I can recall getting up to take a look. I'm afraid," he said very quietly, "I'm afraid I remember nothing after that, as hard as I try."

"That's okay, Alex. It explains how whoever it was got in."

"Was a lot taken?"

"Hardly anything at all."

"Then why?"

"Good question, Alex," I said. "Perhaps something scared him or them off before they could take anything." I wondered if he knew about the body. I was determined not to be the one to tell him, at least not while he was in such bad shape. He began to nod off again, and the nurse came and signaled to me that it was time to go.

As I turned to leave, he stirred again. "I'm afraid I have let you down very badly, Lara," he said. "You entrusted the shop to my care, and I have let you down." His hands trembled as he spoke.

"Alex!" I exclaimed. "Don't you ever think that. Ever. It was not your fault. And I promise you we'll be back in business in no time. We are not quitters, you and I. So get better and get out of this place, as fast as you can. We have lots to do."

He smiled very slightly. "No, we're not quitters. I'll be back at work in no time," he said.

I'd thought then of telling him about Lizard, of asking him if there was anything I should know about the events of that evening that he hadn't already told me, whether or not he'd ever been in Peru. In the end, though, I decided that you have to trust both your friends and your instincts. I could not bring myself to consider that he was even remotely connected to any of the recent events.

"Need anything? Anything I can bring you?" was all I said, but he had already fallen asleep. I limped out of the room as quietly as I could.

I had much to think about that evening. Through a set of rather silly circumstances, I'd become the owner of a box of objects, sent in the first instance by someone by the name of Edmund Edwards in New York to A. J. Smythson in Toronto. Smythson hadn't received it, perhaps because he was dead. And he was murdered, possibly because of his lifestyle, but also possibly because he may have dealt in the black market in antiquities.

The box had made its way to Molesworth & Cox, where it went on the auction block. Two people went after it, had wanted it very, very badly: Lizard and Clive. I got it, they didn't. Lizard, if I was reading Lewis's questions correctly, was from Peru. Lizard might even, I surmised, be a customs agent, since Lewis had mentioned that as well. That meant it was not the snuff bottle he was after, but the replica pre-Columbian vase, now missing, and possibly the ear spool, also a replica, I had hidden away at home.

But Lizard was dead. Murdered. That left Clive. I knew he wanted the snuff bottle, but hadn't he raised his offer considerably if I'd throw in the rest of the contents of the box? And hadn't the peanut disappeared about the time Clive had been in the shop? I might not be prepared to think ill of Alex, but the same did not hold true about Clive.

I brooded on that for a while. The fact is, though, that in those moments when I'm being brutally honest with myself, which I have as infrequently as the next person, I know that Clive is not quite the ogre I make him out to be and that it is a lot easier to be angry with him than to think about why our marriage failed. I know that the reason he lost interest in the shop early in our marriage, the reason he fought me so fiercely for it during our divorce, and why he forced me to sell it to give him half the money, and maybe even why he'd set himself up in business right across the street was that he always felt I'd loved the shop more than I'd loved him. And maybe I had.

Clive might be up to stealing the odd customer away, but he would not have murdered to get something. Not ever. The fact that he had been interested in the box was, I decided, immaterial. Something much more sinister than Clive was capable of was going on.

On a more mundane level, even with Alex and Clive out of the equation, cleared of any wrongdoing as I was convinced they would be, as long as there was a police investigation under way, my insurance company was not going to pay up, and if they didn't pay soon, we would go bankrupt.

If that happened, my dear friend Alex would never forgive himself, no matter what I said to him. I took the gold and turquoise ear ornament out of my bag and, unwrapping it carefully, turned it over and over again in my hand. It was the only lead I had, that and a letter from a gallery in New York written to a dead man.

Well, I thought, I told Alex I'm not a quitter, and I'm not. I was not going to sit around waiting for the worst to happen. I picked up the telephone and called Rob's house. I got the answering machine. I told it everything I knew to this point: the stuff about Smythson, my silly bid at the auction, my lingering feelings about Clive, my anxiety about Alex and the store, and how I was afraid my words were being used to condemn him, my curiosity about the vase, the peanut, everything. And as the beeps sounded when my time on the answering machine was running out, I said how sorry I was about the position I had put Rob in. I wondered if he'd hear that part before the machine cut me off. I hoped he would.

Then I picked up the telephone again and called American Airlines.

Spider

THE BURIAL CEREMONY *is soon to begin. All is in readiness. The Great Warrior's body is prepared, clothed in a shirt woven of the finest white cotton, his face painted red, color of blood, color of life.*

In the huaca, the chamber is completed, walls lined with adobe bricks, the thick boards of the coffin floor already in place.

The others who will go with him on his journey, the women, dead long ago and bone brittle in their shrouds and cane coffins, are taken from the palace. Soon they will be placed in the tomb.

The fishermen and the sea lion warriors have come in from the sea with their spondylus shells and their offering vessels. They assemble at the foot of the huaca, in the great courtyard, surrounded by the murals of a thousand other ceremonies.

The procession of llamas, backpacks laden with

conch shells, draws near. Iguana awaits them. The plumes of his bird headdress shimmer, his lizard face and almond eyes are watchful.

The Decapitator also waits.

5

I WAS IN Manhattan before ten the next morning. I'd left a brief note for Moira, walked out to Parliament Street, and hailed a cab for the airport. There I'd taken all the money the bank machine would let me have, not nearly enough as it turned out, and caught the first flight of the day to New York, boarding at the last minute and feeling like a fugitive, which I guess I was in some ways.

I suppose, looking back on what I did from that moment on, that a stranger could be forgiven for thinking that I, not Alex, was the one with the serious bump on the head. Be that as it may, irrationally or not, I did the only thing I could think of. I went to find the origin of the box of objects that I was convinced was at the root of all my problems. I had packed only a small carry-on bag, fully intending to be back in Toronto by early evening, before anyone, most particularly Sergeant Lewis, had noticed I was gone.

Ancient Ways Gallery was located on the West

Side, close to the American Museum of Natural History. Cautiously I had the cab drive past it (there was no sign of life at the place at this hour) and then let me out at the museum. I'd called from the airport: A recording told me gallery hours were noon to six Tuesday to Friday, noon to five on Saturday. Closed Sunday and Monday.

Partly to kill time, and partly to do research—I was not, after all, in Manhattan to take in the sights—I went into the museum and headed for the Americas section.

The card had said that the stolen pot was a pre-Columbian replica. That covered a lot of territory. Even the words "made in Peru" on it didn't narrow it down completely. The only Peruvian pre-Columbian civilization I knew anything about was the Inca, but I knew enough to understand that there had been lots of civilizations in that part of the world before the Inca empire had its heyday. I worked my way quickly through the Mexican and Central American sections, pausing just long enough to confirm that the pot, as I remembered it, didn't fit there. The artifacts from South American cultures were located at the end of the section.

It took about an hour, but eventually I had a name I felt reasonably comfortable with. Just to make sure, I took a quick cab ride across Central Park to the Metropolitan Museum of Art and took in the art of the Americas section there as well. By the time I'd seen what there was to see there, I was convinced I was on the right track.

I went to the museum bookstore, purchased a couple of books on the subject, and headed for the cafe for a coffee, a muffin, and a quick read. I had what I wanted.

Moche.

The Moche, I learned, were a people who ruled over the north coast of Peru during the first 500 years of the Common Era, long before the Inca had ever been heard from. The empire stretched from the Piura Valley in the north to the Huarmey Valley in the south, from a capital city which is now called Cerro Blanco. The Moche culture is known in archaeological circles for its engineering feats, primarily the building of fabulous adobe pyramids and lengthy canals which brought water from the mountains to the coastal desert where their empire was located; its political mastery of a large area as one of the first definable states in that part of the world; and artistically for masterpieces of craftsmanship in pottery and metals.

There was now absolutely no question in my mind about it. I had seen with my own eyes pottery that matched the stolen pot in style and execution, and ear flares of gold and turquoise that were, to my untrained eye, identical in style to the little ear flare I had in my handbag. And if I needed further corroboration, I had it. The books I had purchased showed photographs of a magnificent necklace of gold and silver beads, each bead in the shape of a perfect peanut.

As carefully as I could, I took the little ear flare out of my bag to take a better look at it. The little gold man with his gold scepter stared back at me mutely. I turned the piece over and over again in my hand. "So what do you have to say for yourself?" I softly asked the little man.

In my business, you learn to spot fakes. You have to. The point is that you can take as many courses about antiques as you like, and I have taken several, but when it comes right down to it, you just have to develop a sixth sense about objects. I've learned to look at furniture, for example, to look at the metal hardware, the way the boards are planed, the kinds of nails and other fastenings that are used. But a really good craftsman can fool even a museum curator, and in the end you rely on your gut on some of the things you see. Sometimes, even after you've checked out everything you can think of, objects still just don't feel right, and, taught by an expert, my friend Sam Feldman, I've learned to go with this feeling.

Before he opened his own gallery, Sam was a museum conservator. He told me that in his early days at the institution, a mere neophyte, he'd gotten the feeling a particular artifact, the centerpiece in an exhibit, was a fake. He tried to tell the curator of the exhibit and was roundly chastised. On his last day of employment at the museum, now a noted expert in his field, he went back to the curator and told him again. Once again Sam was told he was wrong, but he found on his next casual visit to the museum that the offending piece had been removed from the exhibit. "You see!" he told his students. "I was right. They will never admit it, but I was right. That's why you go with your gut."

This time the process was reversed. This object was supposed to be a fake. Maybe it wasn't.

The piece looked in pretty good condition for something that was at least 1500 years old. Generally I would have said it looked way too good. The gold was nice and shiny, and overall the piece was in very good repair. But there were places where the gold, probably hammered on, was worn away, and the turquoise inlay was not of a uniform color. Carefully I edged a fingernail into one of the cracks between the inlays. There was dirt, but I wasn't sure that proved anything. A good forger would know enough to rub a little dirt into the piece.

The question was, where had my little friend been for 1500 years? If he'd been well cared for in a museum, that might explain his relatively pristine condition. Or if he'd been hidden away somewhere, in a tomb for example. This might explain it. The Moche lived in the coastal desert, and arid conditions would limit corrosion.

For a while I just sat there looking at him. He was really sweet, if it's possible to say such a thing about a little gold man on a pre-Columbian ear flare. His eyes bulged out of carefully cut eye sockets, and around his neck he had a necklace, ceremonial I would have thought, made up of tiny heads: owls most likely. Each of the beads had been made separately, then strung together, so they moved when you touched them. The scepter could easily be removed from his hand. His sturdy little legs showed muscle markings that were quite extraordinary. Under his nose was an ornament in the shape of a crescent, and it too moved when you touched it. I thought you could easily imagine the body under the garments, and that my little man could even be said to have a personality.

I reached my conclusion, and I couldn't really explain why I hadn't done so before this, except, of course, that I'd purchased it from a reputable auction house. The point was, no one could afford to make such a little masterpiece these days, replica or not. No one could afford to forge it, either. And even if someone had the patience and time and resources to do so, most of us couldn't afford to buy it. The vase and the peanut might or might not be genuine. I didn't have them anymore, so I couldn't say. This little man, however, was genuine Moche, and Edmund Edwards had some explaining to do.

Before I left the museum, I went into the gift shop and bought a large pin in a Celtic pattern. I asked the saleswoman for a box—a big box—for it, saying it was a gift. She was very obliging in finding the right size box. On the steps outside, I put the brooch on my shirt and took the little gold man, carefully wrapped in tissue, and put him into the box with the card identifying it as a reproduction Celtic brooch. It wouldn't fool anyone who knew anything whatsoever, but I was getting nervous walking around with this potentially very valuable antiquity in my purse.

By ten to twelve I was in position across the street and down a bit from Ancient Ways. It was a very warm August day in Manhattan, and it felt as if rain, perhaps a thunderstorm, would soon blow through. About five minutes to noon, an older man, grey of hair and unsteady of gait, shuffled down the street and opened the security gate with some difficulty. He had on way too many clothes for the heat of the day, as older people often do. It looked from that distance as if he had seriously arthritic hands and knees. He opened the door, but closed it immediately behind him, and the closed sign remained hanging in the door for several minutes.

Finally, at about twenty after twelve, he came and unlocked the front door, and turned the sign around to show the place was open for business. I crossed the street and entered.

Even by my standards of housekeeping, which let's

just say will never earn me a Nancy Neatness Award, the place was a mess. The carpet was old and worn, and quite frankly dirty. The desk at the back, where the old man sat, was covered in junk, papers strewn haphazardly about, coffee stains on his invoice book and everything else. He fit right in: His jacket looked as if it had gravy stains on the lapel, and his hair, what was left of it, was unkempt and unclean. Under his jacket, he wore a grey knit vest, a moth hole prominently featured. As I stood there, the phone rang, and the old man pushed stacks of paper around to find it. By the time he'd located it, on the floor under the desk, it had stopped ringing.

The merchandise was impressive enough, what you could see of it. Glass cases lined the walls, each of them packed with treasures. On top of each of the cases were various objects too large to be placed within: some very impressive African sculptures, including what looked to be a Benin bronze figure, and some really lovely wood carvings. There was no particular theme that I could see, except that everything was old, very old, and to my eye at least, authentic. In the middle of the room was a large table, also piled high with merchandise.

I idly picked up a small figure, a lovely little blue faience statue about six inches high, and had a closer look. It was, I knew, a *ushabti*, a representation of a deceased person, probably one of some importance, that would have been placed in an Egyptian tomb many hundreds if not thousands of years ago, to be a servant of sorts to the deceased. It is always fascinating to hold a few thousand years of history in the palm of your hand, but one always has to ask the question in these circumstances: Is it legal? I turned the figure over. On the back were tiny little numbers in black ink: museum catalogue number, I thought. Possibly deaccessioned, possibly not.

I turned toward the desk to see the proprietor's eyes, almost hidden behind thick, thick glasses, focused on me. On the wall behind him were a couple of old prints and right over his head an extraordinary blade mounted on black fabric and framed in gold. It was not a knife as we know it, with a thin blade and handle. Rather it was one piece, almost bell-shaped, with a thick handle that led to a crescent-shaped blade. It was about six inches high, gold in color, with a string of tiny turquoise beads threaded through a hole in the handle. It was, I was almost certain, a *tumi*, a ceremonial blade used by the ancient peoples of Peru, perhaps for sacrificial purposes.

"Hi," I said, moving over to the desk. "Are you Edmund Edwards?"

"Who wants to know?" he asked irritably.

I handed him my business card. I don't know why I did that, exactly, other than that I felt I had to establish my credentials before proceeding. It was a gesture, however, that in retrospect I would come to regard with profound regret. The old man looked at the card very carefully, then peered back at me. "I'm a dealer from Toronto," I said, just in case he was unable to read the card. "I'm in New York on a buying trip for a client of mine, who shall, if you don't mind, remain nameless."

"Anything in particular you're interested in?" he asked, apparently satisfied.

"My client collects pre-Columbian art almost exclusively," I replied.

"Big field. Hard to get. Expensive," he replied.

"Money is no object here," I said. He opened a small card case of the recipe box variety and thumbed laboriously through it, peering at each card myopically. The box was overstuffed, and at one point, as he tried to pull a card up, several of them flew up and scattered across the desk. Finally, he arose from his chair with some difficulty and shuffled over to the table in the middle of the room. There did not appear to be any particular system for cataloguing what he had, but he seemed to know where everything was. He started to look under the table, leaning heavily on the side of it, but wasn't up to the task.

"Under there," he grunted. "In the middle. The stone. Part of a stela from Copán. Nice piece."

I bent down and pulled the object out from under the table. It was a very heavy stone piece, beautifully carved, and it was probably what he said it was, I decided: Maya, from Copán. I also decided that he shouldn't have had it.

"Very nice," I said, "but . . . "

"Or this," he said, opening one of the glass cabinets and removing a splendid terra-cotta of an Aztec god, also probably authentic.

"Very nice as well," I said. "However, my client has a specific interest. Moche. Anything Moche: terracotta, metals. Do you ever come across that kind of thing?"

"Very hard to get," he mumbled.

"Well, yes," I said. "That's why I'm here. A. J. Smythson sent me. From Toronto. Do you remember him? Anton James Smythson?"

The phone rang again, and the old man started shuffling around looking for it.

"It's on the floor," I said. "Under the desk." He

just looked at me. "The phone," I said. Light dawned, and the old man leaned over. The phone stopped ringing as he grasped it and wheezed into the old headset. The caller had evidently hung up again. Once again he turned to a second card box and started rifling through it. I decided he was not looking for objects this time, he was checking the name Smythson. He paused at a card. This is hopeless, I thought.

"How is Anton?" he asked at last.

Oh, dear, I thought, what now? "Not quite as peppy as he used to be," I replied.

"Not many of us are," he said. That was true, of course, but most of us were a little more energetic than A. J. Smythson at this very moment, even Edmund Edwards.

"No, I guess not," I replied. We looked at each other. Already I knew more about Edwards than I had a few moments ago: He wasn't a close friend of Smythson. Sam Feldman had told me Smythson's friends called him A. J., not Anton. "Anton told me you were once able to get him some Moche. You mailed him a couple of pieces, three actually, in with some other stuff, a couple of years ago."

The old man looked very wary now. "Don't know what you're talking about," he said. "It's illegal. Moche. Can't take it out of Peru."

"As I said, that's why I'm here," I said, giving him what I hoped was a conspiratorial look. "How about that tumi?" I said, pointing to the blade on the wall behind the desk. "Is that Moche, or later, Inca, maybe?" I asked, trying to sound somewhat knowledgeable.

He looked me up and down. The phone rang again. "Come back later," he ordered. "About three."

There did not seem to be much else I could do. "The floor," I called back to him as I left the shop. "The phone is on the floor."

It's not often I would comment on the freshness of the air in New York, but after a few minutes in that shop, even the oppressively heavy air of the city felt good. As I turned back to look at the shop, I could see the old man at the door. He changed the sign to closed and locked the door behind him. I watched for a few minutes, but the closed sign remained firmly in place. Either he kept the world's shortest business hours, or I'd upset Edmund Edwards.

It was by now about one P.M., and I had a couple of hours to kill. I turned back toward Central Park West, determined to find somewhere to have lunch, in the park perhaps. I found a bench to perch on for a few minutes while I figured out where to go. As I sat there I watched a middle-aged woman dressed up in what appeared to be a Viking costume, a long plait of blond hair tumbling from a helmet with plastic horns on it, harangue passersby. Some Norse cult apparently. She was suggesting that we repent our sins, most notably by offering her money, I gathered, so that we'd all go up to heaven when the end of the world, now very imminent, came upon us. How nice, I thought, just like home.

As I idly looked about me, I was very surprised to see the old man shuffling across the street. He hadn't come from the direction I would have expected, which probably only meant there was a back door to his shop. Cautiously I arose from the seat and, keeping well back, began to follow him.

As we both shuffled along, I began to feel really silly. It was difficult for me to move slowly enough that I didn't catch up with him, and he stopped frequently and looked behind him, forcing me to turn and pretend I was going the other way. The only thing that was saving me, I thought, was his vision, which judging from his glasses, which looked like the proverbial pop bottle bottoms, was not very good.

After a block or two, he turned into the park, and I did the same. It was easier here. There were lots of people just strolling along, and the trees afforded me some cover. Finally the old man stopped and sat down on a bench. He took a bag from his pocket and started throwing crumbs in the general direction of a couple of birds.

Wonderful, I thought. Here I am in Manhattan, one of the most fabulous cities in the world, and instead of lunching somewhere elegant, I'm hiding behind a tree, watching an old man with bad eyes and flat feet feed pigeons. I felt like a fool. What I really should be doing, I knew, was flying home before the Toronto police figured out I had left.

I started to leave and indeed had traveled several yards in the opposite direction before something made me turn back. I saw that someone had come over to the old man and, standing with his back to me, was leaning over to talk to him. I wondered if this was a coincidence, or if the old man had arranged to meet someone. And if this meeting was planned, had it anything to do with my visit to the shop?

Suddenly the visitor straightened up and turned to look around him. I pulled back to where I hoped I couldn't be seen. What I saw made me at once nervous, but also certain I was onto something. It was the man who'd reminded me of a spider when I'd last seen him, lurking behind a potted palm at Molesworth &

Cox and watching as Lizard, now deceased, had tried to buy the box of what was supposed to have been junk, but which might have been almost priceless treasure. If the Spider was here, and talking to Edmund Edwards, a return visit to Ancient Ways was definitely called for.

I found a cafe for a bit of lunch and did a little more reading on the Moche while I waited. Shortly before three I was back in position across the road from the gallery. The closed sign was still in the door.

About three-thirty, the closed sign hadn't moved, and I was beginning to get impatient in the oppressive air. I walked across the street and tried the door, but it was locked. I couldn't see inside. I decided to take a bit of a walk to try to find the back entrance, which I was certain must exist because of where I'd seen Edwards, and eventually found an alleyway. I'd counted the doorways from the corner, so I was able to conclude which building was Ancient Ways. All the others had gates that were securely locked, but the gate to the back door of the gallery was slightly ajar. I walked in. The back door was closed but not locked, and I knocked a couple of times before opening it and calling inside. "Is there anyone here? Mr. Edwards?" I called out.

I stepped inside. I was in a tiny vestibule, beside a flight of stairs leading to the second floor, the wall of which blocked my view of the desk at the back of the showroom. I noticed a security system panel inside the door, and a red light was flashing. Did that mean I'd just tripped the alarm? If I had, it was a silent one. Indeed, the store was eerily silent, considering the noise of the busy city outside. I could hear an old clock ticking away, and as I looked toward the window in the front, dust motes swirled in the light.

I listened very carefully. There was no other sound. How careless to go out and leave the back door open like this, I thought. There were some quite lovely pieces hidden amongst the junk, and it struck me that leaving the back door open was an even poorer idea in New York than it was in Toronto, and I knew first-hand just what a bad idea it was in Toronto. "Mr. Edwards?" I called out again. It occurred to me that perhaps he was a little deaf, so I called out even louder. Nothing.

I took three or four steps forward into the show-room.

What I saw then I will never forget as long as I live, a ghastly little tableau that will remain with me forever: Edmund Edwards was dead, throat slit. Blood had spattered across the desk and onto the carpet in front of it. An overturned teacup had spilled its contents, and the tea and the blood had mingled, creating little rivers of brownish pink all over the desk. There was no need to wonder about the weapon that had been used for this atrocity. The gold *tumi,* wrenched from its mounting, was gone.

I felt as if I'd been standing there for some time, unable to tear my eyes away from the awful sight, but it was probably only for a few seconds. I was pulled back to reality by the tiniest of sounds: a very slight creak over my head, as if someone, upstairs, had shifted his weight slightly. I stood very quietly, then heard it again, this time closer to the stairs. I ran across the room, unlocked the front door, and dashed into the street, footsteps now pounding down the stairs behind me.

I flagged a cab and leapt in.

"Bit of a hurry, lady?" the driver said. "Where to?"

The truth was, I didn't have a clue. I got him to take me to the Plaza Hotel, thinking in my overheated brain that it would be unthinkable for anyone to kill me in the Plaza Hotel, and ran into the lobby, cutting through it and out the side door by the Oyster Bar in my idea of a diversionary tactic. Then for an hour or two, I just tried to blend into the crowd.

An observation I would make about New York is that you can always tell the natives from the visitors. I don't know what it is, a way of walking, perhaps, or more likely a style of dressing. Moira would know. She has the kind of job that requires knowing what's in and what's not. Mine isn't, which is just as well, because under normal circumstances I wouldn't know haute mode from a hot fudge sundae. I just know that New Yorkers look like New Yorkers, and the rest of us don't.

Whatever the reason, I felt that I stuck out like a sore thumb. I'd brought only a change of underwear, a cosmetics bag with a few essentials, and a clean shirt, which I changed into in the ladies' room in the Trump Tower, the elegant sound of a grand piano and a waterfall tinkling in the background. Then I bought a New York Yankees baseball cap from a street vendor, and pulled it over my head. I wore my sunglasses even though it was now raining. Haute mode indeed.

I realized after a couple of hours of this that I really had to pull myself together and think what I would do. A baseball cap and sunglasses would hardly be sufficient cover, and obviously I had to go somewhere. Home was my first choice. There was one small problem with that. I knew I'd left my business card with

Edmund Edwards, now deceased. I tried visualizing the desk again, to see if I could recall if the card was where I left it. I couldn't remember, the rivers of blood blotting everything else out. If it was still there, and the police found it, I could be implicated in the murder. Even if I could talk my way out of that one, the Spider—if indeed it was he who had killed the old man, and I was quite convinced that he had—would have my name too. Perhaps the Spider already knew it, I thought, from Molesworth & Cox. They were known to be discreet, but it wouldn't take much to read the list of auction attendees at the front desk. I'd done it myself more than once. But of course he knew it, I thought. He'd found the shop already: Who else could have killed Lizard?

The upshot was I couldn't stay there and I couldn't go home. I knew that the police, Rob in particular, would try to protect me as a witness to this horrific event. But the Spider, I was quite sure, was a truly brutal and determined killer. And not just brutal, I thought, although he was that. I thought of the pathetic body of Lizard, hands tied behind his back, looking as if he'd begged his executioner to spare him. And Edwards, a shortsighted, rather befuddled old man, whose throat had been slit with a ceremonial knife. To my mind, the Spider was someone who enjoyed killing. He knew where I worked, and could easily find out where I lived. Even if he worked alone, which I very much doubted, the police couldn't protect me forever. That pretty well left me one destination, if I hoped to figure out enough about the situation in which I found myself to extricate myself from it. There was, however, one stop along the way. I raced to the curb and hurled myself in front of another cab—

perhaps I was beginning to look like a New Yorker at last—and jumped inside.

"The airport, JFK," I gasped. "As fast as you can."

Once there, I checked the departures and approached a counter. "Mexico City. I'd like a ticket for the next flight to Mexico City," I said. After all, what good are old loves, if you can't call upon them in a crisis?

6

IF ANY ONE of my acquaintances would know how to shake a tail, police or otherwise, it was the former love of my life, Mexican archaeologist Lucas May. Make that Congressman Lucas May.

One quick phone call was all it took to persuade him to meet me at the Museo Nacional de Antropologia e Historia, a place we'd frequented many times on our trips to Mexico City when we'd been together. We'd go to see the exhibits, then find ourselves some lunch to eat in the park surrounding the building.

I cut through the strikingly handsome courtyard and, picking the Maya section, began to look carefully at the exhibits, as if I were a real tourist. I felt his presence immediately. It's amazing really, how you can do that, when you've been as close as he and I once were.

"Hi," I said, turning around.

He looked completely different. I hadn't seen him for almost two years, not since he'd dumped me—

there is no other word for it—to pursue a political career, getting himself elected to the Mexican Congress. Then he'd been an archaeologist, his hair too long to be fashionable, and dressed almost always in black jeans and T-shirts, wearing his work boots most of the time. Now he wore a grey tropical-weight suit, white shirt, and grey and silver tie. His hair was cut short, and he looked very businesslike and almost a little prosperous, maybe just a tiny bit heavier than he'd been when I knew him. He took my arm and led me out of the museum and into the park.

"I'm in a bit of a jam, Lucas," I said.

"I know," he said. "They've called already."

"They?"

"The Canadian authorities. Fellow by the name of Sergeant Robert something or other I can't pronounce. RCMP."

"Luczka," I said, pronouncing it Looch-ka. He nodded. "How did he find me before I even got here?"

"He didn't say. Did you use a credit card for the ticket?" I nodded. "Bad idea," he said.

"Yes, but there was this small problem called lack of cash. I know it's my turn to treat lunch," I said, "but I'm trying to be frugal, being a fugitive and all." He went and bought us enchiladas from a stand.

"Tell me about it," he said.

I took the little gold man out of my bag and handed it to him.

He looked at it carefully. "Funny," he said finally. I just looked at him. If there was something funny about all this, I'd be more than glad to hear it.

"Funny how it happens," he said again. "Didn't know much of anything about this stuff," he went on, "until a couple of weeks ago. I read about it in an archaeology newsletter. Then a day or two ago, an old friend, a fellow archaeologist, mentioned it too." He looked at me. "Ear spool. Moche, I would think," he said. He looked at it again. "Real Moche, that is."

"I figured," I said.

"These are, apparently, much in demand on the black market. A pair of ear spools like this sold for about $150,000 U.S. not so long ago in Asia, according to this friend of mine. It's illegal to take Moche artifacts out of Peru," he added.

"I figured that too. But obviously someone did it. Not very successfully perhaps. It ended up in a box of junk at an auction. But someone did get it out of Peru." I told all that had happened. "I don't want to do anything that would put you in a bad position, Lucas. You're an important person now. But I need a new identity, and I need to get to Peru. I want to take the little Moche man back to Peru, and figure this all out. It's the only way I can think of to extricate myself from this situation."

He sat very quietly, looking off in the distance. As I watched him, I felt such a pang of regret. His hair had a lot more grey in it, and he looked so tired, and perhaps more than a little disillusioned, the exhaustion of a highly moral man in a line of work in a country not noted for its morality, I thought. I wanted to reach out and touch his face and stroke his hair and tell him everything would be all right. He'd always been such a crusader for the rights of the indigenous people of the Yucatán; he'd even, I was reasonably sure, been a member of a local guerrilla group operating out of the forests outside of Mérida where we'd met. But then he'd been persuaded to take the political route, to get himself elected, and to work for his people that way. Never one to do anything by halves, he'd told me he couldn't do that and maintain our relationship, and I'd been the part of his life that was sacrificed.

"This maybe is not working out as well as you'd hoped," I said hesitantly. "The life of a politician, I mean."

He just looked at me, then turned away again, his gaze focused on the treetops, and when he finally spoke again, his voice was bleak. "Perhaps not," he said. "I'm not making many friends, that's for sure. And the things you see sometimes..." His voice trailed off. I didn't probe anymore. The thing about Lucas was that he told you what he wanted to tell you. I'd learned to live with that.

"You were always very good about not asking me about my secret life," he said finally. "But I suppose you know I was not above a little resistance, shall we say, from time to time."

I waited.

"I really appreciate the fact that you didn't ask about it, and that you didn't try to argue with me when I told you our relationship had to end. I've deluded myself into thinking you would have regretted that decision," he said.

"You didn't delude yourself," I said. Actually I'd been more than a little upset with him.

"The thing is, when you do the kind of work I used to do, you have to have a plan. An escape plan, if you follow me."

"Lucas," I said. "You're in politics now. I don't want you to do anything that would compromise you."

He laughed, but it was a laugh with no humor in

it. "Compromise me? When I think of what I have seen some of my fellow elected representatives do! Helping someone on the run from the police is a minor indiscretion barely worth noticing, believe me," he said bitterly.

"Here," he said, taking an old silver coin out of his pocket. "Take this. I'll give you the money for the cab. Go to this address," he said, scribbling an address on a piece of paper, "and go to the flat on the main floor. There will be an old woman there. Show her the coin. She'll take care of you. Do whatever she tells you, even if you don't like the idea, okay? It will take a few days, but if you really want to go to Peru, we'll get you there."

"I know this is pushing it a little, but could you get me as close as possible to a place called Campina Vieja?" I asked.

He actually smiled slightly. "I'll do my best," he said.

He stood up. It was time to go. He walked me to the street and a cab stand, and gave the driver an address. I got into the cab. His black mood softening, he leaned in the back window and planted a gentle little kiss on my lips.

"If this political stuff doesn't work out," he said with a tired little smile, "I may need to leave Mexico in a hurry myself. I've heard Canada is good. Hard to get citizenship, though. Would you know a nice Canadian woman who'd marry me?"

"Maybe," I said. The cab pulled away. I didn't look back. Moira would be pleased.

• • •

Four days and nights I spent in a tiny room in the back of the building where the old woman lived. The building looked like any other in that part of town, distinguished only by the fading pastels, that had been chosen for the stucco, the color peeling under the hot sun. This building was pale aqua. I gave her the coin, as instructed, and after looking at both it and me very carefully, she led me up three flights of stairs, pulling her bent figure up each step, leaning heavily on the railing.

The room was small but adequate: a small bed, a desk and chair with one tiny lamp, a ceiling fan. The shutters were pulled against the heat of the day. There was a shower, for which I was grateful. The old lady did not speak to me, whether because she could not or would not, I do not know. But she saw to my comfort. A tray of food arrived regularly: fresh warm tortillas, always, and eggs or *sopa*, and cheese, sometimes a little wine or beer.

At night, before the little lamp was turned on, she pulled heavy dark curtains across in front of the shutters. No one was to know I was there. After I turned out the light, I opened the curtains and lay on the bed, watching through the cracks in the shutter, a soft pink glow which I think must have come from the neon sign of a cantina, because I heard music and voices and the clatter of dishes until very late at night.

The days and nights blurred together, the days known by the sunlight against the shutter, the night by the pink neon. Mainly I slept, exhausted, feeling safe for the first time in days, confident that neither the police nor the Spider would find me there. Sometimes I dreamt, though, and the horrible pictures of Edmund Edwards and Lizard hovered on the edges of my sleep.

Sometimes my dreams were of an arid desert, where bleached skeletons and blackened brush dotted the landscape, where no living thing could be seen.

On the second day a man came to see me. He told me to sit on the edge of the bed, and pulled the desk and the chair up to me, so that he could sit across from me. He turned the little lamp on my face and looked at me very carefully, turning my head one way and the other. He asked me to stand up and walk around. Then he got up and left, as suddenly and silently as he'd arrived.

He was back again the next night with another, a hunched over old man, a serape and hat making him indistinguishable, who stood out of the light in a corner. The first man pulled up the desk and chair as usual, but then took my handbag and emptied it onto the desk in front of us.

He went through everything in my purse, everything. He took my wallet and emptied it. He took the U.S. money and carefully divided it into two piles, putting half back on my side of the table and half in his pocket. "Credit cards," he said, and cut them up one at a time. "Passport," he said, then, "driver's license." These he didn't cut up, but tucked them away carefully in his pocket.

On the fourth night, the man arrived with his companion once again, but this time I knew who it was and smiled into the darkness in the corner. The first man handed me a package of hair color, and gestured for me to go into the bathroom and use it. In a few minutes my strawberry blond hair was brown. I stared at a stranger in the mirror.

He handed me a U.S. passport, and the picture in it looked more or less like the stranger in the mirror.

I had a driver's license, Kansas, and the exit part of a Mexican tourist card already filled in. I also had a wallet bulging with money I didn't recognize, Peruvian soles. And no credit cards.

Suddenly the man in the corner threw off his poncho. It was Lucas. "I have a message for you from a friend of yours, the policeman. Not a bad fellow really, for a policeman." He looked at me.

"He says that should I be speaking to you—I said I would be surprised if I did—I should tell you that you should come home. That he will do his best to straighten everything out. He also says to tell you Alex will be all right.

"We could get you home too, you know. Send you north rather than south."

"I don't think so," I said. "I've come this far, and I think I'll see it through."

"So you're still set on doing this." He sighed. I told him I couldn't really think what else to do, although I had a pang of doubt as I said it. He handed me a sealed envelope. "Do not open this," he said. "Give it to the person it is addressed to without opening it. It will serve as an introduction."

"Where will I find this person?" I asked.

"Just follow the instructions," he said. "You will find what you need to know, when you need to know it. We will get you to the land of the Moche. After that you are on your own. Can you do this?"

"I think so," I said "Can you find some way of telling Moira where I am? Without anyone else knowing, I mean?"

"Yes," he replied. "I will."

"Be careful," I said.

"I think I'm the one who's supposed to say that,"

he said, then he hugged me, pulled the robe back on, and disappeared into the darkness of the stairwell. I had a feeling I might never see him again.

The next morning the old woman handed me a packed suitcase, battered and covered in travel stickers, and then I was driven to the airport. I was told to go to a specific wicket at a specific airline and ask for Antonieta. She handed me a package. In it was a ticket for the next flight to Lima.

Just before I left, I called Clive's store, collect. I reasoned it was the last place anyone would expect me to call, and even if they traced it, I'd be long gone before they could do anything about it. I told Clive I'd be calling back in ten minutes and he was to get a move on, go down the street to Moira's salon and bring her to the phone. For once he did what I asked.

Moira wasted no time. "Heard from Lucas," she said. "I figured you'd find some way to call. This is what I've been able to worm out of Rob so far. The dead man in your storage room's name is, or was, Ramon Cervantes. Señor Cervantes worked for the government. A customs agent, as it turns out, just as you thought. He lived with his family, a wife and three children, in Callao," she continued.

"Where's that?" I interrupted.

"Suburb of Lima, I think. That's as much as I know."

"That's good," I said. "How's Alex?"

"Better. He's out of intensive care, but he still can't remember what happened that night. They're keeping him in the hospital, doing some tests, but I think the doctors are confident he'll recover."

"And the police? Are they still investigating Alex?"

"Alex, and you now too," she replied. "I'm trying to get that awful man Lewis off the case," she added.

"I knew he'd rue the day he got on the wrong side of you, Moira," I said, "but how are you going about this?"

"I've put Rob on it," she replied. "Told him what he needs to do."

"And how did you manage that?"

"I just told him that I considered him to be personally responsible for your disappearance, and that if anything happened to either you or Alex it would be on his head, that's all," she said. "Subtlety is, of course, my middle name."

I laughed, then the enormity of what I was about to do caught up with me.

"You may not hear from me for a while, Moira," I said. "I'm not sure where this will take me."

"I know. Just make sure I hear from you sometime," she said briskly. I guess you don't get to own the most successful salon in the city by being subtle, or sentimental.

Then I, no not I, Rebecca MacCrimmon cleared immigration and customs, and boarded the plane.

7

CARLA MONTOYA CERVANTES sits in the darkened room at the top of the stairs, shutters pulled against the light, her face puffy with tears. She is pretty in a soft way, a slight plumpness hinting at sensuality, eyes and hair dark against skin she shields from the sun in the belief that paleness appeals, rosebud lips held in an almost perpetual pout, except, that is, when she's angry, when her eyes narrow, and the pout flattens out into a thin, hard line.

And she is angry now. Such an ineffective man, that Ramon, no ambition, no drive to better himself or her. Way too old for her too. She needs someone with more energy. Papa told her not to marry Ramon. He warned her Ramon would never amount to anything, that she deserved better. But Ramon adored her, would do whatever she asked, and, when it came right down to it, what was she to do, with the first of three squalling babies on the way? There would have been more than three too, if she hadn't put her foot down, banishing him to the living room. Thank God her sister has taken the children for a few days. They are so noisy, needy. She must have silence, time to think.

What is she to do? He was ineffective to the end, Ramon, left her with the children and no prospects. There is Jorge, his brother, of course. She could marry him. What would that accomplish? More drive, more ambition perhaps, but still, not exactly the match of the century, is he? It's unfortunate Ramon saw her and his brother together, truly unfortunate, though why he should run off like that, to such a far-off place . . . For what? It was harmless enough.

Papa was right. She is meant for better things than this, this hovel, the smell of cooking from below, the smoke of rancid oil permeating everything, the furniture, her hair, her clothes; the children always crying, and the noise of the street, like the bad air, working its way through the cracks in the shutters. She should be living in Miraflores, or San Isidro, perhaps, just off embassy row. A little house with roses in the front yard. Pink, she thinks. Pink roses, the house clean and white and cool, the windows fronted by white wrought iron grillwork, delicate metal tendrils climbing a fence, just like the beautiful homes of Trujillo where she grew up. A nanny for the children.

So if not Jorge, what or whom? She will have to think of something, and soon. Señor Vargas, the landlord, despite his infatuation with her, is too much the businessman to let her stay for long without payment. She had better not open the door. She would kill Ramon, really she would, if he wasn't dead already. Taking all their money—her money, really, he would never have made the arrangements on his own—when they were just beginning to get ahead, with the promise of more to come. And flying off to Canada! How exactly is she to pay to have his body shipped back home? Maybe she'll leave him there. She won't wear black for him, either. It doesn't suit her. She's meant for prettier things. Papa told her.

She sighs. There is only one answer. She'll have to go and talk to the Man. She doesn't like him: There is something about him that frightens her. But what choice does she have? After all, he owes her, doesn't he? Without her pleading, Ramon would never have helped the Man with that little problem he had. Yes, that is the answer. She will go and see the Man.

The sun apparently does shine in Lima from time to time. I didn't see it. For about nine months of the year, the city is blanketed in a grey pall that consists of mist from the sea, the *garua,* and pollution from millions of cars and factories. It is a damp, gritty greyness that burns your throat and lungs and eyes, and oozes its way into your soul.

Lima also, to my eyes at least, has the air of a city besieged. Every building, every parking lot, is watched by at least one guard, some of them armed. Restaurants have guards to watch over patrons' cars while they dine; a home with even the slightest hint, a mere whiff of wealth, has a twenty-four-hour civilian guard. Children are escorted to and from school.

And there is something to fear, make no mistake about it. Terrorists, for example; internationally prominent, like Sendero Luminoso, the Shining Path, and another, named for an Inca leader, Tupac Amaru, responsible for the occasional bombings, hostage takings, and other acts of terrorism. But perhaps even more frightening than terrorists are the desperate, the millions of poor and unemployed who left their homes in the countryside to come to the city in search of a better life, only to find themselves worse off, by far, living in wretched shantytowns on the outskirts of the city, without water, sewage treatment, or electricity.

Perhaps to compensate, Limenos have painted their city the most astonishing hues, colors to banish the greyness and anxiety: sienna, burnt umber, cobalt, and the purest ultramarine, and shades the color of ice cream, soft pistachio, creamy peach, French vanilla, and café au lait.

The central square in every Peruvian town, and Lima is no exception, is called the Plaza de Armas. In Lima, the plaza is a striking yellow ochre broken only by the grey stone of the governor's palace and the intricately carved wood casement windows on the buildings surrounding the square. And like every Plaza de Armas, it is a hive of activity, filled with *ambulantes,* people who come in from the shantytowns to hawk candy and drinks on the sidewalks; money changers with their calculators and wads of bills, giggling schoolgirls weighing themselves, for a small fee, on scales on the corner; street cleaners dressed head to toe in brilliant orange, stooping and sweeping in an almost compulsive rhythm—the hustle and bustle of everyday life in the city.

A large statue of the Spaniard Francisco Pizarro on horseback once graced the center of the square. Spain, its lust for gold and empire unsated by successful conquests in the more northern Americas, sent Pizarro to bring the mighty Inca Empire to its knees, a stroke of history that earned him his position of honor in the Plaza de Armas. As the saying goes, *sic transit gloria mundi:* Pizarro's horse's rear faced the cathedral. The Church was not amused, and so Pizarro and his horse were relegated to a small side square just off one corner of the plaza. Now it is the inhabitants of the building that bears the conqueror's name and the patrons of the cafe at street level who get to look up the backside of Pizarro's horse.

I was in that cafe for what amounted to a job interview, unbelievable though that seemed to me. I was to meet someone by the name of Stephen Neal, archaeologist and former classmate of Lucas's. I'd spoken to him briefly on the telephone, and we'd arranged to meet. He sounded pleasant enough on the phone, but I had no idea what he looked like. To facilitate our meeting, he'd told me he had fair hair, what was left of it, and a beard. I had been about to tell him I was a strawberry blonde when I caught myself. "Brown," I'd told him, "my hair is brown." Being someone else required, I found, eternal vigilance.

Who was Rebecca MacCrimmon? I wondered. Did she really exist? If she did, did she look like me, or at least like the person—pale skin almost transparent against the dark brown hair—that I had really seen for the first time, stared at length at, in the mirror of the tiny, run-down but clean hotel off the Plaza San Martin? If she was a real person, was she still alive, her passport and driver's license taken like mine, or lost perhaps, in some Mexican adventure, then put to other uses? Or was she dead, her identity transferred to me after her demise? No stranger to adventure, I had never felt like this before, cut off from something so personal, so basic, as my name.

It was a disorienting experience in a way I cannot describe, and yet somehow oddly liberating. Rebecca didn't have bills to pay, meetings to go to, and, more importantly, she didn't have an ex-husband she still had rather ambivalent feelings about, who'd had the bad taste to open a shop right across the road from her. She wasn't slowly going bankrupt, and best of all, neither she nor any of her friends were being investigated in a murder case, nor was she being pursued by a cold-blooded killer.

On the other hand, it did have its hazards. I'd assured the airline personnel that I had, indeed, packed my own bag and it had never left my sight, a statement that was patently untrue, and one that constituted a leap of faith in Lucas and his compatriots that left me breathless. What if a security guard asked me to describe its contents? I had no idea what it contained. I was nervous as I cleared immigration on my way out of Mexico, then again as I entered Peru. Would they catch me with some seemingly innocuous question about my life? Even my clothes felt as if they would betray me, although the jeans and the denim shirt fit just fine.

On the plane, I sat, eyes squeezed tightly shut, my hands gripping the seat arms, reciting over and over in my mind, like some feverish mantra, my new name, my birth date, my home. I pretended to sleep, too nervous to eat, and unwilling to hold a conversation with my seatmate, lest I betray myself in some way. When, as the plane began its descent into Lima, the flight attendant touched my arm, calling me Señora Mac-Crimmon and handing me an envelope, my heart leapt into my mouth.

But then there I was in my little hotel room, clean and tidy but threadbare. I circled the bed looking at the suitcase which lay there unopened, like someone else's abandoned bag turning endlessly on an otherwise empty baggage carousel. Inside was the new me: another pair of jeans, two pairs of khaki mid-thigh length shorts, an Indian cotton skirt in blacks, aquas, and rose, a turquoise Indian cotton blouse to go with it, a light cotton sweater, weatherproof jacket, and a pile of T-shirts. There was some utilitarian cotton underwear, including socks, a long T-shirt that would double as a nightie, a pair of sandals, running shoes, and work boots. I regarded the shoes and boots with unease. In my experience, shoes generally fall into one of three categories: almost comfortable, uncomfortable, and excruciating. At home there was a collection of footwear that would give Imelda Marcos pause, testament to an almost obsessive pursuit of the perfectly comfortable pair of shoes. I tried on the sandals and running shoes: They fell into the almost comfortable category, much to my relief. The boots I would leave until later.

Rebecca MacCrimmon was a bit older than I, forty-five to be precise, although with what I'd been through in the past few days, looking older than I was did not seem an insurmountable problem. She was, I decided, a bit of a hippy at heart, a child of the sixties who had not succumbed to the acquisitiveness and self-absorption that had overwhelmed many of our generation. Her T-shirts supported various causes: The first urged one and all to save the rain forest; another, and this one brought a smile to my face, proclaimed archaeologists to be better lovers; the third asked the world to save the whales. I held the whale T-shirt up to me. It was clear my first purchase would be a new shirt. No one with my generous proportions, I decided, should ever have to wear a picture of a whale.

Money was a problem, of course. I couldn't be running out to replace my wardrobe. I had some cash, the equivalent of about $400, but I had no credit cards, the absence of which I felt keenly. Credit cards, I decided, had become my personal security blanket. I would have to be very careful with money, that was certain, but I would buy a new shirt nonetheless. Because, as it turned out, I had job prospects.

The letter I'd received on the plane told me that my application to work at an archaeological site in northern Peru was being seriously considered, and that I was to contact Dr. Stephen Neal, codirector of the project, on my arrival in Lima. The letter informed me that if I were the successful candidate, I would be expected to report for duty on August 28, two days hence. The letter said that my lodging and meals would be covered, but that unfortunately there were no funds available to pay a salary, however small. As compensation, however, there was the privilege of working with someone of the caliber of the other codirector, Dr. Hilda Schwengen, whoever that was. The signature on the letter was that of Stephen Neal, and a postscript added, much to my relief, that the successful candidate would also receive transportation to the site from Lima.

For a moment or two, as I sat in the cafe and waited to meet my soon-to-be employer, my attention was diverted by a crowd of uniformed schoolchildren, wearing red blazers and navy slacks and jumpers, on an outing in the square. "Ms. MacCrimmon, by any chance?" the voice asked, and for a moment I was about to say sorry, no.

I liked Steve Neal immediately. He had a kind of large, rumpled look, a warm handshake, a friendly and open face, with eyes that crinkled at the corners when he laughed, which he did a lot.

"Beer?" he asked as he sat down. *"Dos cervezas, por favor,"* he said to the waiter, as I nodded. "Pilsen Trujillo," he added.

"So how do you like Lima so far?" he asked. "And how is Lucas? I hear he's taken up politics. I suppose archaeology does tend to get a little political from time to time." He laughed.

"Both Lucas and Lima are fine," I replied, handing him the letter Lucas had given me for him. I waited while he read it. As I'd promised, I hadn't looked at it, but my curiosity was piqued as Neal's eyebrows raised ever so slightly at one point in the text.

"Okay," he said, carefully pouring his beer. "Let's talk about the job."

This was the moment I had been dreading. Lucas had done exactly what he said he would do. He had got me to Peru and had provided me with a way to get to Moche country. The rest was up to me. But I was certain the first question would be from which august institution of higher learning had I received my degree in archaeology or anthropology. My degree was in English. The second question would undoubtedly be, tell me what you know about the ancient cultures of the north coast of Peru.

Unfortunately, my experience in archaeology was limited to spending a few pleasant afternoons with Lucas on sites he was digging. He'd let me help with the work, under his supervision, but no one would ever call me an archaeologist.

As for the second topic: As recently as two weeks ago, I had only a passing interest in the ancient cultures of Peru, and that related solely to studies I had done a few years back on the Maya in Mexico and Central America. In a gesture that I knew was futile, I had spent the morning before my job interview dashing around Lima from museum to museum. The sum total of my knowledge to date was that there were a number of cultures that had inhabited the northern coastal desert of Peru long before the Inca and the Spanish conquest, including Chancay, Chimu, Chavin, Moche, and Lambayeque, but that, in my opinion, the Moche were the most brilliant craftspeople of them all. If anyone was capable of the artistry that made the little gold man I still carried with me, it was a Moche craftsman.

I had seen rooms of ceramics, textiles, and metalwork made by these peoples and had been quite overwhelmed by the artistry and technique they had shown. I had even seen rooms filled with Moche erotic ceramics, by and large couples in positions I can only describe as anatomically challenging. Some of these ceramics had depicted one member of the twosome as a death skull and skeleton. The guard on the room had told me this meant the Moche thought too much sex would kill you. The current status of my love life being what it was, I had decided this was not something I needed to spend much time worrying about.

As entertaining as my museum tour might have been, the point was that if I were asked the question, Can you tell late Moche from Lambayeque? the answer quite clearly was no.

The question Neal posed took me completely by surprise.

"I don't suppose you know anything about running a business," he said, speaking in Spanish. "Paying bills, wages, dealing with government authorities, that sort of thing? The point is, I'm an archaeologist, not a businessman, and all the organizational stuff I have to do is getting me down. I've got some really good lab people, good workers on the site, but no one to keep the whole show running smoothly.''

Did I know something about running a business? Of course I did. I'd been running my antiques and design business for about fifteen years, with only one interruption. I needed to approach this with a certain amount of caution, of course. I'd decided that the only way to survive as Rebecca MacCrimmon was to keep her background as close as possible to my own. That way, I would be less likely to get caught out in a contradiction. Rebecca was from Kansas; her driver's license said so, and I had only passed through Kansas once. That one I would have to be very careful about. But running a business? Who was to say Rebecca MacCrimmon didn't have business experience?

''I have a fair amount of business experience,'' I replied carefully in my best Spanish. ''I had my own business for a number of years. Retail. I sold furniture. I didn't have a lot of staff, but I had some, and they always got paid. The bills did too. I am also accustomed to dealing with customs officials and agents, bankers, tax people, accountants, and shippers. I can honestly say that I never missed a shipping deadline through a fault of my own.'' I paused. ''Although I'll admit it was close a few times.'' I laughed.

''You're hired,'' he said.

''I am?'' I replied in surprise.

''Sure,'' he said. ''Your Spanish is good, Lucas says you can be trusted—trusted absolutely, actually—and you can take the work I hate off my hands. That's good enough for me.'' He laughed. ''Lucas says in his letter he is asking me for a favor. Don't tell him, but I think he may have been doing me one!

"You know the terms—transportation to the site, room and board once you get to the site. I know it's not much. Will you do it? Do we have a deal?" he said, extending his hand across the table. I took it.

"We have a deal. When do I start?"

He spread a map out on the table. "We're working at a site here," he said, pointing to what appeared to be a blank spot on the map, "between Trujillo and Chiclayo. Early to middle Moche site. Showing a lot of promise. The closest town is Campina Vieja."

Good old Lucas, I thought: right to Campina Vieja. I must have started, though, because Neal hesitated for a few seconds before continuing. "You can fly to Trujillo, and then you'll have to find the Vulkano bus station and take the Trujillo/Chiclayo bus. The buses run almost hourly, and they'll stop at Campina Vieja if you ask them.

"I'm flying back to Trujillo tonight, so why don't you fly out tomorrow sometime and have a look around Trujillo—there's some interesting Moche and Chimu sites to see there—then take the bus the following morning. I'll be in town for much of the day and I'll keep an eye on the bus stop. Just sit yourself down on the bench if I'm not there when you arrive: I'll be along and drive you out to the site. We've taken over an old hacienda and set up operations there. You can meet the rest of the team, including the boss, Hilda, when you get there.

"Now let's go and see about getting you an airline ticket," he grinned, "before you change your mind. What do you prefer to be called, by the way?"

I almost made a mistake, I felt so relaxed in his

presence, but I caught myself in time. As I hesitated he said, "Do you prefer Rebecca or something like Becky?"

"Rebecca," I said. "Definitely Rebecca."

After Neal and I had parted company, as the sun began its rapid descent into darkness, as it does this close to the equator, I paid a final visit to the place where, according to Rob Luczka, the man I had called Lizard, Ramon Cervantes, had lived. It had not been all that difficult tracking the place down, there being only one Ramon Cervantes listed in Callao. As I had on two previous occasions, I hailed a *colectivo*, that particularly Peruvian mode of public transit, a private minibus or van that plies a regular route, a sign in its front and side windows indicating its destination. In addition to the driver, there is an assistant who opens the sliding door and signals the number of empty seats with his fingers. The van barely stops to pick you up and drop you off, but it's cheap, and it gets you there, weaving its way through Lima's appalling traffic, pollution, and noise.

Ramon Cervantes, I was now certain, was not a wealthy man, living as he had on a dark little street in a part of Lima out near the airport that I would characterize as decidedly modest, a neighborhood that reeked of rancid cooking oil and thwarted aspirations. The streets, unlike many of the streets in the old part of central Lima, were paved, although badly rutted and potholed. Ramon had lived in a flat that one reached by going up a dark and dirty staircase running between a malodorous restaurant and an engine repair shop. At street level, the visitor was overwhelmed by the dinginess of the location, but if one stepped back, across the street, one could see, on the second floor, vestiges of Lima's colonial past in the large windows fronted by wrought iron railings, and the swirling plaster wreaths and garlands along the roofline above them. The shutters on the apartment to the left of the staircase were closed tight.

On my first visit, shortly after my arrival in Lima, I had climbed the dark steps to a second-floor landing. There were two apartments, one on either side of the staircase. On the door to the right was a little nameplate, not Cervantes, and on the other, a black ribbon tied to the door knocker. I knocked, tentatively at first, then louder. No one answered, and there was no sound from within. I waited outside for a few minutes, watched closely by a Chinese woman in a little *chifa*, or Chinese restaurant, across the street.

On my second visit, I was greeted by the same silence and lack of an answer. This time I took a seat in the *chifa* across the road where I could watch the staircase, and ordered a beer. After a few minutes, the Chinese proprietor came over to my table. "Who are you looking for?" she asked. I told her I was looking for Señora Cervantes.

"That tart," she said. "Señora Cervantes you call her. Very fancy. She'd like that. Thinks she's better than the rest of us, always putting on airs. But around here she's just Carla. Or sometimes just the tart." She used the word *fulana*. Spanish has as many words for those who ply the world's oldest profession as we do in English. "She's in there," she went on. "Won't answer the door. Worried it will be the landlord. She can't pay the rent, you know. Or her brother-in-law, who blames her for what happened. Her husband's dead."

"I heard," I said. "Too bad."

"Too bad for her, that's for certain. Maybe not for him. For him, perhaps, a blessing. Left her with three kids. She's sent them away, you know, to her sister in Trujillo. She shouldn't have kids. No patience with them. Too much of a child herself. Took all their money, did that husband of hers, what there was of it, and went off somewhere far, Canada I think, and then up and died."

Clearly my newfound friend didn't miss much, and didn't mind whom she told about it either.

"Why would he do that, I wonder," I said.

She snorted. "Die, you mean? Or go to Canada? The only thing to wonder about is how he got enough money to go there in the first place, and why he didn't go sooner. Found her with someone. His own brother. A fine man, Ramon Cervantes. He didn't deserve that, I can tell you. A real tart, that one."

Dear me, I thought, poor Lizard. But how does finding your wife in flagrante delicto with your brother get you to an auction in Toronto and a gory and premature death in my storage room?

The woman from the *chifa* had more to tell me. She paused only long enough to get me another beer, unasked for. Buying from her was, I gathered, how I was paying for this information.

"But it's no use feeling sorry for Ramon, is there? No use feeling sorry for the dead. It's his brother I feel sorry for now: Jorge. Consumed with guilt. Just consumed with it. Drinks like a fish at the bar down the street, then comes and stands under the window watching for her. I call her a tart, but he calls her a witch, a *bruja*. Claims she bewitched both him and his brother, made them do bad things. His wife has left him now. Taken his kids too. Him, I feel sorry for.

"There," she said, pointing to a young man, obviously drunk and disheveled, passing in front of the *chifa.* "Jorge." We watched him lurch by. She was right: He looked pathetic indeed. A few moments later, when Jorge could no longer be seen, she went on. "As for her, when she does come out, she's not dressed like a widow, that I can tell you. Disgraceful. Lots of loud colors: Pink's her favorite. If she's shedding tears, it's for herself, and not for him. She'll do all right, of course. Men like to look after her. First her father doted on her, then Ramon, the poor man. Not good enough for her, was he? A good man with a steady government job would be enough for most of us, wouldn't it?"

"She goes out these days, does she?" I asked in what I hoped was a disinterested tone. The woman didn't answer. I ordered a cheese sandwich to go with the beer. It was the cheapest bribe on the menu.

"At night," she said, setting the grilled cheese sandwich in front of me. "After the landlord closes up his office down the street and goes home to Montericco. Then she usually goes out. About eight or nine."

And so it was that I was back in Callao at night. I was a little uneasy about being out alone in this part of town, but the *chifa* was still open, and I ordered a coffee and a crème caramel while I waited to see what would happen.

Around seven-thirty, my newfound Chinese friend nudged my arm and pointed to a rather rotund middle-aged man heading down the street. As he passed the Cervantes residence, I saw him look up for a moment or two at the darkened apartment. "The landlord," she whispered. "Going home. Now watch the shutters carefully." I did, and a few minutes later I could see that a dim light had been turned on inside. The *chifa* owner gave me a knowing look.

About three quarters of an hour later, I heard, rather than saw, someone on the stairs, and a young woman entered the street.

"The tart," the Chinese woman hissed, tossing her head in the direction of the woman. I quickly paid the bill and followed the young woman.

As my informant had predicted, Carla Cervantes was not dressed for a funeral. Instead she was wearing a pink dress, sleeveless, with narrow straps and a neckline that swooped rather low. The dress was, in my opinion, a little unfashionable, and more than a little tight on her, although I'll admit I'd give my eyeteeth to be able to look like her in that dress. I could not help but note that all the men in the street gaped at her as she went by, and not one of them took any notice whatsoever of me, despite the fact that I was the only *gringa* on that street at that moment, testament, indeed, to the allure of Señora Cervantes.

At the end of the street was a busy avenue, and after a moment or two, Carla flagged down a *colectivo* headed for Miraflores. I immediately hailed a cab and asked the driver, a young man in jeans and a T-shirt advertising a rock group I'd never heard of, possibly the one on the tape in the car, to follow that *colectivo*. He jumped on the accelerator in his enthusiasm for the project, and whipped into the traffic, horn blaring, bouncing both me and his audiotape collection from side to side in the backseat like dice in a box. From time to time, he would turn to grin at me and quite unnecessarily point out the *colectivo* only one or two car lengths ahead. I held on to the door handle for dear life.

The *colectivo* turned off a side road, took a couple of backstreets, then turned down a ramp that led to what Limenos call the Ditch, a sunken expressway that cuts diagonally across the face of the city. A few minutes later, the *colectivo* pulled off another ramp and then dropped Carla at the door to one of the swankier hotels in Miraflores, in itself one of the poshest parts of Lima. I followed her through the glass doors into the hotel bar to the left of the main door, and took a seat at a table three away, but with a clear view of Carla and the man she had obviously come to meet.

He was much older than she was, sixty perhaps to her late twenty-something. He was not Spanish. He looked European to me, in the way he dressed, although with a Spanish rock video blasting from a large screen at one end of the bar, I could not hear him speak, until he called over the waiter and ordered a martini for his lady friend. French, I decided. I ordered a glass of white wine, and tried to look as if I belonged there. Surveillance, I would have to say, is not something in which I have any expertise.

I do like to think, however, that after fifteen years in retail, I can read body language pretty well, and this particular conversation, although I could not hear it and did not dare move closer, was an interesting one. The man, dressed in a tan suede jacket over charcoal-grey slacks, a yellow shirt, and a rather stylish cravat, leaned well back in his chair at first, distancing himself from his companion and keeping his face in relative shadow. One hand rested on his knee; the other he kept well to his side, between his thigh and the arm of the chair. Throughout most of the conversation, which lasted almost an hour, his body language said that he was not very interested in what Carla had to say.

She, on the other hand, was trying very hard to be persuasive. I had the feeling she had a proposal to make to him, and that she did not know him that well. First there was a lovely smile as she leaned toward him, then, when that appeared to have no impact, dainty tears and blowing of nose into a lace hanky. Still the man remained unmoved. Pouting was next, and then as a last resort she wriggled just enough to let one pink strap slide off her shoulder. The man leaned forward and smiled. It was not, I thought, a nice smile, rather one of victory, or perhaps anticipation.

Through all of this, I nursed my one little glass of white wine, and tried to look as if I were waiting for someone, glancing at my watch from time to time, and pretending to be a little impatient. The price of wine by the glass was so outrageous in this hotel that I had no intention of ordering another, no matter how long the two of them sat there. I ate every peanut from the little crystal bowl on the table, determined to eke out my time there and get my money's worth. Being alone in a foreign country without the comforting presence of a credit card is an experience I would not wish to repeat.

Shortly after the shoulder strap incident, it was apparently time to leave. Carla's companion signed the bill, thereby indicating he could afford to be a guest in this hotel. It was only then that I noticed that his right hand, which he used to hold the bill while he signed with his left, was missing the little and ring fingers.

They left the bar together. I didn't really need to follow them any farther. It didn't take a genius to figure out where they were headed. But I followed them just the same, at least as far as the elevator. As I went past their table, I tried to read the signature on the bill, before the waiter swept it away, but the light was too low and the signature appeared to me to be illegible. I could see the room number quite clearly, however: room 1236. I saw the two of them enter the elevator, then to confirm my suspicions, I watched the numbers over the door. It went directly to the twelfth floor. The widow Cervantes appeared to be dealing with her grief quite well.

I left the hotel and looked for a *colectivo* to take me back downtown, catching as I did so a brief glimpse of a man standing to the side of the entrance-way, who slipped into the darkness when I looked his way. Although I couldn't say with any certainty, I could have sworn it was Ramon's brother, Jorge.

The question was, what now? In my impulsive and one might well say ill-advised journey to solve the nasty situation in which I found myself, I had only two clues: a name, that of Ramon Cervantes, whose widow was now upstairs behaving badly—one could only assume—with a man I'd never seen before, and whom I had no reason to suspect had anything whatsoever to do with all this; and a little piece of jewelry that was probably genuine Moche. I could continue to follow the name—that is, I could wait and see where, and with whom, the widow Cervantes went next; I could go and search out Jorge, to see what light he could shed on what had happened to his brother; or I could follow the artifact, take the job in Moche territory and see what I could find.

I chose to follow the artifact. As some would say, when you don't know where you're going, any road will get you there. Personally, I prefer a line penned by the poet Robert Browning: *Everyone soon or late comes round by Rome,* he wrote. Rome, in this instance, was a little town in northern Peru called Campina Vieja.

The Priestess

STILL THE DECAPITATOR *waits, tumi blade in one hand, the other still empty. And with him the Priestess, with hair of snakes, she who holds the golden cup that soon will contain the sacred liquid, the blood of sacrifice.*

While they wait at the huaca, we prepare the Warrior's shroud. Three woven cloths will cradle him. The golden helmet with its feathered plumes, the gold and silver back flaps, the gilded bells, are placed first.

The litter that will support him on his descent lies beneath him. He rests on a second headdress, a gold crescent crowned by flamingo feathers. In his right hand we place the golden scepter, symbol of his earthly power, in his left, the silver, smaller. A gold ingot rests on his right hand, a silver on his left.

On his face we place five gold masks, on his feet, silver sandals. Three pairs of ear flares accompany him: one pair the sacred white-tailed deer, the second golden spiders, the third a feline head that represents the creature that can cross the line between the two worlds marked by the double-headed serpent—the world of now, the world of the ancestors.

Three pectorals of shell beads, thousands of them, in cream and green, pink and white, we have placed on his chest, wristbands to match on his arms.

Next comes his necklace of peanut beads, as always gold on his right, silver his left, sun/moon, earth/sea duality; then a second necklace of gold spiders and a third of discs of gold and turquoise.

To cover him we place his banners, his standards, symbols of his earthly powers: rough cotton onto which we have sewn golden discs and his image, the image of the warrior god. Then the shroud is wrapped around him.

The offerings are all assembled; the guardians, those among us who will accompany him, have been chosen.

Soon the ceremony in the great plaza will begin.

8

Even as I pondered which path to take, all the players in this macabre little drama, as if moved by some invisible director's hand, were, like me, being drawn to take their place upon the stage. Some were driven by desperation, others compelled by avarice and greed, still others by obsession, and there were those still blissfully unaware of the role others, more malevolent, had chosen for them. Like stock characters in a modern morality tale—the Hero, the Villain, the Temptress, the Witch, the Magician, the Fool—from the four corners of the globe, we assembled in Campina Vieja to play the roles assigned us.

It was a concept, I've since thought, that would have resonated with the Inca, who called their huge, yet short-lived empire, Tahuantinsuyo, Land of the Four Quarters. At the time of the first European contact with the Americas, Tahuantinsuyo was the largest nation on earth. At its center was the glittering city of Cuzco, the navel of the Inca universe, just as Campina

Vieja was to become the heart of this drama.

From the northern quarter, if you count my point of origin, Chinchaysuyu for the Inca, came I, the Narrator perhaps, or worse yet, the Fool. For me, the journey from the comforting cocoon of Lima, possessing as it does that essence that all large cities share, was an exercise in shedding my old identity, along with preconceptions, as a snake sheds its skin. It was not so much that the journey was extraordinary, just one filled with quirky moments, that made it clear that Rebecca wasn't in Kansas anymore.

The flight to Trujillo had been uneventful, unless you count playing bingo rather than watching a movie an event, and I found the Vulkano bus station without difficulty. A bus trip in that part of the country, apparently, is an exercise in participative democracy. Passengers preoccupied themselves with shouting instructions to the driver, telling him he was lingering too long at any given stop, or that he wasn't driving to their particular specifications.

We were on the Panamericana Norte, the Pan-American highway, that hugs a narrow strip of desert crisscrossed by river valleys, most of them dry, between the sea on one side and the Andes on the other. From time to time we'd pass a little town, sometimes a small forest or some farmland, but by and large the land on either side of the highway was desert, very dry. Sometimes I could see tire tracks leading off the highway, in what appeared to be a straight line to nowhere. In the distance are the mountains, looming up out of the sand. As austere as it may sound, it was actually quite beautiful, the colors of the desert, the golds, browns, the burnt greens, cinnamons, and dusty rose, playing against the blue-green of the sea, and the hundreds of greys, greens, navy blues, and purples of the mountains.

And what of the other characters? the other quarters? From the south, Collasuyu, comes the Magician.

With the help of several vocal backseat drivers, the bus driver stopped regularly to disgorge passengers and pick up others, sometimes in little towns, more often than not at a marker—a little stand or a sign— at the side of the highway.

At one of these stops, a young couple loaded down with enormous backpacks got on. They both looked about fifteen to me, but to be realistic I'd put them in their early twenties. Gringos. She wore jeans with holes at the knees; a halter top that revealed her suntanned middle and a hint of navel; lots of jewelry, most notably silver rings on every finger and a pair of long silver earrings that looked vaguely Navaho; and a halo of long wavy hair around a small face that gave her the appearance of a Titian Madonna. He had hair almost as long as hers, cutoff jeans, a T-shirt frayed at the shoulders where the sleeves had been removed, and a neat little row of tiny safety pins in one ear. On one arm he had a large tattoo with a skull and crossbones and a succinct suggestion that the Establishment—such an antiquated term—perform an anatomical impossibility on itself. As they passed my seat, I idly wondered if their parents, particularly hers, knew where they were and what they were doing. Advancing middle age can be tiresome.

Several moments after the bus started rolling again, the young man walked to the front of the bus and, turning to face the crowd, pulled out a deck of cards. He spoke no Spanish, and, with the exception of me, no one else on the bus spoke English, but he kept up a patter that would have made a showman proud, and soon had everyone's attention as he demonstrated several card tricks. After that, he took a newspaper, asked in sign language for one of the men sitting in the front seats to check it out carefully, folded it into a cone shape, and then, pulling a bottle of water out of a bag he carried with him, poured the water into the cone. He then very quickly inverted the cone over the head of the nearest passenger, who ducked away, much to the amusement of the other passengers. No water came out of the cone. There was a smattering of applause. He grinned, and then, still talking, poured water out of the cone and back into the jar.

There was even louder applause this time and I could certainly see why. While I'm not exactly a fan of magic acts, I had to admit the young man was very good. He had no sleeves in which to hide anything, and I was close enough to be able to watch him pretty carefully. I could not see how he had done it. He did a couple of other tricks, one with a coin, and another with a plastic tube, both of them equally baffling. As he came to the end of his performance, the young woman made her way from the back of the bus with a baseball cap and began to collect tips. I could see that those ahead of me had given very small coins, brown ones which I knew to be almost worthless by North American standards, and although I knew I had to be careful with money, I gave the Peruvian equivalent of about three dollars. The young woman looked suitably impressed with my generosity as my coins dropped into the hat, and a few minutes after the act was finished, the young man plopped into the seat beside me.

"Speak English?" he asked. I nodded. He was an American.

"The name's Puma, after the wild cat that roams around here," he said. "My girlfriend's name is Pachamama. That's the native word for Mother Earth. They aren't our real names," he added, "just ones we're using for now."

I would never have guessed. Not that I could be judgmental. "I'm Rebecca," I said, taking his proffered handshake and complimenting him on his magic act.

"What are you doin' in the back of beyond?" he said. "If you don't mind my asking."

"I'm going to work at an archaeological site," I replied.

"Wow!" he exclaimed. "Amazing!"

"How about you?" I asked politely.

"We've been doin' the sites, Inca mainly, down south. But now we're gonna join a bunch of people, a commune sorta, not too far from here. We're gonna grow our own food and stuff."

How sixties, I thought. "What a lovely idea," I said.

He looked carefully at me to see if I was kidding, and apparently concluded I was taking him sufficiently seriously. "I'll tell you a secret," he whispered solemnly. "We're here to 'excape' the end of the world." Inwardly, I groaned.

"There's gonna be a huge 'pocalypse, you know," he added. He didn't appear to know or care that apocalypse starts with an "a." "Earthquakes, fire, volcanoes, floods, everything. Followed by nuclear holocaust." It sounded like overkill to me.

"Right at the stroke of midnight on December 31,

1999," he went on. "I seen it, in my head, I mean. All the capitalist countries, the United States, Europe, everything, will be destroyed. You're lucky to be here."

We were silent for a moment or two after that conversation stopper. Then he went on. "I'm a little worried about your archaeology site, now that I think about it. You might find a tomb or something and unleash some terrible curse."

"I'll try not to do that," I replied.

"Good." He grinned, getting up and heading back to his seat. "Thanks for the donation."

I turned back to watch the scenery flashing by. Peru, it seemed to me, was a land of geographic extremes, from the world's driest desert, the Atacama in the south; to some of the richest ocean waters, teeming with marine life, created by the cold Humboldt from Antarctica and the warmer Pacific current coming south; to the Andes, the world's second greatest mountain range. In this part of the world, there are no foothills. You could crawl out of the Pacific, cross a few miles of arid desert, and come upon a wall of rock rising almost vertically from the desert floor. Beyond that is the rain forest, in some cases, in others huge grassy plateaus and jagged valleys.

The area is unstable, geologically speaking, with the oceanic Nazca plate sliding under the South American continental plate at a rate that, while imperceptible to us, is the fastest tectonic activity anywhere. It is this action that created the Andes and an extraordinarily deep ocean trench off the coast. It is also the reason for a geological instability that results in bad earthquakes on a reasonably regular basis and sporadic volcanic activity. Puma's and Pachamama's choice of

Peru as a place to avoid the cataclysmic upheavals of Armageddon was, from that standpoint, a poor one.

This is Moche country, I thought and marveled at it. How could such a remarkable civilization, capable of the art I had seen and held, flourish in such an inhospitable place? I wondered. But it had. Around 100 B.C., some kind of political alliance coalesced in the Rio Moche Valley, then spread north. Enormous complexes were built at Cerro Blanco, a capital city dominated by two enormous pyramids, the Huaca de la Luna and the Huaca del Sol, temples of the Moon and the Sun.

For several centuries, the Moche consolidated their position by building ceremonial and administrative centers in the river valleys—control of water being absolutely critical to their empire in such an arid part of the world—to the north and south of their capital. They had a system of canals, high up in the Andes, that diverted water from the river chasms in the mountains to irrigate the desert lands.

The Moche had a complex social structure, with an elite, a warrior class, artisans, and commoners; they practiced elaborate rituals, many of them involving human sacrifice; buried their most important citizens with treasures that rival the Egyptians; and had a vivid mythology, tantalizing hints of which remain.

Late in the sixth century, though, environmental catastrophe began to wreak havoc on the northern coastal desert. Long periods of blistering drought interrupted by sudden and devastating flooding destroyed much of Cerro Blanco and other Moche cities. There were attempts to rebuild, but the damage to the empire proved irreversible, and gradually the Moche culture faded away to be replaced by others. And it was a very long time before the grandeur of that period became known and appreciated once again.

It occurred to me, as I pondered the rise and fall of civilizations, that I might better spend my time contemplating events a little closer to home. I felt I hadn't always been thinking as clearly as I might like in the last little while, not since I'd found Alex barely conscious in the shop, and the charred body of Lizard, and certainly not since my grisly discovery at the Ancient Ways Gallery in New York.

I could laugh at Puma's notions about " 'pocalypses" and the dangers of unleashing curses from tombs, but there was no question I felt that all the bad things that were happening were linked to some Moche artifacts, and that strange things had started happening right after I'd acquired the so-called replicas. Furthermore, almost everyone who had some association with them, however tenuous, had endured some unfortunate happening in their lives, some of them coming to a very bad end indeed. Even A. J. Smythson, the late owner of the Smythson Gallery, who hadn't actually acquired them but was supposed to, had died a horrible death.

The point was, I didn't believe in curses, not when I was being rational, anyway.

And now here I was on a bus headed for the purported point of origin of at least one of these artifacts, the flared vase from Campina Vieja. I was almost three hours north of Trujillo, four or five hundred miles north of Lima, and a lifetime away from the people I cared about.

This is nuts, I thought. Go home. You can persuade Rob of Alex's innocence and yours. He's angry, but he'll get over it, and he will help put this right.

"Campina Vieja," the driver called out. I'd arrived at my destination, good idea or not. I disembarked. So did my two young friends.

Steve Neal had said that he'd be in town to meet me, and he was as good as his word. For the very few minutes I had to wait for him, I did a quick survey of my surroundings. I was in a reasonably large town and across from a bustling open-air market. I also watched the two young hippies—really there was no other word for them, as outdated as the term might be—try to negotiate their onward journey to the commune.

The preferred method of transport in Campina Vieja appeared to be motorcycle taxi. Puma and Pachamama carefully counted out their change—they were obviously broke, even more so than I—and then tried to negotiate the fare with one of the drivers near the bus station.

They were at a serious disadvantage, not speaking Spanish, and dealing with a destination that was either unknown to the driver, or one which he didn't want to go to. Eventually they picked up their packs and started to walk. Shortly after, Steve Neal pulled up in a grey Nissan truck.

For the next half hour or so, Steve did a few errands around town, giving me a running commentary on the place as he did so. We picked up four large plastic cubes of water, a tank of propane and some kerosene, and then we were headed out of town on the north-bound Pan-American highway once again. A couple of miles out of town, I saw up ahead of us the two young people, trudging along the edge of the road. They were covered in dust, and the young woman, in particular, looked tired.

As reluctant as I was to pursue this relationship—

inhabitants of communes waiting for the end of the world are not exactly my cup of tea—my maternal instincts, usually dormant, were roused, they looked so forlorn. I told Steve about them, and he pulled on the shoulder several yards ahead of them, and I got out and waved. The two of them ran to catch up to us.

"Steve," I said, "these are my new friends Puma and Pachamama."

I could see mirth touching the corners of Steve's eyes and mouth, but he managed to control himself. "How do you do," he said gravely, shaking their hands in turn. I explained where they were headed, and Puma showed him some directions. "Throw your stuff in the back and hop in," he said, gesturing to the backseat. "We have one stop, but it's on our way." The two grinned ear to ear with gratitude.

Puma sat up front with Steve, while I took the backseat with Pachamama. She didn't have very much to say, but I noticed Puma was doing card tricks for Steve, which must have been a little distracting.

A few miles out of town, Steve made a left turn on a dirt road that ran between two buildings. Standing in front of one of them was a tiny woman, skin very brown and wrinkled, wearing a brown felt hat the shape of a lamp shade, an embroidered blouse covered by a brown vest, a short full skirt of navy blue over leggings, and black work boots. Her dark hair, streaked with grey, was twisted into two long, thick plaits. Beside her were two very large woven baskets in bright colors, pink and orange and green. Steve pulled the truck up beside her, loaded the baskets in the back, then helped her up into the back of the truck as well.

"Ines Cardoso," he said, getting back behind the wheel. "Our cook. With our dinner," he added.

About half a mile down the dusty road, he pulled off the road again, and we bumped down what was essentially a cart path in the general direction of a clump of trees. I could see a few primitive huts to one side, some laundry flapping in a breeze, a fenced-in area beside them where a few tired stalks of corn were growing. "Here we are. The commune," Steve said. My heart sank for my two young friends.

We disembarked, and Puma and Steve unloaded the bags from the back of the van. I smiled at Ines, who was staring at me. She didn't smile back.

I hugged both the kids and, in a moment of weakness, slipped the Peruvian equivalent of about twenty dollars to Puma, then watched as they headed toward the encampment. "Don't forget what I told you," Puma called back to me. "About December 31 and everything." How could I forget when I was being reminded about it everywhere I went?

"I won't. And thanks for the advice."

"Thanks for giving them a ride," I said to Steve. We were alone in the truck. Ines, although there was now plenty of room, preferred to sit in the back.

"No problem. They're not much older than my kids, you know. My son's in college, and my daughter is just finishing high school. I know this puts me solidly in the camp of male chauvinist pigs, but I particularly wouldn't like to think of my daughter in that place." He glanced over at me. "By the way, I saw what you did." I feigned innocence. "Feeling flush, are you?"

"No," I replied. "Actually, I'm feeling broke. But it's all relative. You're going to see that there's a roof over my head, and you'll feed me. I'll manage."

He sighed. "I don't much like the idea of their staying at that place," he repeated.

"They'll be okay," I said, somewhat hesitantly. "Is there something other than their general comfort you think they need to worry about?"

"Not really," he replied, just a tad too quickly. "Have I conveyed to you how absolutely delighted I am that you accepted this position?" he went on, changing the subject. I smiled.

"Really, I mean it," he said. "I'm a field man, not a businessman. I'm itching to be out there at the site. But there's so much to be done, just to keep this project running, and I'm second on the totem pole. Hilda, Dr. Schwengen, is the head of this project, really, although she and I are called codirectors. Have you heard of her? No?" he said, looking at my blank expression. "She's the high priestess of field archaeology in this part of the world. Austrian, originally, but she emigrated to the States when she was very young. Done some wonderful work on Inca sites, cleared a whole city up in the mountains almost singlehanded, fighting off banditos in the process. Something of a legend, is our Hilda. She's now turned her attention to the Moche. So far, though, we've come up dry."

"Is this your first year here?" I asked, changing the subject.

"Fourth," Steve replied. "Fourth and last unless we can come up with something spectacular. The grant I got for this dig runs out at the end of this season, and unless we can bring in another sponsor or two—we've got one small one to help out this year—we're done here. I've talked to a couple of the Peruvian banks, but sponsors look for something a little more exciting for their money than what we've found so far. The stuff we've found is all really interesting; we've uncovered a workers' cemetery and what was probably a village populated by craftspeople.''

''But that sounds fascinating,'' I interrupted him.

''Oh, it is,'' he replied. ''But it's not glamorous. We've learned a lot about early Moche times, but sponsors want something more exciting than that, and they know it's possible. There have been terrific finds a little north of here. Sipan, for example. Those tombs were just spectacular. I'm biased, of course, but I think they're the New World equivalent of King Tut's tomb. Enough gold and silver to keep a Croesus happy. That's what sponsors want. I'm still convinced, though, there's something big here, and so's Hilda. I have a feeling in my bones this is the season we'll find it. All the signs are right. Hope so, anyway, as much for Hilda as for myself.''

''That's terrific,'' I said.

''It is. I should warn you about our sponsor, though. One Carlos Montero. He's the mayor's brother and owner of one of the few big businesses in town. This is essentially a one-factory town, by the way.''

My ears pricked up. Steve went on. ''As you can see, there isn't much here. Fishing certainly, some farming. And Carlos and us. As for Carlos . . .'' He paused for a second or two. ''Let's just say that political correctness has not reached the northern coastal desert of Peru. Carlos and a lot of the local men around here think that if a woman is out on her own, she's fair game. I wouldn't take in any of the local bars at night without a guy present, if I were you. The women on the project find Carlos a bit of a pain, I should warn you, always hitting on them. We try to make sure you women aren't left alone with him for long.''

''So what does Carlos do, if anything, when he's not bothering women and being the mayor's brother?'' I asked.

''Owns the local factory, one with the rather amusing name of Fabrica des Artesanias Paraiso, which means paradise as you probably know, the Paradise Crafts Factory,'' Steve said. ''They make reproductions of Moche artifacts, and ship them all over the world.''

Now this is interesting, I thought to myself.

''Montero supports our work here,'' Steve went on. ''I'd be hard-pressed to make ends meet without him. He makes a donation of some substance every year, and lends us tools and workers from time to time. I rent the truck from him, and he gives us a good rate. It's generous of him, but not a bad deal for him either. Let's just say we have a rather symbiotic relationship. He helps us financially and in kind. We agree to let him see whatever we find before it's shipped off to Lima, and we kind of turn our backs while he photographs it in some detail, so he can make reproductions later and be first on the market. Most of the souvenirs of Moche objects that you find around here are manufactured in his plant.''

''Is yours the only dig he does this for?'' I asked.

''The only one this year. He supported a dig the Germans did south of here for a few years. Got some lovely stuff from there. Montero usually does ceramics. He's got a mold maker who can do a quick mold right from the photograph, and then the factory churns them out by the hundreds, if not thousands. He's got a chain of little dealers that sell it for him. They hang around the tourist sites and flog the stuff. You know the sort: Wanna buy a watch, mister? That kind of thing. They look like independent dealers, but they're just as often as not Montero's people. He's doing very well, and thinking about branching out into gold and silver reproductions, because the Germans found the tomb of a Moche priestess, lucky sods." He paused. "Do we detect a hint of professional jealousy here, you're wondering?"

I laughed. "Maybe just a whiff. But go on."

"Okay. Some of Montero's stuff is kind of tacky, I'm afraid. It offends me slightly to take his money, but not enough to stop taking it. The Germans pulled up stakes last year and didn't come back this season, so now we're the recipients of all of Montero's largesse. There's a little work still going on way down south, but essentially we're the only project in these parts this year."

"Does Montero make replicas too? In addition to reproductions, I mean," I asked in what I hoped was a casual tone.

"I suppose he might. Anything to make a buck. He's just a bit obsessed with being big man about town, biggest house, biggest car, that kind of thing. Probably competing since childhood with his brother, the mayor," Steve replied. "But replicas are high ticket items, really expensive to make, as I suppose you know. I kind of see Montero as the mass producer of cheap merchandise, junk, dare I say it."

I didn't probe further, even though I wanted to. The flared vase that was supposed to have originated from Campina Vieja hadn't looked like junk to me, but I decided I'd asked enough about Montero and his Fabrica Paraiso for the time being. If Carlos Montero really was a bigwig in town, I was going to have to be careful with my questioning.

"Why didn't the Germans come back again this year?" I asked out of mild curiosity.

"The weather, I expect," Steve replied. "You've heard of El Niño?" I nodded. El Niño was the name given to a periodic climatic event that caused changes in the currents in the Pacific. The phenomenon is named El Niño for the Christ child, because the warm currents associated with it tend to come around Christmastime. When, for a number of reasons, the warm currents stay around longer than usual, they cause tremendous changes in water temperature, and therefore weather on land, not just in Peru, but all over the world.

"Well, we're in for a big one. I don't think those of us who live in large North American cities truly appreciate the kind of climatic and therefore social changes weather conditions like El Niño cause," he went on. "We catch glimpses of how vulnerable we can be to weather during droughts in the Midwest, flooding or ice storms in other places, but to a certain extent we're protected from major weather patterns. Not so down here.

"In the desert, you can really be at the mercy of the elements. There was terrible flooding here during the last El Niño, people killed in mud slides. And then there's the cholera that tends to come along with the flooding. I should add this is not an entirely new phenomenon. You can see evidence of it in the archaeological record. It may even have been these kinds of weather patterns that ended the Moche empire. Anyway, another El Niño is on its way, and we're seeing the climatic and social changes that come with it. Fish stocks are down. The warmer than normal water is killing the sea plants and fish. One of the Peruvian workers on the site estimates the fishing is off by almost eighty percent. That means that the people who make their living fishing are in a bad way. Some of them are trying to turn to a little farming to keep going.

"At the same time, we've got drought elsewhere, so people are on the move. In some cases, they are just moving in and taking over land near the coast here and starting to farm it.

"Needless to say, the locals are not happy with the new arrivals—they call them *invasores,* invaders—particularly since good land is hard to come by, and fishing is all but gone. The newcomers, unfortunately, are armed in some cases, and there have been a couple of very nasty confrontations. Times like these push people to the limit.

"And the rain hasn't even started here yet. It's winter here, remember. Normally we can get in and out in a season before there's any rain, but it's raining already in Chile, so we may have to pack up early and go home. That's why we're the only team in these parts this season. The others decided to give this year a pass. And I confess it's one of the reasons I worried a bit about those two kids we picked up on the highway. I don't think the *campesinos,* the local farmers, will be any more pleased to see these young *invasores* than they will the people from inland, and even if they don't mind, our young friends could get caught in the cross fire.

"We're being extra careful ourselves. We try to stick together as a group out at the site, and always have at least two of us at the hacienda at any time. It is, as you'll see, a little isolated.

"I haven't scared you with this, have I? We just have to take precautions, that's all. And there is some good news in this, by the way. It's made it a lot easier to get Peruvian workers on the dig, with so many people looking for work. Small as we are, archaeology is getting to be the major employer in this town, what with our project and Montero's crafts factory on the other side of the highway."

We sat in silence for a few minutes, as I digested all this. The road was following what appeared to be a very wide ditch on our left, several hundred yards wide, which I eventually realized was a riverbed, with only a trickle of water in the center of it. We were heading, I knew, in the direction of the sea, so this ditch, it would appear, was near the mouth of the river. The road was deserted. There were no houses lining it, and only the occasional clump of trees to the right. From time to time we would see someone, in one case a man riding a donkey, but otherwise the place was just about empty. Our truck left clouds of dust in its wake.

After a mile or so of bumping along like this, we came up to a small woodland and passing that turned right several hundred yards, then drove across a concrete irrigation canal and over a slight hill.

I don't think I will ever forget my first view of the Hacienda Garua. Steve had said the hacienda was a little isolated, but that didn't come anywhere near describing it. It seemed to me to be overwhelmingly lonely, a huge old house, once very grand, that had fallen into decay. The house was angled, I could see, to take in the breezes and a view across the river's mouth to grassy dunes and the sea beyond. The hacienda was two storeys, with a beautiful carved wood door, the carving now dry and cracked and broken. There were large windows on the main floor only, with wood shutters, several of them pulled tight, a couple of them hanging askew on rusty hinges and banging against the wall in the breeze.

The house had once been yellow ochre, I could tell, but the paint was now faded and cracked. In front of the house was a fountain, a stone cupid holding a conch shell, silent and dry. Off to the right on the edge of the woods were the remains of a small building, a little folly perhaps, a place once used to enjoy the outdoors. Now it was a shell, a row of archways leading nowhere. Dust swirled in the yard as Steve pulled the truck up to the door and cut the engine.

The place had an air of a ghost town, somehow, even though I knew it was inhabited. As I approached the door, I half expected to hear music and voices from within, the clink of silver and crystal from some ghostly party held a century before. Instead, all I could hear was the sound of a dog barking somewhere and the distant crowing of a rooster. I stood there, just looking at it, almost overwhelmed by the desolation, as Steve began to unload the back and help Ines with her baskets.

Slowly, and somewhat reluctantly I'll admit, I walked through the huge door and a large entranceway to find myself in an interior courtyard, open to the sky. If houses can be said to have a personality, this one was introverted, its energy directed inside. While the outside of the house was austere, architectural features were reserved for the interior. The courtyard floor was fashioned of large polished stones—marble,

I thought—under the dust. Several were cracked and worn. There was an open hallway, verandahlike, on all four sides of the courtyard and on both floors, raised slightly above courtyard level and reached by three marble steps on each side of the entranceway and an equal number in the center at the end facing me.

The verandahs were held up by Italianate columns, and lined with wrought iron railings, white paint peeling, and the walls showed signs of the same yellow ochre of the exterior. On all four sides of the main floor, and three on the second, several rooms, judging from the number of doors and windows I could see overlooking the courtyard, led off these verandahs. The second floor, on the end straight ahead of me and opposite to the entranceway, was open at the back to catch the breezes, and I could see the sky, grey and overcast beyond.

I heard footsteps behind me. "Hands up, turn around slowly, or I'll shoot," a voice growled.

9

"For heaven's sake, Lucho! Do you have to be a complete dork?" a woman's voice exclaimed.

I carefully inched my head up and to the right until I could see a young woman leaning over the railing on the floor above. "Put that thing away, you idiot," she said to someone I couldn't see. "Lucho," she said, glancing at me but tossing her head in the general direction of whoever it was behind me, "is practicing to be a terrorist."

"A freedom fighter," the man's voice said peevishly. "And I'm not practicing, I'm training. Training to be a freedom fighter."

"A freedom fighter, of course," she said, grinning at me. "I forgot. You must be Rebecca, aren't you?" she asked.

I nodded, not yet having regained control of my vocal cords.

"Hold on a sec," she said, turning away from the railing.

Hold on a sec? I'd hold on a sec. My feet were still rooted to the ground in sheer terror. I heard sandals clicking on the stairs, and then she reappeared from one corner of the courtyard.

"I'm Tracey. Tracey Dougall. The paleo. Tea?"

The paleo? Tea? After that welcoming party, surely scotch would be more appropriate. But I'd take what I could get. "Sure," I managed to say.

Steve Neal wandered in. "Good. I see you've already met a member of the team." He gave both Tracey and me a nice smile, but the real warmth, regrettably, was directed toward Tracey. No wonder. She was gorgeous. Young—still in her mid-twenties, I'd say—blond, hair cut very short and spiky over a beautifully shaped head, great cheekbones, wide eyes, full mouth, perfect teeth, flawless complexion, she was one of those people who have come out on top in the genetic sweepstakes. She was wearing black tights with a black halter top, sandals with platform soles, and a large denim shirt, a man's probably, open but tied at the waist. It would be easy, I thought, to dislike this woman.

"Tracey's my prize doctoral student," Steve said, still smiling. "She's in charge of the lab." Smart too, I thought. With very little effort on my part, I thought, mere dislike could be elevated to pure hatred.

"Lucho's been playing freedom fighter with Rebecca," she said to Steve.

Steve's shoulders slumped in exasperation. "Lucho, get out here!" he ordered. From behind the door came a short, rather tubby young man, dressed head to toe in camouflage gear, his face speckled with a dark stubble, curly hair barely concealed by a Fidel Castro style hat, a gun belt winding a rather circuitous route around his paunch. As silly as he appeared, though, the gun looked real enough to me.

"Give me that thing," Steve ordered.

Lucho cringed. "How can I guard this place without a gun, Señor Doctor Neal?" he whined.

"You're a soldier, you'll think of something," Steve said in a placating but firm tone. "Now give me the gun." With more than a little reluctance, Lucho handed it over. "Now take Ms. MacCrimmon's bag to her room. The blue one," he added, pointing to a room on the second floor.

"He's a bit slow," Tracey mouthed at me, as Lucho picked up my bag and began shuffling toward the stairs. "And . . ." She tapped her index finger on her forehead. "Cuckoo."

"He's harmless," Steve said as Lucho slunk away. "He wouldn't have hurt you. Really. However, we'd better find someplace safe to put this, somewhere our freedom fighter won't find it. Can you think of a place in the lab, Tracey?"

Tracey eyed the weapon with distaste. "Sure," she said. "Give it to me." She took it very cautiously, holding the grip gingerly between thumb and forefinger well out from her body, barrel pointed toward the ground. Guns did not appear to be Tracey's thing. I liked her better than I had thought I might.

"Come on, Rebecca," Tracey said. "We'll drop this horrid object in the lab, and then we'll get Ines to make us some tea and I'll give you a hand unpacking. My room is next to yours. It'll be fun. Like college."

"Enjoy your last few hours of leisure." Steve grinned at me. "I'm putting you to work first thing tomorrow. Let me know where you hide the you-know-what, Tracey," he said as Lucho shuffled back into view on the balcony above us. Dealing with Lucho, apparently, was like dealing with a very small child. As in let's put the g-u-n in the w-h-a-t-e-v-e-r.

Tracey waited until Lucho was again out of sight before leading me to a room off the courtyard to the right of the main door. The lab was a large room with trestle tables along both walls, plus one large table right in the middle of the room. On the left, what looked to be a complete skeleton was stretched out full length on the table, its head resting on a black velvet pillow. "That's Benji," Tracey said, following my glance. "Super, isn't he?"

"Big Benji," a voice said, and I turned to see a tall, greying man coming through a door off to the right. "As you can see, he is, or was, rather tall. I'm Ralph," he said, extending his hand. "Welcome to the Hacienda Nowhere."

"Ralph Woolsey, Rebecca MacCrimmon," Tracey said, doing the introductions. "Ralph is our ceramicist, University of Southern California. Rebecca—"

"I know who Rebecca is." Ralph laughed. Ralph too was rather tall, with a relaxed and easygoing manner, and a nice firm handshake. "Steve has talked about little else for the last two days except how he's found this wonderful woman who is going to get us all organized. I can only say that if you can get us even remotely organized," he added, his arm sweeping around the room, "you are a wizard indeed."

"It's not as bad as it looks," Tracey said. I looked about me. Actually, it seemed pretty orderly to me, in a chaotic sort of way. On the left there was Big Benji and assorted other bones. "That's my domain," Tracey said, following my glance. "I'm working on my doctoral thesis in paleoanthropology. I'm the bone person on the project. We're learning some interesting things about the state of people's health in Moche times from my friend Benji here. Look," she said, grasping Benji's skull and holding it up to my face. "Nice teeth! The other side of the room, as you can see," she said, waving the skull in Ralph's direction, "is Ralph's."

Ralph's side of the room was covered in pottery shards, some soaking in large pans of water. A couple of pots were being carefully restored, broken piece by piece. About halfway along the wall was a photo setup with a camera on an arm over the table, and a computer, of the laptop variety. "How are you on computers, Rebecca?" Ralph asked. "We're kind of hoping you can help us with the cataloguing of all this stuff."

I took a quick look. It was the computer and software that I used in the shop. How long ago and far away that seemed. "Fine," I replied, collecting myself after a moment or two of incipient homesickness. "This will be no problem." Both of them looked rather delighted. They might not have been quite so thrilled had they known I was thinking how easy this made it for me to check up on their records in search of a flared Moche pot and a turquoise and gold ear ornament.

At the back of the room there was a pile of boxes, each marked with the year, the initials CV for, I assumed, Campina Vieja, and *Caja,* box in Spanish, and then a number. "What are these?" I asked.

"Boxes of catalogued artifacts taken from the site," Tracey replied. "We study them, catalogue and store them in these boxes. At the end of each season, they're packed up and shipped to Lima to the INC, the *Instituto Nacional de Cultura.* One requires a *credencial,* a permit, to do archaeology in Peru," Tracey went on. "*Credenciales* are issued by the INC, and everything found on archaeological projects in Peru becomes INC property."

She walked over to the pile of boxes. "Speaking of storage, how about *Caja ocho*, Box eight?" she said, holding the gun up carefully, then laying it in the box. "Will you two remember that? Remind me to tell Steve too," she said, "and to take it out before we ship, of course. I doubt the INC would be too impressed by finding a very new gun in with the artifacts from our project! Now let's see what we can do about getting you settled, Rebecca. Don't tell Lucho about *Caja ocho*, Ralph," she admonished as we left.

"Wouldn't dream of it," he replied, smiling at her. Ralph too, judging by the warmth of his smile, was an admirer of Tracey.

Tracey led the way to the kitchen and imposed on Ines to make us a cup of tea. Dinner was well under way by now, but Ines seemed to like Tracey and put the kettle on, and the two of them chattered away while it heated. Ines was still not speaking to me.

The kitchen looked reasonably complete. There was an acid-green refrigerator, propane according to Tracey, a range in cobalt blue, with a little propane stove as backup, a sink and all the usual accessories. I don't know what I expected out here, but clearly it was something more primitive. Dinner, whatever it was, smelled delicious.

Armed with cups of tea, Tracey and I had a quick tour of the place, and then went upstairs. The Hacienda Garua was essentially a square, with a ground level courtyard, and rooms opening onto it on two floors, all of them off tiled hallways that were open to the courtyard and lined with beautiful wrought iron railings.

The rooms on the main floor were raised slightly, three steps, from the ground level, for some reason. Esthetics perhaps, or to protect them from floods, which were hard to imagine in such a desert climate, although not, according to Tracey and from what I'd heard from Steve, unprecedented. At the back, opposite the door, was the dining room and the kitchen. To the right was the lab and some storage space. To the left, at the back was a little sitting room, a library of sorts with a few worn but comfortable armchairs, lots of books, and a writing desk. The first room to the left of the main entrance was Lucho's. His door featured a skull and crossbones on it and a warning not to enter. With the exception of the kitchen, which was tucked into a corner at the back of the hacienda, all rooms had not only doors, but windows that opened to the central courtyard, and it was possible to walk all the way around the square on either floor.

Stairs led from the ground floor to the second in the two back corners of the courtyard, at the opposite end from the entrance. The women's rooms were situated on the second floor on the right-hand side as one came through the main door, the men's to the left. My room, the blue room, was at the far end of the right-hand hall, joined to Tracey's, the yellow room, by a shared bathroom. Hilda Schwengen's room was the first on the right from the main door, and featured, according to Tracey, real windows, that is windows that opened to the outside at the front of the hacienda.

The counterpart of Dr. Schwengen's on the men's side was Steve Neal's. Next to him, working toward the back, was Ralph's, and then a room that was used by visiting scholars, and sometimes, Tracey told me, by one Ricardo Ramos, a Peruvian archaeologist who was, I gathered, a friend and colleague of Steve's.

Hilda and Steve, I was told, had private bathrooms, the rest of us shared small bathrooms with toilet and sink. There were communal showers at the back of the second floor, the women's on the right, the men's on the left.

"The hacienda was built in the late 1800s," Tracey said, in answer to my query. "It belonged to a wealthy family, who had, I'm told, the most amazing parties in the courtyard. But the water ran out, and the house had to be abandoned," she said, "until about thirty years ago, when someone opened it for a short period of time as an inn. It was way too isolated to be successful, and the owner went bankrupt."

"Who owns it now?" I asked.

"Carlos Montero," she replied, making a face. "Awful man. An old lech. His father held the mortgage on the place, so he got it when the inn closed. You'll meet Carlos soon enough, maybe too soon for your taste. He likes to hang around. But you're a lucky girl. He's gone to Trujillo and won't be joining us this evening."

As she spoke, I was unpacking Rebecca's duffel bag, placing everything on the bed.

"You didn't bring much," Tracey said dubiously, eyeing my rather pathetic little heap of belongings.

What could I say? That I was on the lam, using someone else's identity and someone else's clothes? "I didn't know I was coming until the last minute, so I didn't have much time to pack," I said lamely. "Even so," I said, peering into the tiny cupboard, "there doesn't seem to be any way to hang this stuff up."

"Oops," Tracey said. "That's because I scoffed all the hangers. I brought more than enough clothes for both of us. I'll lend you some of my stuff. I've got lots. Come on into my room and see."

I smiled nicely, even though it was quite apparent to me that I had about twenty pounds on Tracey, and knew nothing would fit. But she was right about one thing: She'd brought lots of clothes, enough for an army really. Her room was crammed with clothes, shoes, photos, stuffed animals, and trinkets of all kinds.

"I really love my work," she said, noticing me looking around. "But I hate being away from home, so I always pack lots of stuff, so I feel sort of as if I'm home. I miss my mom and my stepfather, my brother, my pals, my boyfriend Jamie," she said, pointing to photos of each in turn. "I phone home once a week, and sometimes twice. I even miss my car," she said, handing me a photo of the vehicle in question. Well, who wouldn't? I thought. A Saab convertible. I too might miss such a car, should I ever make enough money to own one. Tracey was beautiful, smart, and apparently rich as well. But not spoiled somehow, I thought. "Here," she said, tossing some clothes on her bed, "some hangers."

Just then we heard Steve call from below, and went out onto the hallway. "Cocktails," he yelled so all could hear, "now being served in the lounge."

Hilda Schwengen was in the little lounge, sitting ramrod straight in a rather uncomfortable-looking chair, a halo of smoke winding sinuously around her head from the cigarette she held between long, elegant fingers. On the table beside her there was a very large drink, scotch, I thought, no water, no ice. She did not get up as I came in. In fact, she did not so much as lean forward when we were introduced. Instead, she extended her hand, palm turned down slightly, in such a way that for a moment I felt I was expected to lean over and kiss it. Perhaps, I thought, she believes her own publicity, about being a legend, the high priestess of Peruvian archaeology, as Steve had described her. She was tall, I thought, and very slim, with a long neck and aristocratic cheekbones. She was wearing an off-white linen shirt and pants with a silver metal belt. Her hair, silver-grey, was long and worn tied back loosely.

"Welcome to the Hacienda Garua and to our little project," she said to me, her tone gracious, but her voice rubbed raw by the smoke of a million cigarettes. "I understand Lucho pulled a gun on you when you arrived," she said. "I really must apologize on behalf of my staff. You must have been terrified."

"It was certainly an exciting start to my work here," I agreed. Everyone laughed, Steve appeared at my elbow, bottle of scotch in hand, and the party began. Everyone on the directors' team squeezed into the little room and chatted away about the day, what they'd found, what they hadn't. I got to meet Pablo Vela, the foreman, a nice young man, medium height and thin, with a beginning moustache that was quite fetching. He lived in town, he told me, but had dinner at the hacienda every evening to plan the next day. "Better food here than at home." He laughed. In honor of my arrival, the students who lived and normally ate in town had been invited to dinner: Alana, Susie, Janet, and Robert, students from the University of Southern California, George, David, and Fred from Texas A&M. The only person missing was Lucho, who preferred to stand guard outside, preparing himself, apparently, for the rigors of the life of a freedom fighter. Against what or whom he was guarding us, no one said.

Although the tiny room was packed and the scotch flowed freely, cocktails at the hacienda were, that evening and others to follow, a rather subdued affair, more ritual than anything else. Everyone made a point of going over to talk to Hilda, deference in their manner, who always sat the same way in the same chair, cigarette in one hand, glass of scotch in the other. Everyone, I should say, except Tracey, who stayed as far away from the legend as she could in such a small space.

When Ines appeared at the door, we went in to dinner. And what a meal it was. First there was a spicy corn and sweet potato *sopa,* which Ines served from a large tureen on the sideboard, followed by large platters of corvina, a type of sea bass, I was told, in a walnut sauce, avocado slices smooth as silk, marinated vegetables, and sliced potatoes covered in a sauce I didn't recognize but instantly fell in love with. All of us tucked into the food with real gusto, except for Hilda Schwengen, who pushed her food around her plate between gulps of scotch. Several times I saw her look down the table in the general direction of Tracey, who was talking in an animated fashion to Pablo and Steve. There was something in that glance that gave me pause. I couldn't interpret it, but I knew it wasn't friendly. Perhaps it was simple jealousy. Tracey was certainly someone who could arouse envy in almost anyone, were it not for the fact that she seemed to me to be genuinely friendly. But I'd just got here; maybe Hilda knew something I didn't. Ralph too, I noticed, watched Tracey a great deal more than was necessary, confirming my earlier impression that he was more than a little besotted.

In any event, a few minutes into the meal, Hilda arose from her seat at the head of the table, almost all her food left on her plate, and excused herself. Hefting the half filled bottle of scotch off the side table, she left the dining room. I could hear her slow steps on the stairs and on the upper hall as she made her way to her room.

For a moment, no one said anything until Tracey broke the silence. "Ines," she said, "please take a tray up to Dr. Schwengen, will you?"

"She doesn't eat," Ines replied.

"I know," Tracey said quietly, "but take it up anyway."

If Hilda didn't eat, she was missing a good thing, I decided, as Ines's food continued to flow from the kitchen. Then Tracey left the room, and I began to wonder what was really going on here, but she returned minutes later with her hands behind her back.

"I've been saving these for a special occasion," she said, "and I think Rebecca's arrival and her narrow escape from death at the hands of the ferocious freedom fighter Lucho must qualify. Ta dah!" she exclaimed, and produced from behind her back three very fine bottles of wine. Now, how could you dislike someone like that? I thought to myself, and judging by the chorus of cheers that greeted the gesture, we agreed on that. From then on the conversation and the noise level rose considerably. Everyone had an archaeological adventure to tell, each more exciting and more unbelievable than the last. Steve and Tracey told stories of helping the police with their investigations of crimes long hidden; Pablo told tales of townspeople angered by the archaeological digs taking place in their region, robbing them of their livelihood, the illegal traffic in artifacts. The students had funny stories about the primitive conditions under which they'd lived from time to time.

But the best story was reserved for last: the time Hilda Schwengen held off four banditos. Hilda and Steve were heading back to town in an open Jeep on a narrow country road lined by high embankments, not far from one of their dig sites, when four men leapt from the bushes into the path of their car, brandishing metal pipes and, in one case apparently, a sword. Steve and Hilda were ordered to get out of the vehicle. Hilda calmly reached over, pulled a gun out of the glove compartment, and started shooting over their heads. ''I believe they thought she was a poor shot,'' Steve said amid much laughter. ''Even I thought so. I was cowering on the floor of the Jeep . . . if you can imagine someone my size cramming himself into that small a space. Which I did. But Hilda kept firing, and eventually it occurred to them she might get lucky and hit something, so they turned tail and ran.''

It was a story, I could tell, that had been told time and time again until it had reached almost mythic proportions. It was also apparent to me as the story was being recited that there was a great deal of affection as well as reverence for Hilda, no matter how she appeared to me.

It was a really enjoyable evening, the first I'd had in a while, and I began to relax just a little, enough so that I'd kicked off my shoes and sat curled up in the chair. As we all sat around the table enjoying the camaraderie, the power went out. This was, apparently, a reasonably regular occurrence, because candles and matches were right at hand. The evening was getting cool, however, and I decided to get my sweater from my room to cover my shoulders. I padded up the stairs in my bare feet, enjoying the feel of the cool marble on my toes, and careful not to make any noise to disturb Hilda. As I got to my room, I noticed the door was partly open, not as I had left it, and I thought I could see a flicker of candlelight within. Carefully, I eased my way very quietly around the door.

Ines was there, her back to me, a candle flickering on the night table. She was touching each article of clothing I had left on the bed, and I thought I heard her whispering. When each piece had been touched in turn, she straightened, and without turning around, she said, "So you've come at last, as it is spoken." Then turning to look at me, rigid in the doorway, she whispered, *"Cuidado al arbolado!"* Beware of the woods. "If you are to succeed, you must survive the woods."

Suddenly there was a gust of wind, the candle went out, a door banged sharply. I turned, distracted by the noise. When I turned back, she was gone, although I was blocking the door. I looked to see if she had gone through the little bathroom to Tracey's room, but could not see her there. It was perplexing and unsettling.

I went back downstairs a few minutes later, and Ines was there, cleaning up in the kitchen. She didn't say anything to me; in fact, she didn't acknowledge my presence in any way. Shortly thereafter, her brother, Tomas, came to take her home and Steve, Tracey, and I walked her to the door. Tomas had a little motorcycle taxi, a bike with a seat in the back. Ines climbed on and sat primly, her hat pulled down firmly, her bag clutched in front of her. As her brother, whom I'd not met, wheeled the bike around to head back into town, I saw a figure caught for a moment in the beam of the headlight, standing under one of the ghostly arches of the little folly outside. He was a workman, a *campesino* or farmer, perhaps, judging from his clothes, and he was holding something in a sack—burlap, I thought, or plastic—a rice sack most likely. He quickly melted back into the shadow of the arches as the beam passed by.

Strange place, I thought.

Later that night, I lay in bed unable to sleep, although perhaps I dozed. The episode with Ines preyed on my mind, as did the vision of the man under the arches, and so I started at every little noise. At some point, I began to realize that the breeze had begun to whisper, and I got up quietly and went to the door, opening it just a crack. There were indeed voices, whispers, down below. I sensed, rather than saw, the big front door open a little and someone slip in. A match flared for a second or two just as I moved to the railing to see who was down there. Steve, I thought, a stranger and someone else I couldn't see. The conversation was short and it seemed, an angry one, and then the second person, whoever he was— the man of the arches perhaps?—slipped out again. I was back in my bed, door closed tight, before Steve reached the second floor.

A moment or two later, I thought I heard Tracey's door, next to mine, click shut. I got up once again and looked out. The night sky was fairly bright, despite the haze, and I caught a glimpse of Tracey gliding

along the balcony on the opposite side of the courtyard. She went right down to the end, and although I
waited for a few minutes more, didn't return. Steve
and Tracey. I wasn't surprised, but it was a little dis-
appointing just the same.

10

I FIRST MADE the acquaintance of Señor Carlos Montero, owner of the rather preciously named Paradise Crafts Factory, and my personal choice for man most likely to have smuggled Moche artifacts out of Peru, a few days after I'd arrived. It was not an auspicious start to the relationship, as I recall, and certainly not one that improved his standing in my eyes, Montero more than living up to his advance billing from the women on the project. But at least it afforded me an excuse to visit the factory, something I'd been trying to accomplish since I'd first arrived.

The problem was that my life as Rebecca was seriously cutting into the time I needed to solve the problems of my real life. In the morning I rose to the crowing of the rooster in the yard outside the hacienda, not long after five A.M. By six, I'd washed, the degree to which I did so dictated by the state of the water supply, I had the coffee on, some fruit, bread, and peanut butter out on the table, as the team, yawning, made their way to the kitchen, such as it was. Shortly after six, I drove into town, picked up Pablo, the foreman, at one end of town, and a group of students studying with Steve and Hilda who were billeted in a small apartment building right in town. Some piled in the back of the truck, others in the cab. I then drove them to the site, a dusty area just a few hundred yards off the Panamericana, dropped them off, and headed back for a marker on the highway, where I picked up the team of Peruvian workers, eight in all, and ferried them to the site. Then I returned to the hacienda. By that time, Steve would be eager to get going, and Hilda, who apparently thought there were three food groups—caffeine, nicotine, and alcohol—would be well into the cigarettes and coffee she lived on all day. I'd take them out to the site to join the others.

At seven-thirty or so, I picked up Ines Cardoso at the highway and took her to the market in Campina Vieja to buy groceries. While she was doing that, I picked up whatever supplies were needed for the hacienda and the dig: scotch every day, drinking water almost always, film for the cameras, rope, wood, chains, propane for the refrigerator, whatever. As soon as that was done, I headed out to the site to assist with the work there, dropping Ines and her bundle of groceries off at her home. She didn't mention the incident in my room in the whole time I was there, and neither did I. I didn't think she'd explain herself if I asked, and furthermore it was difficult to take a warning about the woods very seriously when there were so few trees around.

When I wasn't running errands, I worked in the lab. Every single artifact at the site, no matter how small or insignificant they might look to me, was sent back, usually in a plastic baggie with a tag on it with details of where it had been found. Each article had to be entered into the computer on a template designed for that purpose: the first cut at information included location, depth in ground, size, material, and a description of some sort. Then there a more detailed template, depending on the type of material, which was much more specific. Here Ralph and Tracey tried to classify the material by period and culture—middle Moche for example. It was painstakingly detailed work for them. For me it was a kind of mindless activity, simply taking the information given me and entering it in the appropriate place on the template.

At some point every day, and sometimes more than once, I'd pick up the little bags of whatever artifacts had been found at the site, delivering them to Tracey and Ralph, who worked all day in the lab.

If I had a moment to spare, I worked at the site, sometimes as what is called a digger assistant, working under the supervision of Steve or Hilda. The excavation site was about twelve feet square marked off in sections by a grid of string. I was occasionally allowed to clear areas of the site, but usually I either helped with the recording of the artifacts that had been found—by and large, ceramic shards—or carried debris from the pit to the sieve. The sieve was made of a large piece of mesh, about two and a half feet square, framed and mounted on legs, so that it was about waist height. The debris was placed on top, and then the frame was rocked back and forth on its legs so that the dirt fell through, leaving tiny artifacts on the top. These were recorded and bagged to take back to the lab. Nothing, I learned, is removed from a site until it's been mapped on a grid of the site, recorded, and often photographed.

On a hot day, I was supposed to be out at the site between two and two-thirty to bring everyone back; on a cooler day they worked a little later. Not much though. In the afternoon, the breeze, which would normally be welcomed in the heat, gained in intensity until the dust whipped and swirled around the site. It got in your eyes, your clothes, your hair. You could taste it in your mouth. Worse yet, on a bad day, it drifted back into the excavation, covering up much of the day's work.

At five every day, I'd be back out at the highway to pick up Ines at her place, to bring her to the hacienda to finish preparing dinner. In between I ferried people and supplies between the site, town, and the hacienda as needed.

At some point every day I went to the commune to check on my two young charges, as I quickly came to think of them, Puma and Pachamama. I rather surprised myself with this sentimental attachment to the two kids. I didn't quite know how they had wormed themselves into my affections, but it seemed they had.

They'd been assigned a little hut, and Pachamama, with the help of the other members of the group, very quickly made it quite habitable, for a hut, that is. They'd found some woven rugs somewhere which were nailed to the walls to keep the dust and sand out, and someone had lent them a little wooden table and a couple of stools. They were still sleeping in their sleeping bags but had a little platform to put them on. Puma immediately set himself the task of learning Spanish, although it was hardly necessary for life on the commune, the inhabitants being, by and large,

Americans. He spoke Spanish to me whenever I visited, and while it was certainly rudimentary at this stage, I thought he showed some real facility for the language.

The head of the commune was a man, who, in a fit of hubris, had named himself Manco Capac, after the first Inca king, said to be the son of the Sun and the Moon. When I asked him why he'd chosen the name, he replied, "Whatever works," a statement I began to realize was the motto of the commune. That, and "go with the flow."

Manco Capac was not a tall man, rather short, in fact, about my height, but what he lacked in stature, he made up for in presence. He'd been an actor at one time, apparently, before he became the original Inca reincarnated, and it showed. He had a large head, in proportion to his body, moved with a certain grace, as if he'd studied dance, and had a voice that commanded attention. He had piercing eyes, an unusual shade of blue; rather splendid cheekbones; and grey hair pulled back into a very long braid at the back. I'd have put him in his early fifties. One of the other commune members, a middle-aged man who had inexplicably chosen the name Moonray—I gathered that taking an alias was part of the ritual of leaving one's past life behind—told me that Manco Capac had been on the verge of a brilliant career in Hollywood, when he'd become sickened by the excess, and come to Peru to get back to basics. I could certainly understand someone being sickened by Hollywood, but Manco Capac, imposing though he might be, didn't look familiar to me, so how close to the verge of success he had actually been was debatable. Failed actor seemed more likely.

The commune consisted of a group of small huts, where most lived, and a main building, with water and electricity, where the kitchen and eating area were located, and in the back of which Manco Capac resided. About twenty people, of all ages, shapes, and sizes lived there, and everyone was given a job. Pachamama worked in the kitchen, and Puma, who struck me as not being particularly bright, but a sweet kid, was assigned a lot of the grunt work, such as finding wood, or clearing more land for the primary activity which, according to Moonray, was farming. At least they called it farming. Gardening is what I'd call it, and difficult gardening at that. The soil was very sandy, and the commune sat on the edge of a clump of trees, algarroba or carob trees with beautiful spreading branches, but some of the nastiest thorns I'd ever seen. They covered the ground beneath the trees and would tear through thin soles in a flash. All in all, it had an indelible air of the sixties, right down to the faint whiff of marijuana.

Never having been one inclined to togetherness, I'd often wondered what people saw in such a lifestyle, and for some reason I decided that in Puma I'd found a kindred spirit in that regard. Pachamama liked the bustle of the main house and the kitchen, made friends easily, and seemed to regard all of this as a bit of a lark. I had a feeling that when she'd had enough of the life of the commune, she'd just blithely move on. But on more than one occasion I'd found Puma alone on the edge of the property, deep in thought. Not wanting to startle him, I'd watched him from a distance.

The place was peaceful and very quiet, the silence broken only by some distant voices singing in the commune and the chink and scraping of a trowel nearby. Puma looked up finally and saw me. "Hear that sound? Farmer over there," he said, gesturing behind the commune. "Putting up a wall between us and him. Not too keen on us, I'd say. I offered to help, but either he didn't understand me, or he didn't like me. I'm not sure which. He should learn to go with the flow like Manco Capac says. I told him about the 'pocalypse too, but I don't think he understood that either."

Lucky man, I thought.

He smiled slightly, as if he could read my thoughts. "Reminds me of home, that sound. I lived near a quarry."

For a moment I saw him for what he probably was: a homesick kid a long way from home. It was a feeling I could understand. "Why don't you pack up and go home, Puma?" I asked him. "Is it the money? Do you need money to get home?"

He looked at me for a moment, and I thought, as the rims of his eyes went red, that he might cry. "I can't go home right now. I don't have any money, but it's not that. I just can't go home right now."

"Neither can I," I said. We sat in silence for quite a while.

"Is there any chance you'd have any time to help me out with the work I have to do at the project, Puma?" I said at last. "I have a little trouble loading the water cubes and the propane tanks into the back of the truck, and could sure use some help." It was hardly subtle, and Puma, bright though he wasn't, saw through it immediately, but he agreed right away.

After that I stopped regularly at the commune, not once a day, but often enough, and if he didn't have any communal chores to perform, I drove him into town. Town with Puma was an experience, particularly the market, where all was grist to his mill. Avocados, oranges, bananas, pots, pans, scarves disappeared and reappeared to the amazement of all, particularly the children. No matter his Spanish was rudimentary, his magic spoke for him, and we were never without a little crowd about us.

I decided I'd been wrong in thinking him not very bright. He was poorly educated, yes, and a little weird, marched to a different drummer as it were, but he had a phenomenal knowledge of history, and regaled me with stories of the conquistadores and the Inca, in particular, that breathed life into textbook history. On a few of these trips, he tried to engage me in conversation about the 'pocalypse,' and whether or not I believed in past lives, but I refused to be drawn into the discussion. Neither of us spoke of home.

I offered to pay him to help me with my work, but he refused. So I sent him on errands, to pick up the water, several yards of rope, or whatever, and told him to keep the change from the bills I gave him. That seemed to be acceptable to him, didn't offend his pride. It was a silent pact of some kind, I think, between two people who, for their own reasons, in both cases unstated, couldn't go home just then.

It was on one of those many trips to town that I met Carlos Montero. On that particular occasion I'd driven Puma and Pachamama into town so they could spend a little of Puma's hard-earned cash on some ice cream, and Tracey to the Telefónico del Peru office to call home. After her phone call, Tracey and I left Puma juggling oranges for the children, and went to the market to search out some supplies she needed for the lab. I was rather enjoying myself, I recall, taking in all the smells, sights, and sounds of a busy marketplace.

Campina Vieja is a pleasant place, not pretty, perhaps, but always interesting, one of many such towns strung like little beads along the Panamericana. It has the requisite Plaza de Armas in front of the church, this one so small it is difficult to get back far enough to fully appreciate the statue of the conquering hero at its center, in this case, Simón Bolívar, one of the liberators of Peru. Day and night, the little square is a hive of activity. In the evenings, couples come to pass the time, strolling in tight little circles around Bolívar. A rabbit warren of streets, more lanes really, radiates out from the square. Not wide enough for our truck, many of them, they are the domain of little motorcycle taxis that ply their trade up and down and around the town.

The market is more expansive than the rest of the town, situated as it is in a large open area. But once inside, the aisles take on the character of the laneways elsewhere: crowded, noisy, busy all the time, almost claustrophobic in their closeness.

We were wandering around on the upper level of the market, munching happily on *alfajores,* sublime little shortbread sandwiches with a sweetened condensed milk filling, as we walked about.

"Yuk!" Tracey said. "He's back!"

Yuk? I turned to see a round-faced, middle-aged man in grey slacks and a pink, short-sleeved shirt, the buttons of which strained against a belly of some proportions. He was waving and yahooing at Tracey from two aisles away.

At closer range, Carlos Montero, our sponsoring angel, proved to be a man with bad teeth, his smile a flash of gold fillings, and what can only be described as roving hands. No wonder all the women on the project had winced when they heard from Lucho that his uncle's return from Trujillo was imminent.

If I thought at my age I was immune, I was soon disabused of that. Any female, no matter her age, size, or general disposition, was apparently appealing to Señor Montero.

"Rebecca, this is Señor Montero, our sponsor, to whom we owe so much," Tracey said brightly. From where I was standing, I could see her fingers crossed behind her back. "Señor Montero, this is Señora MacCrimmon, the latest addition to our team."

"Señor Montero," I said, trying to sound enthusiastic, "I've heard so much about you." That much was true. "Steve has told me about the wonderful reproductions you make at Paraíso," I went on. "I do hope I'll have a chance to come and see your factory sometime."

Montero gave me a smile that was essentially a leer and kissed my hand, holding it way too long for comfort. "And are you an archaeologist too, señora? Such an admirable profession. How I wish I had been able to study archaeology myself, but my family was not wealthy, and it was necessary for me to begin working with my father and older brother when I was very young." He shook his head sadly, still holding my hand. I pulled it away and Montero turned his attention to Tracey, who was looking very fetching in white, a cool blond ice princess in white sleeveless tee, linen pants and sandals, thin chains of gold at her wrist and her neck.

Carlos liked what he saw obviously: He was practically salivating. "And how is Señorita Tracey?" he asked in a greasy tone.

"Just ducky!" she replied in as pleasant a manner as she could muster. "And how about you, Señor Montero?"

"Carlos, please. You must call me Carlos," he oozed. "I am extremely well. And may I dare hope that in my absence you have been successful in finding some excellent artifacts, or God willing, even, perhaps, a tomb?"

"Nothing really exciting, Señor Montero," Tracey said, assiduously avoiding his attempts at familiarity. "You won't have got your money's worth this week, I'm afraid."

"But it is not the money," he said unctuously, making a pretense of appearing pained at the mere thought. "My sponsorship is all in the name of scholarship."

"Of course," we both muttered.

Getting nowhere with Tracey, he turned back to me. "It would be a great honor to personally show you around Paraiso, señora. I do hope I will have that pleasure very soon."

Tracey began to make excuses, and after a few more minutes of expressions of appreciation for Señor Montero's great generosity and commitment to scholarship, and a promise of mine that I would come for a visit, we began to take our leave. Tracey, wisely as I was to learn, backed away from him. Naively, I turned around, bringing my first encounter with Montero to a close with a sharp pinch on my derriere. So unfamiliar was I to such treatment—I hadn't had my bum pinched since I'd been backpacking my way through Italy at the age of eighteen—I actually said nothing. Being a quick study, however, I vowed to back out of Señor Montero's presence thereafter.

"The word yuk, colorful though it may be, does not begin to describe that man. Carlos Montero goes way beyond yuk!" I hissed at Tracey when we were out of earshot. "Now I see why you don't think Lucho is so bad. I mean, he only points a gun at you. This fellow drowns you in drivel and then pinches your rear."

Tracey giggled. "Oops. Should have warned you about that." I glared at her, but then I had to laugh.

Armed with Montero's invitation, I found an excuse to visit Paradise the following day. The hacienda didn't have a telephone, and part of Montero's so-called sponsorship included the use of his telephone and fax machine. Steve asked me to send a fax to one of his colleagues back home to ask him to try to find an X-ray machine he could borrow to help in the study of Benji.

The Fabrica Paraiso was on the far side of the high-way, just a little north of the turnoff to the road to the hacienda. It was a sprawling complex of faded pink buildings that housed the factory, a body shop, and a small gas station. Montero was quite the local busi-nessman.

There was no sign of Montero in the body shop or at the gas pumps, so I entered the farthermost building through a doorway marked on either side by rather large ceramic pots decorated with Moche-style draw-ings. Just inside the door, in the dark little entrance-way, was a table on which were displayed a number of ceramic items, including three or four pots with stirrup-shaped handles, and various ceramic animals, most notably sea lions and deer. The entranceway led to the right, and I turned into a row of three little rooms, one leading into the next.

The second room had been set up as a little exhibit, with large poster boards on the walls that explained how Moche ceramics were made. Before I had time to look around, however, a timid little woman approached me quietly, as I glanced in the cabinets. "Can I help you?" she asked.

"I'm looking for Carlos Montero," I said. "Steve Neal has sent me, from the archaeology project," I added. Heaven forbid Montero should think I'd come for personal reasons. I heard Montero grunt as he hefted his not inconsiderable paunch out of a chair in the next room and came to see who was looking for him.

"Señora MacCrimmon," he exclaimed, his face breaking into a smile. "What a great pleasure!" I stayed well back as I asked him if he wouldn't mind sending the fax for us.

"Consuelo," he ordered, "get Señora MacCrimmon a soft drink. Have a seat," he said, gesturing toward a chair as Consuelo, who I decided was Montero's wife, poor thing, brought me an Inca Cola, a drink that is very popular in Peru, but which tastes to me like bubble gum in a glass. One sip was enough from my perspective. To cover up this lack of social graces on my part, I asked Montero if I could have a look around the factory while he took care of the fax.

At Montero's "of course" and gesture toward the back, Consuelo led me past Montero's desk and through a door into a very large work area where maybe twenty people turned from their work to look at me as I came in. It looked like any large industrial building anywhere: very high ceilings, open to the rafters, with louvered windows high up for light and ventilation. Ventilation in particular was needed, because at one end of the place, to my right, there was a very large kiln blasting away. On either side of the kiln were large doors open to cool the room.

Filling about half the room, opposite the kiln, were several long tables at which workers, a number of them young women, were painting ceramic vessels in preparation for firing. At the far end of the room, to the left, there was a drafting table set up at which worked a middle-aged man.

I wasn't really quite sure what to look for, now that I'd got there. Earlier I'd decided, sitting in the museum cafe in New York, that Campina Vieja was the point of origin of some Moche artifacts that were being passed off as fakes, but which were, in fact, authentic. There was only one crafts factory in town, and I was in it. So I looked around for anything suspicious, for locked doors, large pieces of equipment or packing that would cover up a trapdoor, some telltale sign of a hidden room. I couldn't see a thing. Other than the two garage-type doors on either side of the kiln, there were only three others: One was open to the back to let in some air—the kiln made the place stifling, another door was the one I'd come through from Montero's office and the rooms at the front, the other led to the washroom.

The storage area, situated in the same area as the kiln, was quite open; rows of metal industrial shelving about eight feet high were lined with various ceramic objects arranged by type. One cabinet had rows of identical fish, another had rows of Moche warriors, still others were plants, animals, and so on in various stages of finishing. Nearer the kiln there were some figures that were still wet clay, others with a first firing only, others decorated but not yet finished, and then a packing area for the finished product. I've visited similar places in my line of work, and it looked perfectly normal to me.

I took a quick look through one of the doors to the outside and saw what was left of a building about 500 yards away, four brick walls in various states of decay, no roof on it, and no windows on this side. It might have been a storage area at one time, I supposed, or a very small house, but now it could serve no useful purpose, whatever it once was.

Montero joined Consuelo and I shortly thereafter. He shooed his wife away and took over her duties as tour guide. He proved to be very knowledgeable about Moche ceramics, and how they'd originally been made. He told me that the Moche were the first in this part of the world to use molds, that the most common form of Moche pottery were vessels that had spouts in the shape of stirrups, and how it was possible to date the pottery, particularly in the southern part of the Moche empire, by the length of the spout and the type of lip on it.

He also explained in detail how his operation worked, with evident pride. "This is the starting point," he said, standing beside his draftsman, who he referred to as Antonio. "Antonio here does drawings from photographs of artifacts, and designs the molds. You see, he is drawing a beaker with scenes of a deer hunt. Over here," he said, moving to another part of the shop, "the molds are made, and here," he said, gesturing expansively about the room, "are my artists who decorate the pieces in accordance with the drawings.

"I'm very proud of my people," he went on. "They do wonderful work. Here, see this stirrup-shaped vessel in the shape of a fish, the detail." The young woman working on it smiled shyly. "Some pieces we make are inexpensive, for the tourists, but in other cases, such as this one, what we do are not strictly speaking reproductions: Rather they are original pieces done in the Moche style. I think these are works of art, really. Don't you agree?"

I did, and I said so. Carlos's people were very talented artists, and watching their deft strokes as they drew intricate designs on the ceramic surface was a pleasure, albeit one I'd have enjoyed more under different circumstances. "Do you do replicas at all, Carlos?" I asked. "Exact copies of Moche ceramics?"

"You mean use the original methods of manufacturing?" he asked. "No, we like our electric kiln far too much for that." He smiled. "In reality, we can't afford to make replicas. I can't make money on them, because they're so labor-intensive and expensive to do."

We walked the full length of the room, Montero chattering away as we went. He showed me where the shipments were packed, told me what museum shops carried some of his work, and so on. It was a revelation to me, not so much what Montero was telling me about Moche craftsmanship—Ralph had already told me a great deal about ceramics—but that he was so knowledgeable and so proud of the work that was being done. I suppose I'd assumed on the basis of his previous behavior that he was an ignorant man, but he wasn't at all. He was obviously a much more complex person than I'd thought.

He spoiled it all, right at the end, of course, with a

lecherous little squeeze, but I suppose I was already getting used to his particular way of dealing with the opposite sex. I merely extracted myself from his clutches and said my good-byes.

As I left the place, I had a very quick look in the body shop. It looked like a body shop just about anywhere, a storey and a half, open right to the roof, two service bays, and lots of mess. Nothing whatsoever looked suspicious.

That night, as usual, Hilda Schwengen disappeared soon after dinner commenced, not to be seen again all evening. Lucho continued to creep around the place, looking, I was sure, for his gun. I'd caught him in the lab, looking through the boxes, earlier in the day. Also as usual, after everyone had turned in for the night, I heard whispered conversations below me, and the creak of the main door, the click and squeak of doors on the second floor opening and closing.

I thought of the visit I'd had that day to Paraiso. I could find absolutely nothing wrong with the place. I could see no places to hide caches of priceless Moche artifacts, although I supposed someone could deliver them at the last minute and slip them into the packing cases. But then what? How did they get them out of the country? I thought about all the shipping I'd done from foreign countries for the shop. I regularly filled containers for shipping by sea, and I supposed I could have put illegal objects in the containers if I chose to. But it would be a risk at both ends I'd get caught. Lizard, of course, had been a customs agent, but surely he couldn't be the one to check every single box from Paraiso through customs. Was there someone somewhere in a museum shop waiting for the shipment and whisking the real thing out? How difficult would this be to organize, I wondered, and my conclusion was very difficult. And how, then, did the objects end up at Molesworth & Cox?

Perhaps it wasn't Paraiso, after all, I thought. If not, though, then the only other prospect in these parts was the archaeological project I was working on. I decided I needed to know a lot more about what was going on at the Hacienda Garua. On the face of it they were a friendly and relaxed group. Just beneath the surface, though, there were tensions. Hilda disliked Tracey, that I could tell, but why, I didn't know. Ralph was more than a little entranced by Tracey, but Tracey was with Steve, and Ralph could hardly help but know it. Was this just all the stuff of soap opera, the result of a small group of people isolated together far from home, or was it something more than that?

Then there was the nocturnal visitor and the man in the arches who might or might not be the same person. I decided I needed to attack this problem on two fronts: to go back to Paraiso when no one was there, and to learn a lot more about this project. It was time Steve and I had a little heart-to-heart chat.

11

*I*T HAUNTS ME *still. Sometimes I dream I am standing on a distant planet, or a desolate moon, perhaps, or some spent asteroid hurtling erratically through space. The dusty surface is pockmarked with the craters of a thousand meteorites. A single hill rises from the surface, its sides streaked, ravaged, by some ancient storm. There is no one there. Someone once inhabited this lonely place, I know, a very long time ago. The cratered surface is littered with their bones. There are other reminders too: here and there a scrap of ancient fabric, and at my feet a plait of dark hair, bleached red by the light of a distant sun seen dimly through the haze. In my dream I hear their ghostly whispers in the mist; I feel their touch in the wind-whipped dust that stings my face. Cerro de las Ruinas.*

My plans to interrogate Steve were delayed by an incident in the market that heralded the arrival in Campina Vieja of one of the most unprincipled people I have ever met. Pond scum, Steve called him. It was a chance enounter that hurled us headlong on a collision course with disaster. At the time I didn't know whether the events that unfolded were diverting me from my course, or were instead another strand in the tangled web that I was attempting to unravel. Not that it mattered what I thought: I found myself drawn along with everyone else.

When it happened, Steve, Tracey, and I were on the upper level of the market, surrounded by clusters of bananas piled five or six feet high, searching for the perfect avocados to bring back to the hacienda to serve on Ines's day off. We'd come into town to shop, for Tracey to make one of her telephone calls home (I thought all these calls were a little obsessive, but perhaps I was jealous), and for a little R&R. We were wandering around together, just enjoying ourselves, when Steve stopped so suddenly, Tracey almost ran into him.

"Shit!" I heard him mutter as he squinted off into the distance. "Tell me I'm seeing things. Shit!" he said again.

Then, as Tracey and I stared after him, he broke into a trot and, calling back over his shoulder to us, said, "I'll meet you at the El Mo in an hour." We watched as he dodged through the crowds, down some steps to the market's lower level, and then, ducking under a tarpaulin that flapped behind one of the stalls, disappeared from view.

"What was that all about?" I asked Tracey.

"Haven't a clue," she said blithely. It took a lot to worry Tracey, I noticed.

Perhaps growing up beautiful, rich, and smart gives you a feeling of invincibility. "Not a happy camper, though, is he?'' she asked. ''What'll we do now?''

''Finish the shopping, I guess, then we'll go have a beer and wait for him.'' I shrugged. If Tracey wasn't worried, then why should I be?

It took us quite a bit longer than we'd anticipated to get to the cafe cum bar and restaurant we were to meet at, El Mochica, better known as the El Mo. We still had a bit of shopping to do, and a couple of times we ran into some of the students—it was a day off for everyone—then Puma and Pachamama, and stopped to chat. When we entered the bar, Steve was already there. He was slumped in his chair and didn't even look up as we came in.

After beers were ordered, and Steve still hadn't said much of anything, Tracey prodded him. ''Talk to us, Steve! What's the problem? Who or what were you chasing?''

He made a face, a sort of tired grimace. ''In a word,'' he sighed, ''or I guess two words, *el Hombre*. The fellow the folks around here refer to as *el Hombre*.''

El Hombre? The Man. There was someone wandering around here who called himself the Man? I wanted to laugh out loud, but something in Steve's manner stopped me.

''What a dopey name!'' Tracey exclaimed. ''Who is he really, and why would anyone want to call himself that?'' she queried, undeterred by the expression on Steve's face.

He sighed. ''*El Hombre?* Beats me. Maybe he doesn't want people around here to know his real name although why he should care, when he's so open about what he does, I couldn't really say. Perhaps he just thinks it makes him sound rather grand. His name is Etienne Laforet. French. From Paris. He's an art dealer, owns a swank Parisian gallery on the Left Bank. He's also sleaze, big-time. I haven't seen him around here in a couple of years, but he used to come at least once a year, and sometimes twice. His modus operandi is always the same. Blows into town in a big, expensive car, visits a few bars and restaurants making a big show of throwing money around. Once he's made sure everyone sees he's got wads of cash, he finds himself a place to stay, parks his very flashy and expensive car—this year it's a gold Mercedes—right out front so everyone will know where he is, and then he just sits and waits.''

"Waits for what?'' I asked. "And isn't that a little dangerous, showing off your wealth like that around here? Isn't he asking for trouble?''

Steve looked at me as if I was naivete personified. "He's not asking for trouble. He *is* trouble. No one messes with him. He's waiting for people to bring him stolen artifacts, of course. They have to know he's here, that he's ready to buy, and where to find him.''

"By stolen artifacts, you mean . . . ?'' I asked.

"Pretty much anything pre-Columbian. He specializes in Moche.''

"Are you saying that he sits around waiting for people to bring their stolen goods to him, right out in the open? Like in a hotel lobby or something?''

"A house. He usually rents a house, and that's what he's done this time. The little white one with the round window on the second floor over on Calle seven near the hardware store. I followed him there this afternoon. It has a high wall surrounding it, with a large tree in the front yard, and no windows overlooking it from the other side of the street. So no one can see what's going on in the patio or the door. But there's a place to park out front, so everyone can see his car and know he's there. Perfect setup.''

''Where are the police in all this? Can't they do something about it?''

''Perhaps they could. But they don't. Maybe it's can't, maybe it's won't. This guy has a reputation for being ruthless, and people around here are really afraid to take him on.''

''But they deal with him!''

''Yes,'' he sighed. ''They do.''

''But you can't take Moche artifacts out of the country,'' I offered.

Steve gave me another are-you-new-to-this-planet look. ''Obviously there are ways,'' he said. ''He's never been caught with anything on him when he flies home to Paris, I can assure you.''

We all thought about that for a while, Steve staring moodily into his beer. ''I thought maybe he wasn't going to show up here anymore,'' he said finally. ''He's been farther south the last couple of years, and nothing much of any interest has turned up in these parts that I've heard about. I wonder what it means that he's here again. I'll have to make some enquiries, I guess.''

I wasn't sure what making enquiries meant, but I didn't have long to think about it. There was a bit of a stir in the entrance to El Mochica, and Steve turned to look at the door.

''Let's get out of here,'' he said, throwing money on the table to cover the bill, his beer still unfinished. ''This place just lost its charm.''

I was sitting with my back to the doorway, and turned my head slightly to see what had brought on this abrupt gesture on Steve's part. Out of the corner of my eye, I saw silhouetted against the bright light from outside, the figure of a man. I looked back at Steve to ask if the shadow I'd seen was *el Hombre,* but I didn't need to speak. Steve's face said it all. By the time we'd reached the door, *el Hombre* had disappeared into the lounge off to the right of the entrance and was not to be seen.

Dinner that night was more subdued than usual, Steve's black mood affecting us all. On Ines's day off, which corresponded with our break from the dig as well, the team, minus Pablo, who spent his time off in town with his family, and Hilda, who spent the day in her room, drinking herself into a stupor, no doubt, and sometimes with the addition of a student or two, crowded into the little kitchen to prepare the evening meal together, and it was normally a rather rowdy affair.

Ralph, a bachelor, liked to cook, and did it reasonably well. His responsibility was the main course, *pollo,* chicken, which he cooked in what he always referred to as the "devil's handmaid," the propane oven, because of its propensity to shut off at the critical moment. I was responsible for the appetizer, and tried to master Ines's *papas a la Huancaina,* potatoes in a cheese, onion, and hot pepper sauce that I'd found so appealing the first night. Tracey's specialty was flan, or crème caramel, so she made dessert. Steve supervised, a responsibility that included keeping the cooks' glasses filled. While the results never measured up to Ines's feasts, on the couple of occasions we'd done this, we invariably declared the meal a triumph, and in a way it was. Sometimes the power went off, usually the stove quit: There was always some obstacle to be overcome to carry it off. Tracey, as always, had one of us take a tray up to Hilda, to leave outside her door, but as often as not it was not touched by morning.

That night, for the first time since I'd arrived at the Hacienda Garua, when everyone had retired for the night, I took the little Moche man out of his tissue wrapping and studied him once again. Every time I looked at him, I saw more to admire. He was exquisite really. The workmanship was extraordinary, the more so every time I looked at him. His necklace of tiny beads, each one handmade, and each just a little bit different, was so beautifully done, it almost took my breath away. I couldn't imagine the attention to detail, the amount of time that must have been spent by some artisan, in making just one ear spool for someone, someone important no doubt. I wrapped it very carefully again and put it in its hiding place, behind a loose board in the cupboard. Was Etienne Laforet, I wondered, the connection I was looking for?

Later I heard the whispers again, and this time I got up quietly and went out to the railing. Three people were talking by candlelight at the front door. Steve was one, the other was the man I'd caught sight of for only a moment in the headlight of Ines's brother's motorcycle, the man of the arches, and the third figure, I saw this time to my surprise, was Hilda. Straining, I could pick up only snippets of their conversation.

"We can't let him get away with this," I heard Hilda say. Then, "Get Montero. Get him to talk to his brother."

More murmuring. "I'll go to Lima if I have to," Steve said.

Then, something apparently settled, the man of the

arches slipped back out into the darkness, the candle was extinguished, and Hilda and Steve headed for the stairs. I quickly pulled back into my room and pushed the door almost shut. I heard Hilda's footsteps a minute or two later, limping slightly.

Very early the next morning, well before dawn, I wakened to a quiet but persistent tapping at my door. "Rebecca, it's Hilda," she whispered. "Get dressed quickly and come downstairs."

I staggered out of bed—all this wandering around in the night was robbing me of my rest—threw water on my face, pulled on my jeans and a T-shirt, and headed downstairs. Steve, Hilda, and Ralph were already downstairs, and even Carlos Montero was there. Only Tracey was nowhere to be seen.

"Ralph, you come with me," Hilda barked. "Carlos has brought us another van, and we'll use that. Rebecca, you go with Steve. Carlos, have you got the letter?" Carlos nodded and handed an envelope to Steve.

"Okay, let's get cracking," Hilda ordered. "Steve, you and Rebecca can get something to eat on the way."

I looked at Steve, more than one question forming in my sleep-drugged mind. "I'll explain as we go," he said as we headed for the truck.

Within minutes we were heading south on the Panamericana. Steve was driving at a good clip, but fortunately the road was relatively clear this early. "We're going to Trujillo," he said. "I need to be at the INC offices when they open."

The INC. The *Instituto Nacional de Cultura*. All this to call on a government office?

"We're moving," he said. "The site, I mean.

We're closing up shop where we are and moving to another site about a mile away. At least I hope we are. I need to get a *credencial*, a license, for the new dig. Carlos got a letter from his brother, the mayor, supporting us, and the mayor and Carlos have called ahead, so the people at the INC will be expecting us.

"I may have to fly to Lima, though, to the head office, so that's why you're with me. You can drive the truck back today if need be."

"I thought you were pleased with the way the project is going," I said. "And why the big rush all of a sudden?" Steve slowed only slightly as we pulled into Campina Vieja. Local farmers were beginning to bring their products to market, and Steve had to dodge a few carts and motorcycles as we blasted through town.

"I have a," he hesitated for a second, "an informant, shall we say, a *huaquero* by the name of Arturo—I won't give you his last name, it's not important—who . . ."

"Huaquero?" I interrupted. "Is that what I think it is? A tomb robber?"

"Right. The Incas didn't have a word for god, just a word for sacred—*huaca,* hence *huaqueros,* robbers of sacred places. Long tradition in these parts. Could be the Incas themselves engaged in it, plundering the tombs of earlier cultures. Whole families around here are involved in it, and have been for generations. They're really good at it too, I'd have to say. Know what to look for, maybe better than we do, and are experts at the techniques for recovering the stuff. Pablo, our foreman, used to be a *huaquero par excellence* as a matter of fact. We've won him over, and now he's a real asset to us. A couple of his men were *huaqueros* as well. We hope by giving them a job and teaching them about their culture, we'll keep them on the straight and narrow.''

That seemed to be a somewhat risky assumption, I thought.

''So what do they—the *huaqueros*, I mean—do with what they find? Sell it on the black market?''

''Yes, in some cases; in others it's considered legit, in a manner of speaking. What I mean to say is that there are ways to own artifacts in this country quite openly, and *huaqueros* profit from it.''

''But doesn't letting people own antiquities here just encourage looting?'' I asked.

''It does. Drives me crazy. But you have to understand looting a little, don't you? You've seen how poor this area is. If you're lucky, you can make a lot more money at looting than you can fishing or farming, that's for sure. It's easy for us, coming from nice rich nations, to tell people they should donate whatever they find to a museum. The people I really blame are the buyers, especially the dealers. They're the ones who encourage this kind of thing, the ones who make the big money on the finds too, I might add. Scum, in my opinion. At least some of them, Laforet first among them. But don't get me going on this subject,'' he said, looking as if he was in serious danger of diving into a depression again.

''You were telling me about Arturo,'' I prodded.

''Right,'' he said. ''Arturo first came to me last season with some artifacts he'd found. I'd seen him hanging around watching, and eventually he showed up at the hacienda and asked me to assess some stuff for him, give him some idea of what it was worth.

''He had a couple of really nice ceramic pieces: Moche, a stirrup-spout vessel in the shape of a sea lion, complete with shell eyes, and another beaker with fine-line drawings. Most certainly genuine. They were looted, of course. There was no other way he could have got them. But he offered to tell me where he'd found them in exchange for my assessment of them. So I made a deal to get to study the fine-line vase for a day or two, before giving him my assessment.''

I said nothing. "I know what you're thinking," he went on. "But looting goes on all the time, and I'm powerless to stop it. I figure this way at least I get a chance to study the stuff before it disappears into the black market.''

I thought that one over for a minute. There were pros and cons to this argument, and the ethics seemed a little murky to me, but what did I know? After all, I was misrepresenting myself to these people, and had all along. I was also the proud possessor of a genuine Moche artifact that I had not yet got around to donating to a museum.

"Anyway, Arturo's back again this season, and brought me another couple of pieces to look at. This time he's got a real find: a little copper figure of a warrior, judging from the attire, and a really beautiful ceramic in the shape of a duck.

"Last night Arturo came to tell me that one of the local farmers, guy by the name of Rolando Guerra, is building a wall around a piece of property on the edge of the *algarrobal*, the carob tree forest. He's told the locals that he's just protecting his land from *invasores*, but Arturo tells me he's almost certain the fellow has found something, and that he's building a wall around it so that no one will see him looting it. The fact that the Guerra family are known *huaqueros*, have been forever, would be proof enough, but add to that the fact that Arturo's ceramic and warrior come from that same area, and that pretty well clinches it. The *campesino* may indeed have found the big one.''

''And the big one is?''

''A tomb. An undisturbed tomb of an upper-class person, someone important. That's the most exciting find of all in our field, and down here, it could be really spectacular. For years people studied the scenes on Moche pottery, not realizing that the scenes depicted real occurrences or rituals. For example, a lot of Moche pottery shows a scene in which captives are brought before a god, or a warrior king or priest of some kind, who often sits on a litter. In front of him there is another warrior who is half man, half bird. Behind him there is a woman, a priestess, holding a cup. Behind her there is often another figure with an animal face, usually feline.

''What's interesting is that no matter how often this scene is depicted and no matter the artist, the figures in it are similar. It's been compared to the Crucifixion or the Nativity in our culture, something that's been depicted by many people over the centuries, but always with common elements that we all recognize. In the same way, the scene I've described is obviously a ritual of some importance to the Moche, and although they had no written language, and we therefore have to surmise what's happening, it's usually referred to as the Sacrifice theme. It's a little gory: Captives have their throats slit, and it is probably their blood in the cup.''

For a second or two an unbidden image of Edmund Edwards, blood streaming all over his desk, and Lizard, Ramon Cervantes, garroted, leapt into my mind, but I resolutely stuffed the images back down into my subconscious and concentrated on what Steve was saying.

"The first warrior, for example, always wears a cone-shaped headdress with a crescent on it and rays coming out of his headdress and shoulders, a crescent-shaped nose ornament, and large round ear ornaments. He almost always has a dog at his feet.

"The priestess always wears a headdress with two large plumes, and her hair is in long plaits that end with serpent heads. The fourth warrior wears a headdress with long flares that have serrated edges. You get the idea.

"The extraordinary thing is that these people have been found," he enthused. "Walter Alva came across the tomb of the warrior priest and the bird priest at a place called Sipan. Christopher Donnan and Luis Jaime Castillo found the priestess at San Jose de Moro. They'd been buried in exactly the same regalia as that depicted on the ceramics!"

"I'm not sure I understand this," I said. "Do I understand you to say that the people depicted on the pots were real people? And if so, you're telling me they've been found. So why keep looking?"

"Good question. For certain the rituals on the ceramics were carried out in real life, and yes, real people held the positions. But the rituals were probably repeated over a very long period of time. Think of them as the British monarchy: the king or queen with the ermine cape, scepter, orb, the crown jewels. If you were new to this planet, it wouldn't take you long to figure out that these people whose picture you saw in post offices and government offices were something special. You might even realize, if you looked at historical photos, or if you stuck around awhile, that more than one person held this position, because they all wore the same regalia. In other words, the crown goes with the position. Now imagine that when one of these monarchs died, all that stuff, the crowns, the scepter, everything, was buried with them. Then—''

''Then you'd have to make all these things over for the next one!'' I exclaimed.

''Exactly.''

''Good heavens,'' I said. ''That would mean a lot of gold and silver over five centuries or so.''

''It would indeed.'' Steve smiled. ''And I just want to find a little of it. Not to keep, of course, but Hilda's and my reputations would be secure, there'd be years of research to be done on what we found, and we'd not have nearly as much trouble finding the money for our research.''

''Are there many undisturbed tombs left to be found?'' I asked. ''You've told me about the *hua-queros*, the tomb robbers, and it sounds as if they're not only good at it, but have been at it forever.''

''That's true. Thousands of Moche tombs have probably been looted since the Europeans arrived on the scene, and relatively few, maybe in the low hundreds, have been professionally excavated. So much has been lost to us permanently. But there is some good news on that front. The Inca have a story about their origins that says that before the Inca, the world was populated by savages essentially, people who lived in caves, clothed themselves in animal skins, had no religion, no villages, and so on. The Sun God is supposed to have been pretty disgusted by this, and sent one of his sons and one of his daughters to earth—they arrived in Lake Titicaca. They're told to put a rod in the ground and wherever it sinks right in they are to settle. This they do, and they eventually arrive in the area of Cuzco, build the city, and teach the people how to farm and weave and so on—civilize them, in other words.

"Now, whether or not they believed that story, the Inca were somewhat successful in persuading the Spanish that the Inca empire was the first, and that before it there were only these primitive, unorganized people. This was patently untrue, of course, as we now know. There were lots of very sophisticated cultures long before the Inca were even heard of. But what that meant was that the Spanish were not out there looking for gold beyond what could be found in the Inca cities. Not that they needed to, either. There was plenty of gold there to keep them occupied. So that helped a little.

"As for now, it's just a battle against time, which we—the good guys, I mean—are losing, in my opinion, despite the fact that the Peruvian government has made it illegal to export any Moche artifacts, and a number of countries, including the U.S., have signed agreements supporting this. So we keep on looking, and sometimes we find what the *huaqueros* have missed, or we get a chance like this one.

"So I'm going to the INC to try to get a *credencial*, or extend the one I've got, for that site, and start digging before the wall goes up. I figure this may explain why Laforet's in town. Guerra must have some way of contacting him, and told him he'd found a tomb. And I'm just not prepared to lose another one to pond scum!"

"Didn't you tell me that it takes a year or two to get a license?" I asked.

"It usually does, hence the letter from the mayor

to support the application. I'm stopping off in town to pick up a friend of mine, a Peruvian archaeologist by the name of Ricardo Ramos, who I hope will come with me and help me plead my case. Hilda is heading to Carlos's place to use his telephone to try to get in touch with Ramos. Hopefully he's in town, and we'll be able to find him.

"God, I'd like to find one for Hilda," he said a moment later. "You aren't seeing her at her best, you know. She can be a lot of fun. But she had a terrible accident last year; she fell off a ladder into a pit we were digging. Hurt her back very badly. This will be her last season. I'm not sure she should be here at all, she's in such pain. That's why she drinks. I assume you can't have helped notice how much she drinks."

"I've noticed," I said. "She and Tracey don't seem to get along too well," I added. If Steve was feeling this talkative, I figured I'd keep going.

"No," Steve sighed. "Tracey's an up-and-comer, that's for sure. Knows what she wants and gets it. Hilda may consider her a bit of a threat under the circumstances. That's the only thing I can think of that would explain it. Tracey wanted to do fieldwork this year, but Hilda said her services were required in the lab. Tracey's disappointed and probably said so. I don't want you to think badly of Hilda, no matter what it looks· like. She's done absolutely dynamite work down here, from a scholarly perspective. What happened to her is really unfortunate, and it's one of the reasons we're all working hard this year. We'd like to find something really great for her."

We made really good time to Trujillo, stopping only once to get gas at a Shell station. It was barely nine o'clock when we roared around Trujillo's Plaza de Armas, with its brightly painted buildings and a rather extraordinary, and disproportionate, statue of an athlete atop a column. Steve soon pulled up to the door of a dark red building. A tall, angular man with an incipient beard was leaning against the doorjamb. He walked toward the truck as we pulled up, and climbed into the backseat.

"Buenos días," he said.

Steve reached into the backseat and shook his hand. "Hilda found you, I see," he said. "Ricardo, this is Rebecca MacCrimmon, Rebecca, this is Dr. Ricardo Ramos." We smiled at each other. I liked him immediately. "Did Hilda give you the details?"

"Some." Ramos looked at his watch. "Let's go get a coffee. The INC office doesn't open until nine-thirty. You can fill me in, in the meantime."

We found a little *chifa* and got some coffee, and for Steve and me, toast with marmalade. Steve told Ramos all about his visitations from Arturo. Ramos didn't seem to find anything unusual in an archaeologist dealing with a *huaquero*, I noticed. Then Steve unfolded a map and spread it out on the table. "Hacienda," he said, stabbing his finger on the map. "Current site." He pointed again. "And here, the new site. Arturo says the locals call it *Cerro de las Ruinas*."

Cerro de las Ruinas, hill of ruins. Steve pulled an aerial photograph out of his briefcase. "Let's have a closer look," he said. "This was taken recently, about two months ago." We all peered at the aerial photograph. I could follow the riverbed, and soon found the hacienda and the site we were currently working on. Where Cerro de las Ruinas was concerned, we had to do some searching.

"Got it!" Ramos exclaimed finally. "Right here," he said, pointing. I looked at the spot he was indicating. I could make out the trees quite easily, and then, right beside them, a shadow that indicated there might be a wall. On one side of the wall, shaded by the trees, there was a dark outline that Ramos said was a hill. It was difficult for me to make it out, but they had the training, I didn't, so I just tried to get my bearings. A little farther along, on the other side of the wall, I could see the roofs of some little huts. The commune, I thought suddenly. So Guerra was Puma's farmer, the fellow he thought was building a wall between himself and the commune. Presumably it wasn't having a commune in his backyard that was bothering Guerra so much. It was the prospect of anyone at all nearby seeing him hauling treasures out of the ground.

"So what do you think?" Steve asked.

"Well," Ramos said, rubbing the stubble on his chin, "it's hard to be certain there's anything worthwhile there from this photograph. On the other hand, you're right about the Guerra family. I certainly wouldn't mind being a burr in their saddle for a change, instead of the other way around." He paused, then shrugged. "Let's go for it!" he said. Steve grinned.

"We'll have to go for the preemptive strike," Ramos added. "With the Guerras, one whisper about this, and they'll have the whole family out digging the place up and destroying everything in their path before we can get there."

"So let's go, then," said Steve, looking at his watch.

At 9:30 the two men disappeared into the INC offices, and I was left to mind the truck.

About an hour later the two men emerged. "Let's roll," Steve said, getting behind the wheel. "The airport. We're going to Lima! The people here are calling ahead. They'll see us as soon as we can get there." I could sense his excitement.

At the airport, I saw them right to the gate. There was a flight already boarding.

"Head back for Campina Vieja, will you, and tell Hilda. I'll get a message to you sometime tonight via Montero. If it's a no, then I'll make my own way back from Trujillo on the bus. If it's a yes, time will be of the essence, and I'll need you to meet the plane, okay?" I nodded.

"Are you okay with this, really?" he asked.

"I am. I'll stand by," I replied.

"Don't speak to anyone except Hilda, Ralph, or Tracey about this, will you?" he said.

"Of course not," I said.

"You're a gem!" he said, hugging me. "See you tomorrow one way or the other." He turned toward the aircraft, but then turned back, and much to my surprise, hugged me again. I watched as the two men crossed the tarmac and went up the steps to the aircraft.

I drove carefully back to Campina Vieja, not wishing a run-in with the police for any reason. I went first to the site, and Hilda came over to the truck as soon as I pulled up, dust swirling. I told her what had happened.

"We're trying to look nonchalant," she said, irony in her voice. "So no one will guess anything's up, not even the students. We've told them that Steve had to go to Trujillo on business, so you drove him, and that Ralph and I are filling in for him for the day. I took

Ines into the market this morning, but I'll leave it to you to pick her up as usual. Don't say anything at dinner while Pablo's there, will you?''

I could feel myself getting caught up in the excitement. It was almost impossible to avoid. All this secrecy and plotting, the rush to Trujillo. Tracey, for some reason, wasn't looking as interested as I would have expected; in fact she was a little withdrawn. I wondered whether the hug from Steve meant all was not well with the two of them. The rest of us could barely do justice to Ines's meal of *sopa* and fish and brown sugar pudding while we waited.

Pablo and Ines eventually left for home, and as soon as they were gone, we got down to planning how we would approach closing down one site and moving to the next with the greatest of speed. The idea was to spring the *credencial* on Guerra before he knew what was happening. Superstitiously, we kept saying we'll do this and that, *if* we get the *credencial*, as if planning for it might prevent it from happening.

"I think I hear a truck!" Ralph exclaimed, and we all strained to listen. The front door creaked open, and Lucho's shuffling steps could be heard crossing the courtyard at the slowest pace imaginable. Tracey, I saw, had her fingers crossed. Lucho handed Hilda an envelope. "My uncle sent me over with this," he said.

We all stared at the envelope, Hilda included, for a moment or two. I felt like an actor at the Academy Awards. Then she ripped it open, scanned it quickly, and raised her fist in triumph.

"We're on the move!" she exclaimed. A spontaneous roar of approval erupted from our lips.

I didn't get much sleep that night. There were so many things to think about: the next day's plans, of course, but also the arrival in town of a known buyer of antiquities. After a few hours' tossing and turning, and reaching no conclusions, I crept quietly down the stairs, shoes in hand, and eased my way out the door. It was still dark, about 5:30 in the morning. As quickly and as quietly as I could, I started the truck, threw it into gear, and swung it around to head out. As I did so, the beam caught Hilda in her upstairs window, her arm raised as if in a benediction, a curious sort of blessing. I gunned the engine. Operation Atahualpa was under way.

12

DID HE HEAR it? The soft swish of the sand as it began its descent, slowly, first a trickle, then faster and faster, filling the void. Did he turn from his work at the sound, now a soft rumble, to see his fate sealed, or, dazzled by what he had found, did he work on, oblivious of what was to befall him? Did he scrabble at it, not comprehending at first, thinking that with a few short strokes he'd be free? Or trapped, did he curse fate, as the air slowly ebbed away?

I'd gassed up the truck in town on my way back to the site the previous day, so, throwing caution to the winds, I just floored it, trimming a full twenty minutes off the drive to Trujillo. By 8:10 I was at the gate, impatiently scanning the skies for the incoming aircraft. Steve and Ricardo were on standby for the flight, so I wasn't sure they'd made it. If they hadn't, I was to wait there until they did. The flight was a few minutes late, but as soon as the steps were rolled up and the door opened, Steve and Ricardo, who'd maneuvered themselves to the front of the plane, bolted down the steps and across the tarmac.

Seeing them coming, I headed for a Telefónico del Peru booth, where, upon my arrival, and in what I considered a stroke of brilliance, I'd posted an out of service sign. Using Hilda's phone card, I called Montero. "We're on our way," was all I said before slamming down the receiver and waving to the two men.

By nine we were back on the highway. I drove again. Steve and Ricardo hadn't had even as much sleep as I had, so they dozed while I drove. The trip back was slower, with lots more traffic, and I had to ease up considerably in the towns, now crowded with people. A couple of times I caught myself pounding the wheel in frustration.

Just a little before noon, I pulled the truck up in front of a yellow building on the main street of Campina Vieja. Waiting there were Carlos Montero and an older, slimmer version of the man, His Honor, the mayor, Cesar Montero. They climbed into the backseat of the truck, and to make room Steve climbed into the back. Two policemen on motorcycles, exactly one half the town's police force, pulled ahead of me, and I wheeled the truck away from the curb and back onto the highway until we reached the dirt road which led to the site. Hilda, Tracey, and Ralph all saw our dust and were waiting for us when we got there.

The truck had barely come to rest when Steve was up and out the back, yelling, "Okay, let's roll!"

Ralph and Hilda had briefed the students just a few minutes earlier, and the place was abuzz. Three students—Susan, George, and Robert—and a couple of the Peruvian workers crammed into the back of the truck with Steve, and the cavalcade pulled away again. Ricardo sat up front with me, Tracey sat in the backseat with the two Monteros (one could only hope the mayor was not as bad as his brother), and, as we pulled away, I heard Hilda and Ralph begin directing the remaining students and crew to start filling in the excavation with the back dirt just as fast as they could.

The truck and its police escort pulled out onto the highway again, heading north. About a mile farther along, we turned left off the highway at a small marker and bounced along what was not, to my way of thinking, a road, just a dusty trail in the sand. I just concentrated on not getting off the track and bogged down. Ahead of us I could see the *algarrobal,* the thorn tree thicket. We circled to the right around it, and on the far side pulled to a stop, police lights flashing. Then everyone was out of the truck and running— all of us, that is, except Carlos and Cesar, who hung way back—toward what appeared to be a very ordinary hill.

Two things about that moment I will never forget: the expression on Rolando Guerra's face, and my first sight of Cerro de las Ruinas.

Seeing what must have looked like a horde of howling banshees, Guerra reached for a rifle, but before he could do that, the police, guns out, shouted at him to get his hands up. Steve and Ricardo went up to him and shoved their *credencial* in his face. The police quickly searched Guerra's truck and a little lean-to on the property, and looked along the wall. There was nothing. No mounds of looted artifacts, just a pile of bricks, a trowel, a shovel, a jacket.

For a moment or two, I thought that we'd made a mistake, that we were terrorizing a simple farmer trying to protect a little piece of land. Then, for just an instant, I saw a look of pure hatred, then sly cunning flash across Guerra's face. He was guilty of something, all right. Whatever it was he was up to, he was up to no good.

But there was no reason to detain him. The police told him the archaeologists had the right to dig the land, and that he would have to leave. In a bit of an anticlimax, Guerra picked up his tools, his rifle, and jacket, and pulled away in a beat-up old Chevy truck, without so much as a backward glance.

All of us, exhausted from the waiting, the anticipation, the adrenaline rush, looked about.

"What a mess!" Ramos said.

Over to our right was what appeared to be a bare hill, only one small bush clinging to life on the slope. I shaded my eyes to see the top. It was flattened irregularly, and the sides were streaked with deep vertical cuts that appeared to be the result of torrents of water in a time long before.

There was a large flat area in front of the hill, its surface marred by depressions of all sizes that made me think of the pockmarked surface of the moon. Scattered across the sand, which now in the late afternoon was swirling about the site, were shards of pottery, black and terra-cotta, and almost unbelievably, fragments of bone. A plait of dark hair, bleached red, lay forlornly on the edge of a crater.

"What is this?" I gasped.

"*Huaqueros,*" Steve said. "They've been digging here. That's what the depressions are, the places they've dug. Some are very old, others very recent. Looters look for metals, so if they come across ceramics, or bones, they just toss them."

"Such disrespect for the dead!" I exclaimed.

Steve nodded. "The Anasazi in the States call looters robbers of the dead. A good name, isn't it? You aren't entirely right about their disrespect for the dead, though," he said, reaching down and picking up a couple of unsmoked cigarettes. "They left these, you see. Seriously," he said, sensing my skepticism. "*Huaqueros* often leave an offering like this so they won't be cursed."

For some reason I couldn't take my eyes off the plait of hair. It seemed so vulnerable, pathetic almost, lying there on the surface like that. Steve watched me. "Human hair lasts for thousands of years in the ground," was all he said. It should never have been disturbed, I thought. For some reason, seeing that plait of hair affected me in a way that Ines's warning hadn't.

Cuidado al arbolada! To succeed, you must beware of the woods. Slowly I turned my head to the left. There was a wooded area, filled with carob trees, or algarroba, the branches heavy with thorns. Were these the woods? Don't be ridiculous, I told myself.

"Do you think we're too late?" Tracey asked, leaning down and picking up a small piece of bone. The sound of her voice pulled me back to reality. "Do you think they found and looted the tomb?"

"Don't know," Steve replied, shielding his eyes, as I had, and scanning the hill. "It's a huaca, all right. They've been digging on the top. You can see the depressions. Practically flattened it too. But if they found something, and removed everything, then what was Guerra doing putting up that wall? Let's have a look around. Maybe we'll try a couple of test trenches at the foot of the huaca."

"Are you saying that hill is a huaca?" I asked.

"Yup," Steve replied. "To you it looks like a hill. But remember, the people of this area built their structures of adobe brick, which is essentially mud brick, not stone. So this was once a pyramid-shaped building. The furrows you see running down the sides would be caused by torrential rains, past El Niños, perhaps, over the intervening centuries, which would, in a sense, melt the brick. See, there's another little one over there, and there." I looked in the direction he was pointing. There was indeed a smaller hill, or huaca, off in the distance, a couple more even farther away.

"Okay, let's take a quick look around," Steve called to the group. "We'll start in earnest tomorrow."

The group had barely started out when what proved to be the first of many accidents happened. "Ouch!" Tracey yelled, and started hopping around. We all went to her aid, and it was quickly apparent what was causing her distress. She'd stepped on one end of a dead branch of a thorn tree; the branch had swung up, and one of the thorns had imbedded itself in her leg, a little above the ankle, just over the top of her boot. It had gone right through her sock and into her leg. Tracey was hurting, that was obvious. Both Steve and I tried to remove it, but we couldn't dislodge it.

We took her in to the doctor in Campina Vieja. He had to freeze the spot and cut the thorn out. She hobbled out of the office, white-faced, a large bandage on her leg. "Very nasty, those thorns," the doctor said. "Keep the foot elevated as much as possible, and if the redness and swelling moves past here," he said, pointing to a spot a few inches up her leg, "bring her back. Had to put two stitches in, so she'll have to come back in ten days to get them out."

"Sorry about this." Tracey grimaced. "I mustn't have been paying attention."

By ten o'clock that night, Tracey was running a fever and her ankle was badly swollen and red. I took a tray up to her at dinnertime, but she was unable to eat. In the night, she called out a couple of times, once for her mother, the second time for Steve, and I rushed to her bedside. After that, I took a candle into her room and sat at her bedside for an hour or two. Around about three, Steve tapped on the door. "Saw the light," he whispered. "How is she doing?"

"She's running a temperature and having bad dreams, I think. We'd better get her back to the doctor first thing in the morning."

"See if you can get her to take a couple of these," Steve said, handing in a bottle of pills, antibiotics. I woke Tracey and managed to get her to take two, along with a couple of aspirin for the fever.

I sat with her awhile longer, hoping she would rest better, but she continued to sleep fitfully. There wasn't enough light to read, so I entertained myself by looking around the room, which was jam-packed with reminders of home. There were photos everywhere: her darling car, top down, Tracey behind the wheel waving; a very attractive photo of her with a nice-looking young man, Jamie, her boyfriend; a dog looking playful in a Santa hat; and a family photo with Tracey, a young man who was probably her brother, the dog again, and an attractive couple I knew to be her mother and stepfather. She called them Ted and Mary Anne, although I noticed she'd reverted to Mommy in her dreams. They were all standing in front of a very elegant home, two storey, red brick, pillars at the entrance, and what was probably a sweeping, circular drive. There was also a photo of Tracey, Ted, and her mother at a podium with a Save Our Museum, Save Our Community sign above them, with her father presenting a check, it looked to me.

Pillars of the community, that family, I decided. I didn't really know much about them, of course. I was a little old for the college dorm thing, and while we got along just fine, I hadn't encouraged the sharing of little confidences with Tracey, because, as Rebecca, I didn't have any to share. I wondered if it had occurred to Tracey that I didn't have a single photograph of anyone with me, and if it had, if she found that strange.

By the next morning she wasn't any better, and Steve asked me to stay around the hacienda as much as possible to keep an eye on her. I did pick up Ines as usual and took her in to the market. When I told her how ill Tracey was, Ines insisted on going to a part of the market I'd never been, known to the locals as that of the witch doctors. This section of the market was darker than the rest, and smelled very strongly, but not unpleasantly, of herbs. The stalls had bunches of dried herbs hanging from every rafter, fresh ones piled high on tables. Some, like the tiny flowers of chamomile, I recognized, others I did not. There were vials of various herbs and roots in some kind of liquid, and various objects, talismans of some sort, offered for sale. Ines stopped at one stall, which appeared to be unstaffed, until a very old man, skin wrinkled more than I would have thought possible, hobbled out of the darkness at the back. Ines explained the problem, and he mixed up a packet of various dried herbs and gave them to Ines with instructions.

Tracey was no better when we got back, and the

swelling was getting perilously near to the point where the doctor had said to bring her back in. By this time she'd had another round of antibiotics, but I knew they'd take a while to kick in and I was getting really worried. Ines carefully measured out some of the herbs, made a tea of them, which she then strained, and got Tracey to drink it. Within twenty minutes, Tracey had fallen into a sound sleep. "She'll be fine now," was all Ines said.

And she was. Partway through dinner that night, she appeared at the dining room door. "I'm starving," she said, and we all beamed.

"Wonderful stuff, that penicillin," Steve exclaimed, but I knew better. In a pinch, I was sticking with Ines.

By the following day we were more or less back to normal. Ricardo Ramos had headed back for Trujillo, saying he'd come back and give us a hand in a few days. Tracey and Ralph were at work in the lab, and I went back to the site in the *algarrobal*. The team had very quickly dug a couple of test pits at the foot of the huaca but had come across nothing that would warrant more extensive work, and thus had begun work on the huaca, the hill itself. I heard a shout and, shielding my eyes from the very bright sun, could make out Steve, a black shadow against the light, waving at me from the top. "Come on up!" he called, and I climbed up the forty or fifty feet to the summit. Here too was massive evidence of looting, large pits, some of them reasonably fresh-looking, marring the surface.

"I'd have to say someone's been here before us," I said ruefully, picking up a potsherd that looked recently broken even to my untrained eye. "Does this mean we're too late?"

"Not necessarily," Steve said. "The Moche built their huacas in stages, platforms on top of platforms. So even if *huaqueros* have found a tomb here and cleared it out, it doesn't mean there isn't another below that, which would be an even earlier burial. We're starting to clear this area now," he said, gesturing toward the activity around us. "Jose," he said, stopping for a moment, "move that back dirt farther away, please. We don't want any cave-ins. And, people," he added, "remember, go for the *mancha*."

"The *mancha*?" I asked dubiously. "What kind of stain would we be looking for?"

"From what we've been able to glean from Moche art, and from what we've seen on previous digs, we know the Moche had particular ways of burying their dead. It varied a little depending on the status of the particular individual being buried, but essentially it involved digging a shaft and then a chamber down some distance. On Moche pottery, you can see depictions of bodies being lowered down these shafts and then sideways into the chambers. Once the body—or bodies, as the case may be—was placed in the tomb, the shaft would be sealed up. But its position can be determined by the appearance of the soil which differs from its surroundings. In other words, the *mancha* or stain. So we look for this *mancha*, which, with a little luck, will reveal the presence of a shaft, and hence a tomb."

"We seem to learn a lot about the Moche from their art," I said.

"Well, they had no written language, so they couldn't leave us ritual texts. But I think their art, like the scenes and rituals on their ceramics and the murals in the huacas we've been able to uncover, are an extraordinarily vivid record of the times." Then he grinned. "For some inexplicable reason, and with absolutely no evidence yet to support it, I have a good feeling about this place! Now I gotta get back to work." He waved to Hilda, who was down below, supervising the photography of the two test pits before they were filled in.

I stood at the summit and surveyed the surroundings: the *algarrobal*, the thorn tree forest, dark and brooding, hiding its secrets in the shade of the broad, umbrella-like branches of the trees, and way off in the distance, if I shielded my eyes, the sweep of the dunes and then the sea. In the other direction, I could see the silver thread of the Panamericana, and along the trail that led to the site, a little caravan of motorcycles and a couple of trucks, dust billowing in their wake.

"Steve," I called out. "I think we have company!" Steve looked in the direction I was pointing.

"Trouble!" he yelled down to Hilda, as the convoy moved closer.

The vehicles pulled up, blocking the way out, and a gang of *campesinos,* Rolando Guerra among them, made their way toward the site. They were armed with shovels and axes, which they waved threateningly in Hilda's direction. "Get out of here or you're dead," one of them yelled.

"You get out of here, or you're dead," Steve yelled from the top of the huaca. He had grabbed a short shovel and, balancing it on his shoulder, was holding it as if it were a rifle. The men looked up, but blinded by the sun, would see only what I could just a few minutes ago, a dark figure silhouetted against the light. "I mean it," he yelled. "Get out of here." Pablo, behind Steve, grabbed another shovel and mimicked Steve's stance.

For a moment, nobody moved. I held my breath. Then one of the men, an older man who'd held back a little from the pack, said something I couldn't make out. Slowly they all got back in their trucks or on their motorcycles, and gunning the engines, then circling around menacingly a couple of times, finally pulled away.

"Whew," Steve said, putting down his shovel. "Sure was worried the sun might go behind a cloud!" A titter of nervous laughter swept through the group.

"That was brilliant," I said, admiration in my voice.

"Oh, I'm not just a pretty face." He grinned. "But to think that just a moment or two before they arrived, I was cursing because the sun was so hot. They're just bullies, that's all," he added. "Nothing to worry about, really."

I wanted to believe him, so I did.

For the rest of that day, and the next, the work on the site progressed at a steady pace, with hopeful signs, according to Pablo, all around.

The following day, however, the second accident occurred. While we were working away, there was a crack, and the ladder on which one of the men, Jesus Silva, was standing to set up the camera, collapsed. Jesus was hurled into one of the pits and just lay there, conscious but groaning in pain. It was only with real difficulty that we were able to get him out. We stretched him out on the back of the truck, and I drove as carefully as I could into town. He had, as it turned out, dislocated his shoulder and cracked three ribs, and would be off work for the balance of the season.

It was about then that the rumors of evil spirits began to surface among the Peruvian crew. "This is a bad place," I heard one of the men, Javier Franco, telling the others. "We should not be here."

"I don't believe in evil spirits," Steve told me. "Come over here."

I walked over to where he was examining the ladder that had collapsed under Silva. I looked where he pointed. There was a crack right below the metal hinge which held the two sides of the ladder rigid when opened.

"So it was defective, is that what you're telling me?" I said. "I feel terrible. I bought that ladder, and I thought I'd inspected it pretty carefully before I took it. I must have missed the crack."

"Look again," he said, and after a moment or two I saw what he was getting at. There were no splinters at the break, except right at the end. In fact it was so neat a break that one would have to assume it had been cut, almost all the way through.

"Guerra?" I asked.

"He'd be our number one suspect, wouldn't he?" Steve replied. "Maybe I'll just go have a chat with the mayor and suggest to him that the police have a little talk with our friend Rolando."

After that, though, the accidents came thick and fast. Ernesto Santo, another worker, cut his hand quite badly, a freak accident involving the metal mesh on the sieve that required several stitches. Javier himself, the fellow who thought the place was haunted, accidentally walked backwards too far and slid down the side of the slope, badly scratching his leg.

I put it all down to hysteria, self-induced accidents brought on by the belief in evil spirits, but the effect it had on the group was real enough. They were all petrified. Steve then hired Tomas Cardoso, Ines's brother, who was also a *chaman,* a shaman, to help protect the site from evil spirits. That kept the team working awhile longer.

In contrast to all the drama around the accidents, however, the work on the site was going exceedingly well. About a week into the work on the summit, a loud shout and a cheer went up, and we all rushed up the hill. Even Hilda, who tended to supervise from down below, climbed up painfully but as fast as she could. And there it was, a circle in the earth quite distinct from that around it. "The *mancha*!" Pablo yelled.

"You're right!" Steve exclaimed, after examining it closely. "We start digging down, here!"

I'd have been inclined to just dig straight down the shaft, but that's not the way it works in archaeology. Earth is removed, layer by layer, inch by inch, everything carefully recorded before it's removed. The earth was, as always, taken to the sieve, which we'd set up on top of the hill.

When I expressed some impatience to Hilda, she replied, "As you can see, archaeology is inherently destructive. When we're done here, we will have destroyed a huaca that survived for centuries before we arrived. You can never put it back exactly as it was. So it must be done right the first time, or the whole archaeological record is lost." I could see what she meant. We were removing a large portion of the side of the hill, cutting down from the top. "Safety is of paramount importance," she went on, "particularly when we're working on a slope. The back dirt has to be taken well away from the site, to a place where it can't slide back onto the workers. Cave-ins are a real concern in these conditions. You have to ensure the walls are well shored up as you go.''

I hoped the workers wouldn't hear her saying that. It was all they would need to really set them off.

The really good news was that there was no further sign during the daylight hours of Rolando Guerra and his pals, several of whom, I gathered from the talk among the workers, were members of the Guerra family. But the signs of his presence were evident almost every morning. One day it was a pig's head on a pike stuck into the ground, another time a skull and crossbones painted on the side of the shed. Once the *mancha* had been found, Steve hired Gonzalo Fernandez, brother of one of the other workers, to stay in the little hut at night to watch the site. With Laforet in town, Steve reasoned, there'd be a surge in looting activity. For a few days, at least, the harassment stopped.

But we didn't for a moment think Guerra was gone.

Then one morning, there was the most terrible accident of all. There were signs that morning that someone had come onto the site at night, not from the trail but from the other side, from the road by the commune, climbing over the wall. From the top, a cap and jacket were spotted lying on the sand several yards up the incline. Someone had been digging on the far side of the huaca from where we were working. Fernandez, guarding the way from the trail and the side of the huaca we were working on, had heard nothing. Some of the back dirt from our excavation had been dislodged and had fallen down the back of the hill. Steve climbed down to have a look at the damage, as the rest of us peered over the edge. Then Steve began tearing at the earth with his bare hands, calling for workers with shovels to come right away. They cleared away the sand as quickly as they could. To no avail. Rolando Guerra was unconscious, buried in sand, his hands still clutching a little copper statue of a Moche warrior. He died later that day in the hospital, a victim of his own greed.

The Warrior Priest

THE FANGED GOD, *the Decapitator, steps forward. The tumi is raised; gold flashes through the air. The Priestess raises the cup. Iguana and Wrinkle Face take their places at the head of the shaft. The great ceremony begins.*

In the tomb, the sacrificed llamas, headless, rest on either side of the coffin, the Warrior's dog nearby. The mummies of the female ancestors are placed in the tomb, two at the head of the coffin, two at the foot.

Iguana and Wrinkle Face, masks glinting in the light of torches, take the ropes and slowly lower the Great Warrior way down into the chamber. The body is placed in the coffin, head to the south, toward Cerro Blanco. With proper ceremony, the coffin is sealed with copper straps.

The guardians, those who will protect the Warrior through all time, go before the Decapitator. One is placed beside the Warrior, the other, feet cut off, in a niche above the coffin. Now the chamber can be sealed, the shaft filled.

The new Warrior Priest sits cross-legged on his litter, his standards to either side, his dog at his feet. The Bird Priest takes the cup of sacrifice from the Priestess and passes it to him. May our new Warrior save us from the water that rushes from the mountains, destroying everything in its path. He must: If he cannot, it is the end of our world.

13

Rolando Guerra's journey to his final resting place was more seething mob than funeral procession, the animosity of his friends and relatives barely held in check by the solemnity of the occasion.

It looked as if half the town had crowded into the Plaza de Armas as the casket, carried by six members of the Guerra family, went into the plaza and up the church steps. Guerra's wife and two small children followed the coffin, the woman sobbing, and the children, a little boy and girl, looking perplexed. An older woman—Guerra's mother, I surmised—walked ramrod straight and dry-eyed behind them.

Mayor Montero had sent one of his policemen to the hacienda to urge us not to attend the funeral in order not to inflame the situation, and it was good advice indeed. The crowd was an angry one, threatening to erupt at any moment, I thought, as Puma and I pulled back into a lane and retreated to the market area.

"Bad scene," was all Puma said. It was a bad scene indeed. While the Guerras were, I gathered, considered loners, Rolando's death had played into the anxiety people were feeling about the approaching El Niño, which, together with the *invasores* that came with it, threatened their livelihood and their safety.

The marketplace where I'd taken Ines to get some supplies was abuzz. There seemed to be a general feeling that Rolando shouldn't have been looting, but there was an almost universal resentment of people who came from somewhere else. A few of the shop-keepers glared ominously at me as I went by, and one old woman slapped a flyswatter rather menacingly in my direction as I drew near her.

We had a conference that evening, in what we'd named the war room that heady night, which now seemed so long ago, when, flushed with enthusiasm for what we saw as the absolute rightness of the cause, we'd planned Operation Atahualpa, our invasion of Cerro de las Ruinas.

This time, sitting around the dining room table after Ines had left for home, we had to decide whether to go on, after this latest grisly discovery, or to close up for the season, pack up the lab and head home.

"I don't know," Hilda said, her voice even raspier than usual. "I just don't know. Part of me wants to go on, the other . . ." Her voice trailed off.

"We're so close, Hilda," Steve said. "I can just feel it. We're going to find something big."

"I know you think so. But is it worth the risk?" she replied.

"Of course it's worth it!" Steve exclaimed. "Are you saying we should just give up and let the looters have it all? Hilda, you've been working toward this your whole career!''

"Maybe I picked the wrong career?'' she asked with a tight little smile.

"I'm with Hilda,'' Ralph said. "Yes, it's important, but not worth getting killed over. And just carrying on as if nothing has happened. Unseemly, really. Guerra, for all his bluster, was just trying to make a living.''

"So was Al Capone, Ralph,'' Tracey snorted. "Surely you're not condoning looting.''

"Your comparison is odious,'' Ralph snapped back. Everyone's nerves were on edge. "I'm not condoning it. I just think we have to be sensitive to the people around here. Capone, I can only assume, lived in a nice home in Chicago, ate well. Guerra probably lived in a hut. And it's a terrible way to go, choking on sand. My God.''

Ralph and Tracey glared at each other.

"Enough!'' Steve sighed. "This isn't getting us anywhere. Let's hear some arguments pro and con, lay them out on the table, and then we'll vote, okay? I'll start. On the pro side, I think we're close to finding a tomb, maybe an untouched one.''

"And maybe we're not,'' Ralph said morosely.

"Well, that pro and that con pretty well cancel each other out, I'd say,'' Steve said. "Anyone else?''

Tracey put up her hand. "Guerra's gone, so there should be no more incidents, should there? That's a definite pro, wouldn't you say?''

Everyone nodded, except me that is. I thought they were wrong. I'd seen firsthand the mood in town. In the first place, Guerra was not the only one involved in looting. His whole family was famous for it, and the rest of them were still among the living. It may have been obvious to everyone else what had happened. Guerra had been tunneling into the side of the huaca. His back dirt, the dirt from the tunnel he was digging, was piled up for all to see. He'd been in a hurry, and therefore careless, and hadn't moved the dirt far enough away, or even on the right angle, to prevent it from sliding back into the tunnel. While the police were already calling Guerra's demise death by misadventure, the unfortunate but perhaps predictable end of a careless *huaquero,* I was pretty sure the rest of the Guerra family didn't see it that way.

By the end of the evening, everyone agreed to stay on, except Ralph, who was wavering. He said he'd think about it overnight.

Later there was a light tapping at my door. Steve stood outside with two glasses and a bottle of scotch. ''Can we talk?'' he whispered. ''Downstairs?''

I nodded and followed him down the steps. The power was out again, so I lit a couple of candles while he poured the drinks.

''What do you think of all this?'' he asked as we settled into armchairs.

''I'm not sure what to think,'' I said. ''The mood in town is pretty ugly.''

''It is,'' he agreed. ''Do you think I'm crazy to encourage everybody to stay? Or do you think I'm just plain crazy?'' He smiled wearily.

''Maybe,'' I said. ''To both.'' I was kidding, of course, but he looked so pained, I felt bad. ''Look,'' I said. ''They're grown-ups. They can make up their own minds.'' Why, I wondered, was he talking to me, instead of Tracey?

As if he could read my mind, he said, ''I suppose

you know about Tracey and me." He paused. "You do know we are . . . ?"

"Yes."

"I guess you couldn't have missed all the creeping around in the night." He laughed ruefully. "I feel kind of silly," he went on. "A guy my age with a woman like that, twenty years younger. One of my students to boot!"

"She's very attractive," I said sympathetically. At least I tried to sound sympathetic, a difficult feat.

"My wife left me last year. For a younger man. Twelve years younger, in fact. I don't know why it should be more humiliating to have your wife leave you for a younger man than it would be for one the same age or older, but it is. Maybe humiliating isn't the word. Demoralizing would cover it better, perhaps."

"That's too bad," I said. I thought of the dying days of my marriage to Clive and the parade of younger women I'd put up with for a while. Suddenly I was feeling genuinely sympathetic: humiliating and demoralizing indeed. "Been there," I added.

"Have you? Really?"

I nodded.

"You probably won't believe this, but the affair wasn't my idea. It was hers. I was flattered, of course. I mean, it didn't take much to persuade me. I gave it a couple of nanoseconds' thought, I confess.

"But now . . ." he said softly. "Now I'm wondering why she . . . I mean, maybe this is the anxiety of a middle-aged guy, but I'm wondering if she did it for some other reason, to displace Hilda on the project or something." He stopped. "I'm sorry, I have no business burdening you with this."

"That's okay," I said. "But I don't think you should assume that. You're an attractive man, and you both share the same interests." I couldn't believe I was saying this, actually. Why would I ever try to convince Steve that everything was okay with Tracey, I wondered, when I found him rather appealing myself? But the fragility of the middle-aged man's ego never ceases to amaze me, and I felt I had to say something to make him feel better, even if it wasn't in my own best interests.

"Thanks," he said. We talked for a few more minutes about the work, about his children of whom he was obviously very proud, about the approaching El Niño. Then he got up from his chair and came over to mine. Leaning over, he kissed me. It was a nice kiss, the kind that makes you think you might not mind making the guy's breakfast for a while. We parted company at the top of the stairs, leaving me wondering what was going on. I like to think I am not lacking in self-confidence, but I try to temper it with a firm grasp on reality. The point was, a contest between me and Tracey for a man was not one I'd expect to win. Was I doing the same thing I'd thought Steve was doing, having self-doubts about a member of the opposite sex, or was there something more calculated happening? There was something about the conversation, I thought, that didn't ring entirely true, but perhaps it was just that there was so much left unsaid.

The Hacienda Garua contingent hung in. Even Ralph decided to stay. The trouble was, most of the Peruvian crew wouldn't come back to work at the site. If they'd thought the place evil with a few relatively harmless accidents, this latest incident hadn't improved their impression of the place one bit. Pablo stuck with us, as did Ernesto, surprisingly enough, the fellow who'd cut himself so badly. I'd heard he had a wife and four children, so maybe a few evil spirits were not enough to deter him from earning his living. Tomas too agreed to stay on. The students all stayed, with the exception of Robert, who said he'd had enough and headed back to Lima.

The one positive aspect of all this was that I was able to get Puma a real paying job. When the Peruvian workers disappeared, Steve tried to carry on with the small team he had, but the work slowed considerably.

"I've just got to get more manpower out here," he groaned. "We'll never get this done."

"I have an idea," I said. "How about Puma? He couldn't do the technical work, but he can carry the dirt and work the sieve. He could sure use some money, if there was some way we could pay him."

"I pay the Peruvian crew," Steve said, "and with several of them gone, there'll be some money. When can he start?"

The answer was right away. "Amazing!" Puma said. "Working on an archaeological site! Do you think we'll find treasure?"

"You never know," I replied. "And even if we don't, this way you'll be able to make sure we don't unleash some terrible curse."

I'd meant it as a joke, of course, but Puma heartily agreed with me.

Puma, as it turned out, was a willing and hard worker—when he showed up. In the first place, he wasn't an early riser. While the rest of us started work as soon as it was light, Puma usually turned up a little rumpled-looking, late in the morning. Some days he didn't show up at all. It was annoying because we were sorely shorthanded, and everyone left had to pitch in. Steve didn't seem terribly perturbed by it: He said it was pretty standard behavior for a boy that age, and that Puma would be paid when he showed up, and not when he didn't.

I tried to talk to Puma about it. He was always very contrite, saying there was something else he'd had to do, and I had a feeling there was something he wasn't telling me, but that was about it. Gradually, we all took the attitude that with Puma, like the magician he was, it was sometimes you see him, sometimes you don't.

I was assigned to help Pablo, working beside him to catalogue all the little pottery shards he uncovered, making notes on the depth, the exact placement, and bagging and tagging them all. We started work right at dawn, and worked until the wind and the dust made it impossible to continue. Then we hauled everything back to the lab, and worked well into the evening cataloguing the day's finds.

Even Lucho was called up for action, made to haul sand and staff the sieve. His complaining and shuffling drove us all crazy, but we needed him to work. What that meant was that the hacienda was left unguarded at least part of the day, before Ines came to make supper.

Tracey's prediction that there would be no more incidents was regrettably not correct. While Rolanda Guerra might be gone, his family was not, and, as I had feared, they took to hanging around the site, watching us work with a real malevolence in their stance. They plainly blamed us for Rolando's death, even though the police had made it clear to them that Rolando was looting illegally: He'd been caught red-handed after all, albeit almost dead at the time. The

Guerra family, however, saw it differently. In their eyes, Rolando had been forced to take desperate measures because of us, measures that had ended his life prematurely.

The situation came to a head one day when I returned to the hacienda with Ines to find an axe through the beautifully carved front door, and a message for us sprayed across the front of the house. What the painter lacked in artistry, he made up for in brevity and clarity. *Asesinos!*—murderers—the message read. Lucho returned to his post as guard of the hacienda forthwith; Cesar Montero, the mayor, had a police guard posted on the site for a couple of days to deter the culprits, and Carlos, the landlord, tutted and clucked, and then sent a crew over to paint it out.

With all this drama and activity, it took me a while to realize that I hadn't seen Puma recently. With some irritation, I headed over to the commune to get him. Nothing appeared amiss when I first got there. The place looked pretty much the same, laundry flapping in the breeze, a couple of the commune members working away at the far end of the garden. I checked the kitchen. Pachamama wasn't there. Then I went to their little hut. There was only one sleeping bag— Puma's, I thought, but he wasn't in it. All of Pachamama's belongings appeared to be gone. Everyone else was out working, so I headed for the main house once again and knocked on Manco Capac's door. He was a minute or two in opening it, but cordial enough when he saw me. "Come on in," he said. "Beer?"

"Not right now, thanks," I replied.

"Mind if I do?" he asked, opening a little refrigerator in his room in anticipation of my reply.

"Of course not," I said, idly thinking as I watched

him reach for the beer that his refrigerator reminded me of the one I had at home, that is, virtually empty. Two thoughts then struck me: one, that this was the first time I'd thought about my home in a rather long time; and two, that there was a significant difference between his refrigerator and mine. While mine tended to yogurt well past its best-before date, various half-empty jars of heaven knows what, a couple of tins of tuna and salmon, and if I was lucky, white wine, his was rather more aristocratic: champagne, Perrier-Jouet if I wasn't mistaken, judging by the flowers on the bottle—I've heard it's lovely—and a couple of jars of a rather distinctive shape and color that I decided held caviar. There were a couple of other tins too, which, on closer examination I was sure, would prove to contain pâté. Not your average supermarket peppercorn pâté, either. Real foie gras, from France. Manco Capac might have come to live a back-to-basics life in Peru, but his definition of basic, in the food department at least, was definitely upmarket. It was also more than a little expensive.

Maybe, I thought, as he opened his beer, he's treated himself to these things because he has a cold. Come to think of it, though, didn't he have the sniffles last time I was here? Maybe he has allergies, or maybe, and now light began to dawn, maybe his expensive tastes also run to cocaine.

When I pulled back from this edifying stream of consciousness—it's amazing what the little light in a refrigerator can do for your thought processes—I found him looking at me closely.

"Would you like something else?" he said. "I have only champagne and, of course, caviar." He laughed. "Birthday present from my family, actually, but it sounds impressive, doesn't it? Don't tell the others, or I'll have to share.''

Good comeback, I thought, and very convincing, but it should be. He's an actor. Apparently he was a good enough actor to fool the other members of the commune into thinking he shared their taste for the simple life.

''I came to see Puma and Pachamama,'' I said, changing the subject. ''But I can't find either of them.''

''Gone,'' he replied.

''What do you mean, gone?'' I asked.

''Just gone. Disappeared. Poof.'' He paused. ''He's a magician. Poof. Get it?''

I got it. ''Very amusing. Would you have any idea of when exactly they went poof?'' I said through clenched teeth. I could hear a certain tone creeping into my voice, one a certain shopkeeper normally reserved for suppliers who didn't deliver on time, and parents who allowed their children to bring drippy ice-cream cones into her store.

''Last night. Maybe the night before, actually. I can't remember exactly.''

My, what a short memory! ''Did you see them go?''

''Nope.''

''And did you report their disappearance?''

''Nope. Why would I? People come and go. There is nothing to stop them. Our philosophy here is go with the flow.''

That expression again. ''Two kids disappear in the night,'' I hissed, ''and all you can say is go with the flow?''

''Well, it beats asking people to commit suicide together so they can beam up to some spaceship or something, doesn't it?'' he snapped, and I thought that for a second I had seen the real person under go-with-the-flow Manco Capac, one who despised what he was doing and the people he was with. ''People are free to do what they wish here,'' he said, his voice returning to normal. ''Those two kids, as you call them, are young adults. People stay here as long as they need to, and if they wish to, they move on.''

''But Puma's sleeping bag is still here.''

''So maybe he's planning to come back!'' The man shrugged.

''Do you know their real names?''

''No. Choosing a new name here is part of casting off our former lives, our former hang-ups, to express the unspoiled part of ourselves. We choose new names so we can go forward.''

There didn't seem much point in continuing a conversation that had gone out of style by the seventies, so I left him to his caviar and champagne, and quite possibly, his drug habit.

I started back to the site, but didn't get very far. It really bothered me, thinking about the kids. I knew they weren't really kids, but they were so naive, and not terribly bright. I couldn't believe they'd just leave, Puma in particular, and not send me a message. He knew where I was, at the hacienda, and I'd have thought he'd have come there if they were in trouble. Maybe Manco Capac, whatever his name was, was right. They'd just decided to move on. They didn't owe me an explanation, really. I wasn't their mother, although occasionally I felt as if I were. I felt some-how bereft, though. It seemed they'd become, when I wasn't looking, an important part of the fabric of my new life.

The fact was I didn't like this Manco Capac, and I didn't trust him at all. It wasn't just that he used an alias. The only difference between him and me in that regard was that he'd gotten to choose his. Mine, I'd been assigned. But anyone who picked the name of the first Inca, son of the Sun God, had a personality disorder of some sort, I felt certain. There was something patently false about the man. Communes weren't really in style anymore, I didn't think, and even if they were, you didn't come to live on a commune to eat caviar. It didn't make sense. The more I thought about him, the more worried about the kids I got, and the worse I felt about not listening to Puma, probing more. Hiding behind my own alias, I hadn't even asked him his real name.

Guilt is a powerful motivator. I turned the truck around and headed back into town to make enquiries. Campina Vieja was far enough off the beaten track as far as tourism went that people like Puma and Pachamama should have been easy to spot, and I hoped someone would recall having seen them.

I checked a couple of cafes I'd seen them in, and then the bus station, where the ticket agent said he had no recollection of them, but that I could check back in a day or two with the other ticket agent who'd been on duty the previous three days. The other alternative, he said, was to wait for the buses to go through and to ask the individual drivers and attendants. There was no time for that: It could take days before I'd checked them all. An ice cream vendor outside the bus station said he'd seen someone who resembled my description of Pachamama, but that she had been alone.

I determined that I'd have a private chat with Steve to see what he could suggest. I didn't want to go to the police personally, not just because I wasn't sure how much scrutiny my passport would stand up to, but also because not knowing what the kids' real names were would make it just a little difficult to fill in a missing persons report. I thought Steve might want to talk to the authorities, though. He'd always shown a more than casual interest in how the two kids were getting along.

When I got back to the site, however, there was no opportunity for that discussion to take place. As I pulled up, I could see the whole bunch of them waving at me from the top of the huaca, and soon, at their instructions, I was heading up there to join them. They were almost dancing with excitement, and with good reason. They had found very promising signs of a tomb, an area about ten feet long and eight feet wide lined with adobe bricks, and what looked to be the outline of timbers, the vigas that would roof the chamber. The center was still filled with earth, but it was clearly a different color and texture.

"This is the lining of a burial chamber, I'm almost certain," Steve explained for my benefit. "With this kind of structure, a large brick-lined chamber, it'll be a tomb for someone important. The Moche didn't build these kinds of chambers for just your average guy. I expect the roof timbers will have collapsed under the weight of all this earth, but I think it may just be an untouched tomb, although we can't be absolutely sure until we get there."

"There'll be flying femurs tomorrow!" Ralph crowed. "Please, please, let there be untouched ceramics for me."

Only Hilda was quiet, perhaps because of the effort it took her to climb the huaca, or because she felt it was almost too much to hope for.

By now it was getting late, and Hilda called a halt to the day's work. I had to run my usual taxi service into town for the workers and students, although I could do it in one trip now with all the defections, while Steve took the others home in our second truck, thereby eliminating another opportunity for me to speak to him.

Dinner was a fairly raucous affair, and for a change Hilda stayed for most of it, helping to plan the next day's work. "What makes everyone so sure they've found an important person's tomb?" I asked Ralph.

"Because of where it is, and the type of tomb it is," he replied. "First of all it's right in the huaca. That says a lot. Also, the Moche appear to have had a range of burial procedures and rituals which depended, by and large, on the individual's status, in much the same way we do. Some of us are buried in simple graves with wooden markers, others with elaborate headstones and the finest coffins," he said.

"For the Moche, the commonest form—the grave with a simple wooden cross, if you will—would be a pit burial, just a shallow grave really, with a few burial goods interred with them. The middle class, if we can use that term, would have had more elaborate burials. A shaft would have been constructed down several feet, then a chamber hollowed out, sometimes to one side, like the foot on a boot. The bodies were lowered down the shaft, either horizontally or vertically depending on the size of the shaft, and placed in the chamber. We know that much from Moche ceramics, my specialty." Ralph smiled. "Burial scenes are depicted on several that we know of, and they show the bodies being lowered into the chambers by two ritual or perhaps mythological beings, Iguana, someone with the face of a lizard, and Wrinkle Face, a being with a very wrinkled face, as the names imply.

"For the higher status individuals, and this is what we're hoping for here, large chambers were constructed, large enough to hold the individual, lots of grave goods, some very elaborate, and other sacrificed animals, like llamas or dogs, and individuals, perhaps their retainers in life. Sometimes there are even guardians, bodies placed in niches above the principal body. So these graves are much larger, they have been known to have adobe walls, and they are more likely to have timber roofs. The presence of these three things, a large chamber, the adobe walls, and the roofing, is what makes us pretty excited about what tomorrow may bring."

"So what will this look like, if we get in?" I asked.

Steve jumped into the conversation with enthusiasm. "Moche dead are normally buried flat on their backs, arms at their sides, with the head usually facing more or less south and away from the shaft. They were wrapped in cloth, then enclosed in some kind of cane sleeve or tube, although there wouldn't be much of the cloth or the cane left, probably. The head normally rests on a plate of some kind, its material related to the status of the individual, a gourd for the lowliest, a gold disc for the most powerful. The feet are often in sandals, silver ones for the big guys, much more humble ones for those of lower status. If we're really lucky and it's a warrior priest or something, he'll be wearing the full regalia—ear spools, the headdress, back flaps, necklaces, everything. Actually, I don't even want to think about this, in case it jinxes us." Steve laughed.

"How do we think the *huaqueros* missed this one?" I asked. "If indeed they did."

"*If* is a good way to put it," Steve replied. "Remember what I told you about Moche pyramids. They were built platform on top of platform. There could be individuals buried in the different levels. It's possible that *huaqueros* found a tomb higher up in the structure and figured that was it."

It was at this point that Hilda decided to retire for the night, this time without the scotch bottle, a development I considered real progress, and perhaps an indication of just how important she felt the next day's work would be. The rest of us sat around for a while waiting to see Ines off. Tomas was a little later than usual, and I figured once Ines had left, everyone would start to head upstairs to get some rest for the big day ahead and I might have an opportunity to have a quiet word with Steve about Puma and Pachamama.

When Tomas came to pick up Ines, however, he brought with him bad news. Gonzalo Fernandez, the night guard at the site, had walked off the job. Just after dark, Fernandez had seen, according to Tomas, an apparition of an owl, a creature associated with death in this part of the world. This was not just any owl, apparently. This one was several feet tall. Furthermore, the Guerra family had paid him a visit after we'd left to go back to the hacienda and told Fernandez he'd be dead by morning if he stayed.

Steve slumped in his chair and sighed. "Well, I guess there's nothing for it. I'm sleeping at the site tonight. Tracey, Rebecca, where'd you put the gun?"

"*Caja Ocho*, in the lab," Tracey replied. But there was no gun in *Caja Ocho*.

"That was the number, wasn't it?" she asked me.

"Definitely," I replied. We searched through several boxes. No gun.

"It must be Lucho," Tracey said. "Where is he?"

But Lucho swore up and down he didn't have it. He even invited us into his room to see, but the place was such a mess, it would have taken us hours to search it.

"Never mind," Steve said. "It was only a precaution. Just thought I might bag me a seven-foot owl. Something for the record books." He grinned as he headed out the door, loaded down with a couple of blankets and a pillow.

"I'll take the second truck, Rebecca," he called back. "Maybe you wouldn't mind bringing me back here for breakfast and a shower after you drop off the students, so I can leave this truck at the site. Don't use all the hot water in the morning, you guys," he called from the cab of the truck as he pulled away.

But in the morning, Steve was gone.

14

CARLOS MONTERO STOOD in his office, beads of sweat breaking out on his brow and upper lip. "Missing!" he exclaimed. "How can that be? I haven't heard from him, no." He looked nervous to me, the way he wiped his brow a couple of times with a large pink handkerchief. It was warm in there, but perhaps not that warm.

"I'll make a couple of calls, why don't I?" he said. You do that, I thought. I was rapidly reaching the conclusion that there was something terribly wrong in Campina Vieja, and that a single sinister thread had been snaking its way through all the events of the past several weeks, from the death of Lizard in my shop, Edmund Edwards in his, to the disappearance now of Steve, Puma, and Pachamama. And Montero, I was convinced, was part of it.

When I had first arrived at the site that morning, I'd thought Steve, while I could not find him, must be somewhere nearby. The bedding he'd taken with him was still there, the pillow still bearing the imprint of his head in a rather endearing sort of way, the blankets tossed aside as if he'd arisen in a hurry. There was certainly no sign of violence or an accident of any kind.

"He's gone to pee in the woods," Pablo said, pointing to faint footsteps in the sand that headed in that direction, and it seemed the obvious conclusion. I waited several minutes, but Steve didn't return. "Maybe he got lost in the woods," Pablo added.

Lost in these woods? "I don't think so," I replied. Where I come from there are woods to get lost in. These woods did not qualify. You'd have to reach either the highway or a side road in fifteen minutes max. And you'd see the mountains or the sea right away to get your bearings.

I drove back to the hacienda to get the rest of the team, watching for Steve as I went. There was a little concern about Steve but nothing serious. By about ten in the morning, however, I could feel a little buzz of anxiety in the group. Hilda sent me back to the hacienda to make sure he hadn't walked back. I was tempted to point out that the easiest and fastest route between the site and the hacienda was the road, and I'd traveled on it three times already. Back I went again. No Steve.

Hilda then sent a small team into the woods, and I went with them. There were lots of footprints in the sandy soil: It was obvious these woods were well traveled, but any discernible footprints stopped at an adobe brick wall. There was evidence someone had had a sort of picnic lunch there recently, but that was all. It could have been one of the workers, or just a passerby. It wasn't Steve: He'd only taken a bottle of water with him. Beyond that was a much-used trail with so many footprints it would be impossible to follow any one of them. We called Steve's name time and time again, and listened carefully for a response, however faint. There was none.

About noon, Hilda pulled me aside. "I don't want to create a panic here, so would you do me a favor? Drive over to Montero's place, the Fabrica Paraiso, and tell him about this. Ask him what he thinks we should do. If I go, it'll look as if I'm really concerned, which I am, incidentally, I will tell you. But you travel around all day, and it's almost time for you to go and get Ines . . ." Her voice trailed off. She looked at me almost beseechingly.

I nodded. It was exactly where I was planning to go anyway. "Do you think we should call his family?" I whispered.

"Not yet," she replied. "No need to worry them unnecessarily. Maybe tonight, if—" Her voice caught for a second. Pablo and one of his team approached us.

"I'm off to get Ines," I said loudly enough that those nearest us could hear. "I'll take the long way and watch out for Steve as I go." Hilda looked relieved.

Now Montero returned from his phone calls; two of them I'd strained to hear but couldn't. "I don't think we should call the police just yet," he said. "I have contacts, you know, and I've spoken to them, and they'll be on the lookout. They'll make enquiries. Let's wait until tomorrow before we go to the police. Come back and see me again if there's no sign of him."

On the surface, I suppose, that made sense. Steve

had only been missing a few hours, and Montero's advice would be considered rational under normal circumstances. But these weren't normal circumstances, as I knew only too well. I fully intended to come back to Paraiso, but not perhaps when Montero was expecting me. I had two plans for the Montero family when everyone at the hacienda had retired for the night: I was going to search Lucho's room, since lately he hadn't been sleeping there, and I was going to take another look around the Paradise Crafts Factory.

Judging from his room, Lucho was a grown man developmentally stuck in his teens. The place was a mess, clothes tossed everywhere, particularly the floor. Posters covered every available spot on the walls, the only difference from the teenagers I knew being the content. Instead of rock or rap groups, Lucho's tended to military recruitment posters with a somewhat fascist bent.

I began to systematically search the room, checking under the bed, lifting the pillows and bedding and then, nothing found, lifting the mattress as well. No gun.

Next I went through the closet and dresser. It's unpleasant going through someone's underwear drawer when they aren't there, but perhaps it would be worse if they were. Still no gun.

I went through his desk, and even pulled the furniture away from the wall as quietly as I could to check behind it. I shook out the carpet, causing a bout of sneezing that I strained to muffle, but not much else.

Just as I was about to give up my search, I saw the edge of an envelope sticking out slightly from behind one of the posters on Lucho's wall. It was not the gun

I was looking for, obviously, but I wondered what someone would choose to store behind a poster. The envelope was addressed to me. *Rebeca,* the childish scrawl said.

I turned it over to find it sealed, but with the wrinkled look of an envelope that has been steamed open.

Dear Rebeca, the letter began. *First of all you got to excuse my writing. I didn't do very good at school. I was sick alot and got behind.* That was an understatement: The writer, whoever he or she was, was the worst speller I had ever encountered. After momentarily pondering the inadequacy of the education system, I read on.

I no my speling is bad. But please read all of this any way. Your my only hope.

What was this? I wondered.

I no I shoulda told you before, but for a couple years I grew very high grade marigana. Mainly I smoked it myself, altho from time to time I gave it for a small donation to freinds. The police dont no the diference between selling the stuff and acepting a donation, so you could say I am some times on the wrong side of the law. I am not proud of this. I only tell you so you no I am a person who tells the truth, so you will beleive what I have to tell you.

I am not sure how to make you understand but here goes.

Up untill a while ago, I cant remember ecaxtly, I thought all this stuff about recarnation was bull shit, just like you do. But then one time when I was laying on my bed, trying out some of my own home growed product if you take my meaning, something realy amazing happen. I beleive what happen was I got in touch with my spirit self. A bright light arked through my mind like a comet and then I was able to go back and forth through all my lives. Realy.

It was the most amazing mind trip of all time. Do you no what I learnt? I will not keep you in sespense. In all ages I was the prophit. I could always tell what woud happen next. When I opened my mouth, words about the future woud roll off my tounge. It surprised me at first, but now I'm used to it.

First I was that lady—Casandra—who told the Trojins about the big wodden horse. How stupid can you get of course it was full of Greek soldiers. Then I stood on a street in Rome and told Julius Ceasar to beware the Eyes of March. He didnt listen and we no what happened to him. Also I told Napoleon not to go to Russia but he didnt listen either.

It is not a good job let me tell you being a prophit. Becuse they never listen. And if they do, usully they dont like what you say. If your lucky they only put you in a deep dark dundgeon. Maybe I am now thinking that is why I have spent time in jail, bad karma from another life or something. But it gets worse. Sometimes they put out your eyes with red hot pokers other times they burn you at the stake. Like it is not good.

Another nutbar. I sighed. Whatever had I done—in another life, of course—to deserve this? But I read on.

The person I was that was closest to what I am now I think was a freind of Atahualpa (speling?) the Inca king. This freind was called Wayna and my name now is Wayne. Dont you think that is amazing? I told Atahualpa that the Spanish were not gods, just bad guys looking for gold and treasure and in the end I think he beleived me but it was to late.

At the end of this experience which I beleive took

several days I came back to the present, but not the same. People dont beleive me tho. I tried to tell them, but what did they do. They called the police and they put me in the hospital for two weeks.

I told the doctors too. They didnt beleive me nei-ther. I also told them all about histry. Even tho I didnt like school much, I always liked histry. I watch all those programs on TV about ancient mysterys and stuff. I always wondered why I liked it so much but now of course I no. It is on account of my former lives as a prophit.

By now, of course, I knew who had written it. But was there a point to this? I wondered. And if there was, would I ever be able to figure it out?

When I got out of there the police were still pretty interested in me, the writer went on. *So I desided to come to Peru to see if I coud get closer to this Wayna the freind of Atahualpa which as I have explained to you is me. I borrowed some $$$ from my brother, I didnt tell him tho so I guess hes mad at me too like every body else.*

Its worked out good tho. I have the lady freind her real name is Megan. She was Joan of Ark in another life so she nos what its like.

The thing is the realy important part is that since I can remember all these times in histry I no where the treasure is. I have seen cities of gold that you get to thru cracks in the rock. And most especialy I no where Atahualpa hid the most fabulus treasure ever so as the Spanish coudnt find it. You no how I no? Because I helped him do it. And I have seen it with my own eyes I mean in this life time. And it is near here. I found it once but I was on a bit of a bad trip so I have to find it again. I could pay my brother back so he woudnt

*be mad any more but also I coud pay off the deficet
for every country in the world. I coud build houses for
those refujees and feed all those kids you see on TV
with those big bellys and sad eyes.*

*The trouble is Megan is mad because I used the
$$$ I earnt to buy marigana. She doesnt realy under-
stand I need it to fuse with my former life as Wayna
so I can find the treasure. Shell get over it but right
now she is gone and I am alone.*

*To make things even worse I think the Spanish are
after me. Like if I can go back to my former lives then
may be they can come forward to now if you no what
I'm getting at. I think they mean to kill me good this
time. Please help me.*

Your freind Wayne, who you no as Puma, the letter
ended.

What was one to think about a letter like this? I
didn't know whether to just forget it—and perhaps
congratulate Pachamama, or Megan, should our paths
ever cross again, for having the foresight to leave her
somewhat deranged boyfriend when she had a
chance—or, on the other hand, to try to find a thread
of reality in all the madness.

Ever since Puma had disappeared, I'd wondered if
he was connected in some way to Moche artifacts. *I
know where the treasure is. I have seen cities of gold
that you get to thru cracks in the rocks ... the most
fabulous treasure ever ... and it is near here.* It
sounded like the words of a madman, but was it pos-
sible Puma had indeed seen something, in this lifetime,
drunk or drugged though he might have been at the
time? *To make things even worse I think the Spanish
are after me.* If he had, then he might well be right
about the Spanish being after him, not, as he main-

tained, from a different time, but right here and right now. Pachamama—Megan, that is—had left because she didn't believe him. I didn't know what to think, but with all the strange things that were happening, I was beginning to give him the benefit of the doubt.

I was sure about one thing, however, and that was that I was more than a little annoyed with Lucho. I was waiting as he came shuffling back through the main door heading for his room, having chosen tonight of all nights to stay here. I was so irritated, in fact, that I didn't care if he knew I'd been searching through his belongings.

"What were you doing with this letter?" I demanded. "It is very clearly addressed to me!"

Lucho looked wary but said nothing.

"When did it arrive? Did someone deliver it? Well?" I demanded, one foot tapping the floor impatiently. "Answer me!"

"I don't know," Lucho whined.

"It was in your room," I said. I could hear a dangerous tone in my voice.

"I forgot," Lucho said. He was practically sniveling.

"When did it arrive?" I asked again.

"Yesterday," Lucho said hesitantly.

"Are you sure?" Manco Capac had said yesterday that the kids had left one or two days before.

"Maybe the day before," he conceded. This was the second person—Manco Capac being the first— who'd had a serious lapse of memory where Puma's whereabouts were concerned.

"Who brought it?"

"I don't know," he replied. I glared at him. "I don't!" he repeated stubbornly. "It was on the floor inside the front door when I came in. I didn't see any-body.''

''But you opened it,'' I said very quietly.

''No way,'' he said, and that was the last I could get out of him. I stomped upstairs and told myself to sleep. But I couldn't, unbidden images of Lizard and Edmund Edwards, and most of all the Spider, haunting me. Very late, I decided that I should go to plan B, back to the Paradise Crafts Factory and look around one more time, to see if I'd missed anything. Lucho's door was closed and there was no sign of a light on, as I eased my way out the front door.

I hoped, as I started the truck, that Hilda had been well into the scotch and thus sleeping soundly. I pulled the truck off the highway several hundred yards from the factory, concealing it behind an old abandoned hut, and went the rest of the way on foot, thankful, for once, for the covering blanket of the *garua*.

Montero's little industrial complex was in darkness except for one light over the front door of each of the buildings. I headed around to the rear of the factory building, hoping that one or other of the doors had been left ajar to help cool down the work area after the tremendous heat from the kiln.

All were closed and locked, but I had a fallback. I'd noticed during my tour of the place that the back door was old, with a very poor lock of the bathroom door variety, where you simply push a button on the inside doorknob. Montero was not overly worried, it seemed, about intruders. If he'd really been up to no good I'd have expected better locks, for some reason, Having had some experience getting locks of this sort open, I figured I'd be able to get in reasonably easily. In the absence of a credit card, I'd brought a couple of tools from the lab that I thought would do the trick. They did, and with very little effort I let myself in. I locked the door from the inside.

The room was stifling, and I stood for a moment or two, waiting until my eyes adjusted to the dark, as sweat began trickling down my back from the heat and my fear.

I made my way to the end of the room where Antonio's drafting table was located, and, turning the shade down as far as I could, switched on the light. In another minute, I'd unlocked the filing cabinet next to the table.

The top drawer was filled with drawings, the second with photographs. It took me a moment or two to see how the files were organized: in large sections by year, and then within that, by type of artifact.

My purchases from the auction house had been abandoned in customs, and A. J. Smythson, to whom they'd been sent, had died between two and three years earlier. I went back three years in the file and started to search.

There were several bulging files for that year, quite a few for stirrup vessels done by subject, one file for portraits, another for animals, still another for birds. What I was looking for wasn't there. After checking every file for that year, I went back four years, and started working through those files as well. At the very back of the drawer I found a file marked miscellaneous and opened that.

Midway through the file, I almost exclaimed out loud. I'd found what I wanted. Before I could look further, however, I heard the sound of a car engine very nearby. I stuffed the file back into the drawer, closed it, pushed the lock shut and extinguished the light, almost in one motion. Footsteps crunched on the sand and gravel that surrounded the building. Then the back door rattled, and the glare of a flashlight swept the upper windows. Night watchman, I thought, checking the doors and windows. I hoped his patrol did not include searching the interior.

The steps moved on, then the two doors by the kiln were tried in succession.

I waited, barely breathing, until the footsteps died away. The check of the property must have been fairly thorough, because several minutes went by, and I still hadn't heard the sound of the car engine starting, a signal that this inspection was at an end. Did this mean, I wondered, that the watchman was permanently stationed there for the night, or was he checking out the other buildings more carefully? I waited several minutes more, then, deciding I couldn't wait all night, I plotted in my mind a route back to the truck that would take me away from the main buildings.

I remembered the old ruin of a building out back, and after looking carefully about me, and pulling the locked door shut behind me, I headed across the sand in its direction. It was quite a distance away, but I made it, then stood behind it to listen. Absolute silence greeted me. I kept close to the walls of the building and went around to the back where a door was located. That's strange, I thought, but at that moment, a flashlight came around the corner of the main building once again, and I pulled back into the darkness. As soon as the guard, or whoever it was, had made his circuit, I looked again.

Two things caught my attention. First of all there was a padlock on the door of the ruin. That shouldn't have been necessary, I thought. Secondly, an electric cord had been threaded under the door. As unnecessary as a padlock might be on a ruined building, electricity was even less useful, I'd have thought. I picked it up. I couldn't slide under the door, of course, but I decided to follow the cord back to see if it was actually plugged in somewhere. The cord snaked its way along the wall of the building farthest away from the factory. I came to the corner of the building, and followed the cord around it. It was very dark, and I stumbled over an object in my path. A large object. I switched on the flashlight I had brought with me. Carlos Montero was dead. Shot. It was all I could do to keep from screaming.

I thought for a second or two what I should do. Carlos was beyond help. They'd find him soon enough. I angled away from the building and made a large circle back to the truck.

Back at the hacienda, I opened the front door and started across the courtyard in the dark. "Hands up," a voice said. "Turn around very slowly."

This time, it wasn't Lucho playing freedom fighter.

I turned around to face the voice.

15

Hilda stood in shadow, her tall, slight figure barely discernible to my eyes, framed only by the dim light from outside. I on the other hand was the perfect target, caught in the beam of her flashlight. She gestured at me to move into the dining room, then shut the door behind her. "Who are you, and what are you doing here?" she rasped. "And don't tell me you're Rebecca MacCrimmon just trying to catch up on some work in the lab. I've had your passport checked. The name and the number don't match."

What to do? Sometimes in life you have to take a chance, make a choice. Feeling as if I stood on the edge of a precipice, I made my decision, and, taking a deep breath, stepped off.

"My name is Lara McClintoch," I said. "I'm co-owner of an antiques shop called Greenhalgh and McClintoch in Toronto. I'm here because several weeks ago I went to an auction and picked up what I thought was a box of junk, except that there were objects in it, supposedly replicas of pre-Columbian arti-facts, that I later decided were real. One of them came from here, Campina Vieja, at least that's what it said. Two of the objects disappeared; someone was killed, murdered in my shop; our one employee, a dear friend of mine, was attacked; and then the shop was set on fire. The police think my employee has something to do with it all, and if they think that, they'll end up charging him with manslaughter at the very least. And if they clear him, then they'll be after me for arson probably, insurance fraud that went wrong. So I went to New York to find the source of these objects, and someone else got murdered.''

I paused to catch my breath and then continued. ''After that, I headed for the source, or what I thought was the source, and here I am. That's the short version, but you get the general idea,'' I said, trying not to sound terrified.

''That's quite a story,'' she said. Wait till you hear the rest of it, I thought. ''Perhaps the missing details would make it more plausible,'' she went on, more than a hint of sarcasm in her voice. ''What did these objects look like?''

''There was a silver peanut, about life-size; an ear spool of gold, turquoise, and some other materials; and a flared vase with serpents drawn around the rim, sort of like this,'' I said, dropping my hands slightly to indicate the shape.

''It's called a *florero*,'' she said, and then I knew I was safe. You don't correct people's description of things, I decided, if you're planning to shoot them.

''A *florero*,'' I agreed. ''It had *hecho en Peru* stamped on the bottom, and there was a card that said it was a pre-Columbian replica from Campina Vieja.''

Hilda said nothing, so I pressed on. "So now," I said into the shadows, "perhaps you could return the favor and tell me who you are and why you're here."

"What do you mean?" she demanded.

"I don't think the average person would know how to check out a passport," I replied.

"Even fewer average people know how to get a fake one," she snapped.

"Touché," I replied.

"Furthermore," she went on, her voice heavy with rebuke, "my name really is Hilda Schwengen, and I really am an archaeologist."

I said nothing, just waited.

"I am also," she said reluctantly, "from time to time, a consultant to U.S. Customs."

"Consultant? What's a consultant? Are you an agent? And," I added, pushing my luck a little, "could we discuss this in a little more civilized manner? Would you mind putting down the gun—is it the one we're looking for, by the way?"

Another pause. Finally she stepped forward, to the other side of the table, and set the gun in front of her. "Sit down," she ordered. She pulled up a chair and sat facing me: We were like two opponents in a chess match, sizing each other up. Her hair, usually tied back, was down around her shoulders, and she was wearing a bulky cotton terry robe, which emphasized her thinness somehow, and no shoes. I was also in my bare feet, having taken off my shoes to creep in. This encounter was beginning to have the rather endearing air of a pajama party, except for the gun. I could see it was a small pistol of a size that would fit in a hand-bag, not the one I'd been looking for.

"You're an agent?" I prompted after a moment or two of silence.

"No," she said. "I just give them information from time to time."

"An informant?"

"If I'm an informant, I'm not a paid one," she sighed. "I keep my eyes and ears open, that's all."

"Drugs? Artifacts?"

"Artifacts, mostly. You weren't the first person to notice that Campina Vieja seems to be a little hive of activity where artifact smuggling is concerned," she said, irony in her voice. I took this sentence to be very encouraging, though, in that it appeared to signal that she was prepared to believe at least some of my story. We stared at each other across the table. Finally she put the gun down on the floor beside her chair. It was a generous gesture.

"I don't suppose you'd care to tell me how you got a false passport and got down here," she said.

"Nope." We looked at each other, each waiting for the other one to say something. I decided to leap in.

"You say you pass information along from time to time. I don't suppose you know anything that would help me get out of this little pickle I find myself in?"

"Sorry, no," she replied. "Nothing concrete at all."

"Do you think something awful has happened to Steve?" I asked hesitantly.

"I don't want to think about it, but yes, I'm afraid that is a very real possibility." She looked away, perhaps to hide the tears forming at the corners of her eyes but not yet spilling over. She's in love with Steve, I thought, and that's why she doesn't like Tracey. My face, as usual, betrayed my thoughts.

"I know what you're thinking," she said, pulling a cigarette pack out of the pocket of her robe and lighting up. "And you're wrong. I'm not in love with him. I'm extremely fond of him, though. He's been having an affair with Tracey, but I expect you must know that. You can't have missed all that creeping around in the night.

"Steve's separated from his wife, and even if he wasn't, it's none of my business, but I really disapprove of professors having affairs with their students," she continued. "I'm not naive, I know it goes on all the time. But I've insisted she work in the lab and not with Steve at the site, because the others have, or will, figure it out, and I don't think it's good for morale."

I said nothing. I still didn't think I was wrong about her being in love with Steve.

"Are you married?" she asked suddenly.

"No, divorced. You?"

"Single. Married to my work, as they say. Boyfriend?"

"For a while, but he dumped me about a year ago."

"For another woman?"

"Worse than that," I replied. "He left me for politics."

"My gawd!" she exclaimed, and suddenly we both got the giggles. It was part hysteria, but also part relief for both of us, I think, to be able to talk to someone about our hidden selves. It was as if a dam had burst, and suddenly we were sharing confidences one would normally share only with the closest of friends.

She told me about her back injury, the pain, and how she'd found out about Steve and Tracey's affair.

"I blame Tracey," she said. "I think she's a scheming little bitch who is trying to take over from me, and using Steve to do it.'' She made a face. ''You don't have to say it. I know I'm the one who's the bitch. I'm being completely unfair, I realize that. I don't even know her, really. I just met her at the start of this season, and I confess I've made no effort whatsoever to get to know her. In fact, I've acted in such a way to keep her at a distance. Perhaps I am jealous. She's beautiful, isn't she? I hate the way she sits with him at dinner and chatters away. Puts me off my food, although I know that leaving the table with a bottle of scotch halfway through the meal is not exactly a mature way of dealing with it.

''In a way, even though Steve and I have never had that kind of relationship, I feel like the tired old first wife who's being thrown over for a younger woman. Steve and I have been a great team, but this is my last season in the field. My back won't take another.'' I nodded sympathetically. ''So next year it'll be Steve and Tracey instead of Hilda and Steve, and I feel just wretched about it. But let's drop this dreadful topic and talk about why you're here in the first place. Details, please.''

I told her about Clive moving in across the street, and how upset and irrational I'd been at the time. I told her about the auction, about Lizard and Alex, and how everything I'd done since the day of the fire had been an attempt to make amends. ''But the harder I try to fix things, the worse they get.'' I sighed. ''Unless I can figure out what's going on around here, Alex is in big trouble, I've lost the store, and I won't be winning any popularity contests with the police back home.''

I told her about the train of events that had taken me from Toronto to New York and then on to Lima, omitting, for Lucas's sake, the side trip to Mexico. I related how I'd first looked up Lizard's wife, and followed her around Lima.

"That got me nowhere," I conceded, "so I decided to come here, the point of origin of the *florero,* thinking there must be some connection to Montero and the Fabrica Paraiso," I concluded. This was a test. I wanted to know what she'd say about Montero.

"I agree," she said, "that Montero and Paraiso would be the main suspect in all this, but I've looked around there and I can't see anything unusual there."

"Me neither. I looked everywhere except the washroom."

"I've done the washroom," she replied. "Invented tummy trouble so I could stay in there long enough to pull a board out and check behind the pipes even. Nothing. I've also had occasion to check out the body shop."

She sighed. "But maybe I'm grasping at straws here, in desperation. Maybe I want it to be Montero because he's so revolting. I find myself looking for evil in everything he does."

"The *florero* had the words *hecho en Peru* on the bottom. I suppose after all this it really could have been a replica," I said.

Hilda looked at me as if I was quite naive. "It's easy enough to put a light slip over the bottom of the vase and put a stamp on it," she said. "It's done all the time, in fact. When it gets to its destination, you just soak the slip off, and there it is, genuine Moche."

Of course, I thought. "Stay here, I'll be right back," I exclaimed. I went back to the courtyard where I'd dropped my bag when Hilda had startled me. I returned and handed her the photograph I'd taken from the files of the Fabrica Paraiso.

"Nice," she said. "A *florero*."

"Not *a florero*. *The florero*," I replied. "The one from the auction. See, the snakes around the rim? I'm sure it's the same one. I thought when I found it at Paraiso that I'd merely confirmed that my *florero* had come from Paraiso, just as the card that came with it indicated. But as soon as you mentioned the use of the slip and stamp as a way of concealing artifacts, it hit me: This is the way they get the stuff out. Someone photographs a looted object, and sends it over to Paraiso. Antonio does a drawing, then, in the case of ceramics, designs and makes the mold, and several copies are churned out right along with all the regular reproductions. They all get stamped with the made in Peru symbol, including the original in the way you described it to me, with the slip on the bottom. They get packed up together, probably in shipping crates from the Fabrica des Artesanias Paraiso, which would clinch it. Anyone looking at them would assume that they are all reproductions. It would certainly look that way, with rows of identical objects coming from a crafts factory."

"I like it," she said.

"There is, however, one problem with my theory," I said. Hilda looked at me. I took the plunge. "Carlos Montero is dead."

"Dead!" she exclaimed. She seemed genuinely shocked. "When? How?"

I told her what I'd found. She looked aghast. "Who would do this?" She paused. "What does this mean? You must be right about the photograph, but with Montero dead, does this mean . . . ?"

"There are several questions, actually," I said.

"Another is, do you think there could be anything to this?" I pulled Puma's letter out of my T-shirt pocket and handed it across to her. "I know he sounds nuttier than a fruitcake, and there's no question he's a tad, shall we say, delusional," I said, watching the skeptical expression on her face as she read. "But I know him," I went on. "He's not particularly bright, although he's actually quite a talented magician, and he's kind of sweet. I mean, look where he says he wants to find the treasure to feed all the world's hungry children," I said, pointing to the place in the letter. "And when you talk to him, you don't get the impression that he's dangerous or anything, or even that he is totally out of it, by any means."

"So what are you saying?" Hilda asked.

"I'm saying, what if there is a treasure trove around here? And if there is, who knows about it?"

"A better question might be, does this treasure, assuming it exists, have anything to do with Montero and Paraiso?" Hilda said. "I have no idea what the answers to these questions might be."

"I don't either, but I do still think I'm right about the way the artifacts are being taken out of here," I said. "Obviously I'm wrong about the leader. But if not Montero, then who? With Montero dead, we have nothing."

"We're not going to solve this tonight," Hilda said, standing up carefully and stretching. "It's time we got some sleep. But you say we have nothing. That's not entirely true. We have Etienne Laforet, an art dealer and known buyer of illegal artifacts, and he's right here in Campina Vieja, blatant as they come. There has to be a good reason for him to stay a few days. With him we have two problems. We've never been able to catch him with any Moche pieces on his person—and believe me, the Peruvian authorities have searched him more than once when he left the country—nor in his gallery. Plainclothes officers have been in. This means he's probably not in this alone.

"Ideally what I'd like to do is take an artifact to him, get him to buy it, and then watch what he does—a sting, if you get what I mean. Which brings me to the second problem: We don't have a suitable artifact to use. I can't risk a piece from a museum collection, and while I might be able to sneak something out of this lab, we haven't found anything he'd buy, I don't think. He only takes high-end stuff. We don't have anything to deal with," she said, shaking her head.

"Oh, but we do," I replied.

16

Over the Pacific, off Peru's shores, a huge, warm, moist body of air begins to move slowly toward land. As it hits the shore it becomes the garua, *the mist from the sea, swirling over the sand of the desert. But it does not stop there. It moves across the land to the wall of rock called the Andes, and somewhere, high in the mountains, the* garua *turns to rain. Torrents of rain. Slowly at first, then faster and faster, the rocky gorges fill with water, hurtling downward. Waterways, both ancient and modern, built to tame it, now strain to contain it, and fail.*

Just as dark was falling the next evening, Hilda and I were standing in the shadow of the awning of the hardware store, watching Laforet's house. To help conceal ourselves, we'd dressed in dark colors, she in a navy turtleneck and trousers, I in jeans and a large black sweater I'd borrowed from Tracey. There were lights on in the house, but none at the front door, to provide the anonymity Laforet's visitors required, no doubt. We'd told the others we were going into town to call Steve's ex-wife and children, and not to wait up for us.

It had been a rather strange day. Not one word was heard about Carlos Montero. Lucho shuffled around the hacienda as usual. There were no visitations from the police. Around two, Hilda went over to Paraiso. I told her exactly where to look. "Nothing," she said on return. "No cord. No Carlos." She paused. "Are you sure . . . ?"

"Absolutely," I replied.

"I went in and asked Montero's wife, that timid little thing, Consuelo, where he was," Hilda went on. "She said Trujillo. He'd left her a note: typewritten. Anyone could have typed it, of course. Machine sitting right out there."

I thought soon enough alarms would go off, about Montero but also the others. Someone was bound to notice eventually that Campina Vieja was becoming the terrestrial equivalent of a black hole, sucking people into oblivion. Not that day, though, it seemed.

We'd decided I'd be the one to go into Laforet's, Hilda being better known in these parts than I, and with a reputation to protect where archaeological objects were concerned.

After about forty-five minutes of watching, and seeing absolutely nothing, and with Hilda getting uncomfortable standing so still, I whispered to her, "Time to beard the lion in its den." I slipped across the street and up to the door, the Moche ear spool, which Hilda had declared to be the perfect bait, wrapped in a soft handkerchief of Steve's, tucked into a canvas tote bag.

After I'd knocked, the curtains in a dark upstairs room stirred slightly before I heard footsteps inside coming toward the door. It opened a crack, someone looked at me, as I held up my bag and tried to look furtive, which wasn't difficult, and a man's voice farther back in the house said, first in French, "*Entrez. Come in.*"

As the door opened and I saw who was standing there, sheer apprehension almost made me change my mind and run away. A young woman greeted me, dressed in one of those outfits that young women occasionally wear these days, where—and I know this will position me solidly in the camp of old fuddy-duddies—it's difficult to tell whether it's a dress or a slip, a very short pink satin number with shoestring straps, over irridescent silk stockings. Her long nails were painted black, her dark hair was piled up on her head, and she swayed provocatively on very high-heeled, black, patent-leather sandals as she led me toward the back of the house. Carla Cervantes, Lizard's widow, gave no indication she recognized me. Although it was unnerving to see her here, it made me think that while I did not yet understand how or why, the pieces in this puzzle were snapping into place.

I entered a darkened room, an office, with a desk and only one light source, a desk lamp that cast a pool of brightness on the desk in front of me but did nothing much to illuminate the rest of the room. For a second or two I thought I was alone, until I realized that a man was there, *el Hombre,* presumably, his chair swiveled around to face the back wall, so that I was addressing the back of his head. "You may leave us now, Carla," the voice said in heavily accented Spanish, and the young woman shrugged and left, closing the door behind her as she went. I could hear her heels clicking down the hall and then up the stairs to the second floor.

"Are you the man they call *el Hombre*?" I asked. Hilda and I had decided that I should pretend I didn't know his real name.

"I am," the voice replied in English. "Why are you here?"

"I have," I stammered, "something I want to sell, and I'm told in town you might buy."

"Name?" he demanded.

"I'd rather not say," I replied. I heard a soft chuckle.

"Put it on the desk, in the light," he instructed, and I placed the little Moche man in the circle of light.

With a creak, the chair swiveled toward the light, and I caught my first glimpse of the man they called *el Hombre*. Second, actually. Predictably, considering who had opened the door, I found myself face-to-face with Carla Cervantes's pal in the hotel in Lima. I remembered him well. The question was, did he remember me?

Here again there was no flicker of recognition that I could detect. A hand, minus two fingers, which I could see had been cut, maybe even hacked off at the knuckles, reached out and picked up the ear spool. With his other hand, he held a magnifying glass, which he placed against the object, then bent his head to examine it closely. I got to look at a bald spot on the top of his head for a moment or two.

"Very nice," he said finally. "Where did you get it?"

Hilda and I had rehearsed my answers all the way into town. "Near Cerro de las Ruinas," I replied.

"Staying at the Hacienda Garua, are you? I didn't think they'd found much there yet, but the vigas sound promising, don't they?"

I didn't answer his questions, but it made me very nervous to think he knew so much about the project. "I said I found it near, not at, Cerro de las Ruinas," I said. "And I'm not saying exactly where."

"But you didn't find it recently," he replied. "This object has been partially cleaned and restored." Hilda and I had rubbed a little dirt into it before we came, but we couldn't put back the aging of centuries in a matter of hours.

"Of course it has," I said. "We have a lab."

"You're an expert on restoration, are you?"

"I know enough," I replied testily. My nervousness was coming across as annoyance, which was good. "Are you interested or not?"

He chuckled again. "Sensitive type, aren't you? I'm sure you're only selling this to help out a sick friend." He smirked. He paused after he said it, congratulating himself, no doubt, on his deep understanding of the dark side of human nature. "I'm interested," he said at last. "How much?"

This one was tricky. Hilda and I both regarded the ear spool as priceless, and from an academic point of view it was. But it also had a commercial value, and we were not at all sure what that was. I wanted to look neither an expert nor a fool.

"A pair of these might get as much as $100,000, I've heard," Hilda had said. "But half a pair isn't worth half the price, if you understand what I'm saying. So let's assume that rather than $50,000, it's worth $25,000. Ask for ten."

"Ten thousand dollars," I replied.

"Nonsense!" He laughed. "A thousand."

We went back and forth a few times and settled on $2000. What a rip-off, I thought indignantly: My little Moche man was worth more, much more, than that.

"Cash!" I insisted.

"Of course," he replied, opening the drawer in his desk and tossing two little packets of U.S. currency onto the table. As I reached for it, his mangled hand slammed down on mine. "You wouldn't be associated with the police in any way, would you?" he asked, his voice a really menacing whisper. "Because if you are, you will be taken care of, do you understand me?"

"Of course not," I gasped. "I understand." His hand drew back from mine and the money. "Go out the back," he said, pointing to the right. I heard Carla's footsteps on the stairs. I grabbed the money and fled the room, down a hallway toward a back door. I passed the kitchen on the way out, and took a peek in as I went by. It didn't appear to be much used as a kitchen, rather, it looked more like a darkroom. The window was covered over, and there were several photographs hanging up to dry, some of them artistic poses, shall we say, of Carla, the kind you'd have some difficulty, and embarrassment, getting developed at your corner photo shop. Pervert, I thought, as I slipped out the back door into a little garden fragrant with night flowers, then through a gate to the side street. But then I had another idea about Laforet's photographic talents, one more related to the subject at hand, the smuggling of artifacts, and my theory on how it was done. Away from the house, I paused for a moment and took a deep breath, willing myself to relax.

There was a smell of something in the air, ozone, perhaps, and lightning crackled off in the distance. Heat lightning, I thought. It doesn't rain in the desert. There was a feeling, though, a change in the air, that at home I would have thought meant a storm.

I circled back to where Hilda was waiting, and handed her the bag. "Two thousand, can you believe it?" I whispered.

She groaned. "We'd better get it back," she said. "How did you get out?" she added. "Back door?" I nodded.

"I think we need to reposition ourselves slightly so we can see both the front door and the alleyway where I came out. The good news is that the alleyway dead-ends, so there's only one way out of there," I said. We waited to make sure that the curtains didn't move and then stationed ourselves a little farther along the street. While we waited, I filled her in on what had happened, and Laforet's connection with Carla Cervantes, his mini photo studio setup, and his knowledge of our activities, which we both agreed was unnerving. I also told her about Laforet's missing fingers.

"Interesting," Hilda said. "He's a bit of a legend around here, you know. He's slippery as anything, and he always seems to get away, even when his partners in crime do not. There's a story that one time he almost got caught with illegal artifacts at the border with Ecuador, but got away, losing his fingers in the process, and leaving his partner to take the blame. I have no idea of whether or not this is true, of course, but you have confirmed his fingers are missing, and regardless, it does say something about the man, doesn't it?"

"No matter what kind of man he is," I said, "for better or worse, we're in play."

About a half hour later, the front door opened, and two shadowy figures emerged into darkness, Carla and the Man, no doubt. They got into his Mercedes and pulled away.

Unwilling to have the truck seen, we'd parked near the crowds in the Plaza de Armas and made our way through the lanes to Laforet's place on foot. It had been a calculated risk: We knew Laforet had the Mercedes, but we'd decided, wrongly as it turned out, that he wouldn't leave the house. We followed on foot, thinking this was hopeless, but luck was with us. At the end of the little street, the Mercedes pulled into the main square, but the crowds were so thick that they made very little progress, so much so that we passed him on foot, and were in our truck and waiting as the Mercedes edged past us.

They didn't go far, another block or two to El Mochica bar. Personally I wouldn't have taken the car that few blocks, but then I hadn't worn high heels like Carla's in at least fifteen years. I let Hilda out. "Your turn," I said. "Go in and have a look around. I don't think it would be a good idea for him to see me."

While I waited for her, I watched the entrance. A motorcycle taxi pulled up, and someone I knew headed into the bar. It was Manco Capac, eschewing for a while the solidarity and simple life of the commune, and his epicurean tastes, for the smoky conviviality and bar fare of El Mochica.

About forty-five minutes later, Hilda climbed back into the truck, alcohol on her breath. I hoped we weren't into another bout of drinking, but she seemed okay.

"Well, I gave Lucho a bit of a turn," she said in answer to my question. "He was in there holding up the bar with a couple of his young pals. Planning the next invasion of somewhere or other, I think. I don't think he was too pleased to see me. He was the only person in the bar that I recognized. I made a pretense of looking around for a friend, and checked out the dining area. The mayor was there, holding court at one table, bobbing up and down to talk to everybody in the room. I didn't know anyone else, but there was a man there with a young woman who'd forgotten to dress. Pink slip, black lipstick and nail polish. I figured that must be them."

"That's Carla." I laughed. "And *el Hombre*." No wonder I liked Hilda, I thought. We saw life in much the same way.

"They'd just ordered cocktails and were looking at the menu when I looked in, so I think they're there for a while," she went on. "The tables in the dining room were pretty well all taken, except for one, which had a reserved sign on it, so I went back to the bar and ordered a scotch, and nursed it as long as I could. I kept my eye on the dining room entrance, but no one came or went while I was there, except for the mayor who came into the bar to glad-hand a few people, including myself. That was it."

"Did you happen to notice an American, not too tall, big head, long ponytail, white shirt and jeans?"

"Yes. He pulled up a stool at the bar and ordered a beer," she replied.

"Did he speak to anyone?"

"Just the bartender. Why? Do you recognize him?"

"Manco Capac."

"Manco Capac? Are we talking about the spirit of

the first Inca? Or maybe the ghost of one of the later Incas that took that same name? The guy looked pretty substantial to me.''

''Not a ghost. A megalomaniac, maybe, and he has royal tastes: caviar, pâté de foie gras, and champagne. Head of the commune where Puma and Pachamama were staying. I keep thinking that all of these paths keep crossing somehow. It's just that I don't get the connections between all the people involved.''

''Hard to see what a commune has to do with artifact smuggling, I agree. What do you want to do now? Wait and see where they go from here?''

''I guess so, and see if anyone we know shows up. If Laforet is going to do a deal of some kind, do we think it would be in a public place?''

Hilda shrugged, and we settled down to watch.

About twenty minutes later, Pablo and a bunch of young friends came along.

''Everyone we know is showing up,'' I moaned. ''They can't all be in on this, can they? How can we narrow down our suspects, if everyone is here? My, my,'' I added. ''Ralph and Tracey too.''

''Ralph!'' Hilda exclaimed. ''He never goes out at night!'' But he had. Our second borrowed truck had pulled up about a half a block from El Mo, and Ralph also went in.

''I think it's time for another drink, don't you?'' Hilda said. ''I'm going in again.''

A few minutes later she returned. ''I think Laforet and friend are finishing up, and we should be seeing them out here soon. Cesar, the mayor, is in the dining room; Lucho, Pablo, Ralph and Tracey, and that fellow Manco Capac are in the bar. The reserved table is for Carlos Montero, and he is expected, although I gather they keep the table for him every night, and sometimes he just doesn't show. I talked to Ralph briefly while Tracey was chatting up the bartender. He says Tracey insisted on coming into town to phone home, and to enquire around El Mochica for any news of Steve. He said he tried to dissuade her but couldn't. He took her to the Telefónico del Peru office for the call and then brought her here. He's planning to take her back to the hacienda soon, but he's obviously hoping we'll go back and help him manage Tracey. He says she's getting quite worked up about Steve.''

''Not right this minute,'' I said, pointing toward the door to El Mochica. ''Here they come.''

Laforet and Carla left the bar, got into his car, and headed back in the direction they came from. ''I think they're going back home,'' I said. ''We'd better go on foot, or they may start to notice the truck. If I'm wrong and they drive off somewhere, though, I'll be fit to be tied.''

Our luck held out again. We were in position across from the house when they arrived, having taken a shortcut along a tiny little lane. We watched as they went into the house, and then for about another hour. The downstairs lights went out, and soon the upstairs ones did too, leaving the house in complete darkness. I went around the corner and shone the flashlight for a second on my watch. ''Twelve-thirty,'' I whispered to Hilda.

She beckoned me back around the corner. ''Look,'' she said. ''We can't both watch these people twenty-four hours a day. I think they're down for the night, don't you, but just in case, I'll stay here. I think I got more sleep than you did last night, so I'll do the first night shift. Let's go back to the square and get a motorcycle taxi to take you back to the hacienda, and get the truck for me. I'll be perfectly safe in the truck, and you can come and spell me off first thing tomorrow.''

"Okay," I said, "if you're sure you'll be all right. But we'll have to hope that something happens soon. We can't keep this up forever."

"I think something will happen soon," she replied. "After all, he's got a real treasure there now, hasn't he?"

That night, I dreamt that I was at Cerro de las Ruinas. In the dream it was the same night. Ines and Tomas Cardoso, her brother, the shaman, were there. He donned the skin of a puma, she the feathers of a condor. They told me not to look. But I did. I lay face-down in the sand, my head buried in my hands at first, but then I raised my head ever so slightly and looked toward the huaca. First, I saw a condor soaring overhead, a large cat prowling the summit. Then above the huaca, I saw the most horrible figure. At first it looked like a crab, then a giant spider, which metamorphosed into a man, but a man with fangs for teeth. In one hand he held a tumi blade—the one, I knew, from Edmund Edwards's store—in the other a severed head. I covered my eyes in terror. I heard growls and then shrieks, as if a terrible battle was raging. In my dream, I knew it was for control of the huaca, the struggle between evil and good. Then there was silence, and I was back in my room once more.

Still later, Ines Cardoso was standing at the foot of my bed. I was dreaming again. I must have been, although I believed I was awake. Her figure had a luminescence to it, a fuzziness about the edges, that I thought meant I was asleep. *"Cuidado al arbolado!"* she said again, this time very agitated. Beware of the woods.

And then I knew what she had been trying to tell me. Etienne Laforet. *La foret.* French for forest. I was to beware of Etienne Laforet. I understood then, that if Laforet had seen only one ear spool of my Moche warrior, he would be pleased to find the pair. If he had seen both of them before, then he knew I didn't find mine at Cerro de las Ruinas. And if this was the case, then he would do what he thought he had to. He would do what he did when Lizard headed for Canada to reclaim the missing artifacts, what he did when Edmund Edwards made a mistake, perhaps as simple as losing his nerve. Laforet would send for the Spider. I had not bearded the lion in its den. I had put my hand into the viper's nest.

The next morning, we found the summit of the huaca disturbed. Several feathers were lying in the sand.

17

WHAT HAD SEEMED a devilishly clever plan to smoke out a smuggling ring had, by the next afternoon, become an exercise that on the one hand was a logistical nightmare, but on the other, almost defined the word futile. As to the former, Hilda and I had to keep shuttling back and forth between town and the hacienda, one of us always watching Laforet's place. Hilda had declared a day off for everyone, but a couple of the students volunteered to help pack up the lab, and there was the shopping and taxiing around to be done. Even with two vehicles now, it was a chore. No one wanted to be left alone at the hacienda for very long. Tracey was particularly high maintenance in that regard. Understandably, I supposed, with her lover missing, she needed to be taken into town to call home on three separate occasions.

As to our real mission, our surveillance exercise, *el Hombre* never left the house; no one came to visit. The pinnacle of excitement was reached when I followed Carla to the market to watch her buy bananas.

There were two unsettling aspects to the visit to the market, however, neither of which had anything, I thought, to do with Carla. One was that the place was abuzz with talk about the weather, about torrential rains in the mountains that were threatening the irrigation and water control systems. The consensus in the market appeared to be that the government's evacuation plans might need to be put into effect any day. People were stocking up with provisions. It was a little difficult for me to fathom this anxiety, however. The place was as dry as a bone.

Secondly, it was on this trip to the market that I got the first intimations that someone else was watching too. Nothing substantial really, just a sense of someone else being there. A couple of times I had a feeling I was being followed, but when I turned there was no one unusual in sight. At other times I'd have the impression of someone pulling back out of sight, or I'd catch a glimpse of a man disappearing down a lane. In the end, though, I decided I'd been imagining it. I had a deathly fear of the Spider, that he might be around, but quite frankly, if he was, and if I was his target, I didn't think he'd just hang about watching me. So I concentrated on being the spy rather than the spied upon.

When it came right down to it, the trick to surveillance, Hilda and I found, was nothing like trying to keep from being seen. It was trying to keep from falling asleep. Hilda and I took turns napping in the backseat while the other watched the house. Sometimes we watched on foot, at other times we parked the truck down the street where we could watch both doors. We alternated watching posts not just to avoid drawing attention to ourselves by staying in one place for too long, but also to keep ourselves moving.

That evening, as they had before, Carla and the Man drove the three short blocks to El Mochica for dinner. This in itself was not surprising: El Mo boasted the only white tablecloth dining in town. Cesar appeared to eat there once again, and Carlos's reserved table remained vacant. Lucho held up the bar with his friends.

While Laforet and the others dined or drank in style, Hilda and I ate barbecued chicken sandwiches from a *polleria* down the street. If there is a national dish in Peru, I decided, it was chicken, *pollo*. There are as many *pollerias* in Peru as there are pizzerias at home.

"I'm going to grow feathers any minute," Hilda groaned as I handed her another chicken sandwich. We were sitting in the truck outside El Mo. "And the sandwich after this, I'll start to cluck. I sincerely regret I didn't eat Ines's lovely dinners while I had the chance, and if I don't get to sleep in a real bed soon, my back will never recover." I nodded sympathetically.

"For some reason," she went on, waving her sandwich in the direction of the bar, "I thought this smuggling operation would work like a well-oiled machine. I have no idea why I thought that: I know absolutely nothing about smuggling, but nevertheless, that is what I thought. I had this idea we'd hand Laforet the ear spool, and then everyone would spring into action, including us, and we'd follow them, and then call in the local police force, all four of them. I had no idea smuggling could be this boring," she sighed.

"I don't know how well this operation ran at one

time," I replied. "It probably once did run like a well-oiled machine. But it must have gone seriously off the rails just over two years ago, when the parcel containing three pre-Columbian objects was in transit to a Toronto gallery, when the gallery owner—the sole proprietor, I might add—died. And he died under exceptional circumstances, circumstances that guaranteed that the police were all over the place.

"There would be nothing the smugglers could do to recover the antiquities that wouldn't bring suspicion on them. So they did the only thing they could. They waited. I recall Steve saying that Laforet hadn't been seen around here for a couple of years, that he was farther south for a while. They waited, and then the objects finally came up for auction at Molesworth & Cox.

"Theoretically, it should have been straightforward. You send someone to buy them back. It doesn't really matter what you have to pay, as long as they are considered replicas, because they are worth a fortune. But then it went wrong again. Two people, not one, came to get them. Lizard, Ramon Cervantes, a customs agent from Lima, and someone I refer to as the Spider. It's possible they were in this together: Spider didn't have a paddle for bidding that I could see, so perhaps that was Lizard's job. But I don't think so. They didn't look like pals to me. In any event, neither of them got what they wanted. I did, and then the peanut disappeared, and finally Lizard ended up dead in my storage room and the *florero* is gone. The only person that could have killed him is Spider. Who else in Toronto would be after a customs agent from Lima?

"Then I go to Ancient Ways in New York, and after I've been there, mentioned the Toronto dealer's name, and asked for Moche artifacts, Edmund Edwards ends up dead too.

"On the surface, at least, things don't appear to be going too well for our smuggling ring. But now Laforet is back in town. Why? Or more precisely, why is he still here when Carlos is dead, even if no one but us has noticed, and the whole town is in turmoil because of a *huaquero*'s death and because of the impending rain? Is it because the threat to the organization was Lizard, or perhaps the old man in New York, or even Carlos—although I still think Paraiso must figure in this somewhere—and all are now dead, or is it because something very big has been found, something worth taking a risk for? I think we need to keep watch, because something is going to happen."

"You're thinking of Puma's treasure, the one you get to through cracks in the rock, aren't you?" Hilda said.

"I am," I replied.

It was at about this point that Tracey and Ralph showed up, parking the second truck just outside El Mo.

"Seems to me the only person who isn't here tonight is that pal of yours, the Inca reincarnated," Hilda said.

"Manco Capac," I said. "You're right. It's the same crew as last night, except for him. Why don't I, while Tracey and Ralph are in there, take the second truck—I have a set of keys—and go out to the commune to see if he's there? I've also been thinking about Carlos and that little ruined house out back of Paraiso. I think while everyone is here and comfortably settled for an hour or two, I could just take another look."

"Okay," Hilda replied. "I'll hold the fort while you're gone. Be careful."

I was greeted at the commune by a rather wild-eyed teenager who went by the name of Solar Flare. Despite my aversion to these nicknames, I had to admit the name suited her. Her reddish-blond hair radiated straight out from her head in spikes, and she spoke in bursts, seemingly unrelated words strung together as if in challenge to the listener. I asked if Puma and Pachamama had been heard from.

"No!" she replied. "Gone. Manco Capac says they won't be back!" Did he now?

I wondered what would make him so certain of that.

"Is Manco Capac here?"

She shook her head. "New moon."

"And that means?"

"Retreat."

"What's he retreating from?" I asked.

"Not what, to," she replied.

"Okay," I said. "What is he retreating to?"

"Mountains," she replied. "Meditating."

"You're saying he's gone up in the mountains to meditate, are you?" This conversation was hard work.

"Yes," she said. "Preparing for the end of the world. I'm preparing for it too. It's soon. Everywhere but here," she added.

"What a relief," I said. "Do you know exactly where he goes in the mountains?"

"Secret," she said, shaking her head. "A place with special power. Spoil it if others knew about it."

"Of course," I said. "He goes every new moon, does he? How long does he stay away?"

"Two or three days," she replied. "He comes back much refreshed."

I'll bet he does, I thought. Knowing his tastes, I was willing to wager my last dollar—which I was getting close to, come to think of it, unless one counted my ill-gotten gains as a *huaquero*—that every month Manco Capac, using meditation as an excuse, probably headed off somewhere like the Lima Sheraton or its equivalent, and spent a couple of days swilling expensive wines and trying his luck at the slot machines in the lobby. Manco Capac, I was more and more convinced, was a fake.

I left Solar Flare preparing herself for the end of the world, and headed out for the highway, parking the truck in my by now regular space behind a little clump of trees and the old hut. The spot was near the old riverbed, and to my surprise, I could hear the rush of water in what earlier in the day had been the merest trickle of a stream. They must be right about rain up in the mountains, I remember thinking, as I turned away from the water and crossed the sands to the ruin.

It was very dark—the new moon, of course—and, not wanting to use my flashlight, I had to stop from time to time to make sure I was heading in the right direction. All was quiet at Paraiso when I got there. Carlos Montero was, as Hilda had said, nowhere to be seen. The padlock was still on the door to the ruin.

While the walls of the place were not particularly high, the days when I could haul myself up and over even a low wall were long gone, if indeed they'd ever existed. There were a couple of wooden crates, empty, I discovered, very close to the wall, near a place where the wall was lowest, its bricks fallen away in disrepair. There were many footprints there, I could see, as I beamed my flashlight about for a second or two. With a little effort, I moved the crates up against the wall at the lowest point and climbed up on them, then onto the top of the wall itself. On the other side there was a pile of old bricks that provided a step of sorts down.

I turned on my flashlight and swung it around the interior. It looked deserted: a couple of old pop cans, some empty paint cans, and the ubiquitous foam coffee cups were all I could see. In the center of the space was a very large square of woven bamboo matting, the type I'd seen used as fencing to enclose construction sites in town. The only thing that struck me as strange about it was that it looked very pristine and new, unlike the rest of the junk that had been tossed aside in the area.

Just to make sure, I lifted the corner of the matting. Underneath it was an extraordinary sight: a round hole about ten feet across that had around its perimeter man-made stairs, carved into the rock, that spiraled down into the earth. I aimed my light down into the hole, and saw that the steps snaked down about twenty-five feet. At the bottom was a faint glimmer of water. It looked to be a natural formation of some sort, almost a chute down into the ground, into which someone, a very long time ago, had carved steps.

I hesitated for a moment or two, not terribly comfortable with heights. The stairs were very narrow, open on the inside, so one false step would send me plummeting downward. Then I thought of Puma. The commune was within easy walking distance of this place. Had he, in his marijuana haze, come here? Perhaps the footprints outside the wall were his, and he'd got in the same way I had. Cities of gold you get to through cracks in the rocks, he'd said, the greatest treasure ever. I stuck my flashlight in my belt, directing the beam downward, and started my descent, pulling the woven matting back in its place over my head.

After one circuit of the perimeter on the spiral, I could no longer stand upright, but had to sit on the stairs and lower myself step by step, ducking under overhanging rock as I went. At last I stepped into the pool of water only a few inches deep at the bottom.

I was in a rock chamber not that much larger than the chute down which I had come, maybe fifteen feet in diameter, probably naturally formed by the action of water on limestone. To my right was a door, leading where I could not imagine. Against the wall to my left was a table covered in packing materials and three wooden crates, none of them yet sealed shut.

In all three crates were rows and rows of *cresoles,* the little pots found in tombs, each identical, made in the shape of a round man. All of them, as near as I could tell, were fakes, reproductions from the factory above. The workmanship was not particularly good, and they were absolutely identical, each made from the same mold. But why hide these in some subterranean vault? My idea about putting the antiquity in with a number of fakes should have meant that the objects were handled using the normal channels, not hidden away down here. There was also a sizable dolly which could transport the crates. But where from down here would you take them? You'd need a crane rather than a dolly to get them up to the surface.

I looked under the first layer of little pots and found a second, all the same. I checked the third layer. By now it was getting monotonous, rows and rows of not particularly exceptional fake ceramics. There must be something here, I told myself, keep looking. From the bottom layer, I picked a *cresole* at random and took it out to have a better look, turning it around and then looking inside. Small plastic bag, white powder: co-caine. It had to be. Cocaine was being shipped out in little Moche pots. The Paradise Crafts Factory was more aptly named than I ever would have guessed.

I went to the second crate and checked the second layer of pots, all empty, and then the third layer. I could hardly believe what I saw. Gold peanut beads, dozens of them, some of them the size of my fist, gleamed in the beam of my flashlight. Beneath them lay a golden scepter, gold breastplate, back flap, nose flap, and ear spools, not unlike the one I'd held, of gold and turquoise and other stones. I took a look at the shape of the helmet and tried to recall what Steve had told me about Moche rituals. "It's the warrior priest," I gasped at last. "They've found the tomb of a warrior priest!"

I never made it to the third box. As I reached it, I thought I heard a scraping sound above me, and tiny pinpoints of light showed through the matting above. I extinguished my flashlight quickly and moved to-ward the door that shouldn't by any rights lead any-where. There was nowhere else to hide. I heard the matting being pulled off the entrance to the chamber and a grunt as someone lowered themselves onto the steps. I grabbed the door handle and pulled. Nothing happened. Open, please, I said to myself. I yanked and the door opened. I stepped behind it, pulling the door closed behind me. I had no idea where I was, and was afraid to turn on the flashlight even for a second. I just stood there, shivering, partly in fear, but also because the air was cold and damp, with an unmistakable odor of something starting to rot. I heard a splash as the intruder stepped off into the water at the bottom.

Then, much to my surprise, the lights came on. The

electrical cord, I thought. They've strung a cord out from the factory to light this place. There must have been a switch in the chamber which I had not seen, although it would have never occurred to me to look for a light switch in an underground chamber. I was in a long, man-made tunnel heading some distance underground. There were wires strung the length of it, and from time to time a dim bulb.

I felt terribly exposed standing there. I would be seen instantly if whoever was out there chose to open the door. On the plus side, however, I could see where I was going, and I knew where Carlos Montero had gone. His crumpled body had been stuffed into a little niche in the tunnel wall.

I turned and plunged down the tunnel. The ground rose slightly as I went along, and after about 500 yards or so, maybe more, I took a right turn and found myself at the foot of a wooden staircase leading upward. Cautiously I inched my way up to the underside of a trapdoor. I pressed my ear to the wood and listened. I could near nothing. I raised the door an inch or two. Total darkness greeted me. I pushed the door back and climbed up, shutting it behind me. I was in a little hut, about eight by ten, and windowless. There were four other crates there. Listening at the door once more, I again heard nothing, and let myself out.

It took me a second or two to get my bearings, but when my eyes adjusted, I could see the outline of the Andes against the sky. Behind the hut was a grove of trees, and beyond that, presumably, Paraiso, although I couldn't see it for the trees; I could see nothing to the right or the left. I found myself a hiding place not far from the hut and waited. About fifteen minutes later, a dark but familiar shape emerged from the hut with the first of the crates. It was Lucho. After the crates had been stacked, which took about a half hour in all, I'd estimate, Lucho shuffled away from the hut in the direction of the mountains for several yards, and then walked parallel to the mountain range, stopping every few yards to do something I couldn't see. I could smell gasoline. Having walked about fifty yards away from the hut, he turned left, walked about twenty feet, and then turned left and made his way back, then an equal distance past the hut, stooping over at regular intervals again, before making his way back.

Finally he went back into the hut, and I heard the trapdoor slam.

I edged my way out in the direction he had come. It was still very dark, but I could make out two straight rows of painted white stones stretching off in either direction. At regular intervals between them I found, on closer examination, old paint cans stuffed with rags doused in gasoline. It's a runway, I realized, an illegal runway. Lucho, or someone else, would set the paint can contents ablaze at the right moment, and the aircraft would come in. The desert floor was hard, and packed flat, the stone markers were straight as arrows. The Moche artifacts, and the cocaine, would be gone that night, under cover of the new moon, and with the added benefit of everyone being distracted by the possibility of flooding. There would be absolutely no way I would be able to stop them alone.

I headed back for the truck, terrified that I'd run into Lucho. I thought the trees would provide protection, and plunged into them. *Cuidado al arbolado!* be damned, I thought. They were the only cover around. But it was also tough going, the thorns a constant hazard in the dark, slowing my progress, and distorting my sense of direction. Just as I was about to emerge from the forest, someone stepped out from behind a tree and shone a light directly in my eyes.

"Rebecca, it's you!" the voice exclaimed.

"Puma," I hissed. "Turn out that light. Where have you been?" For a moment I caught a glimpse of what it must be to be the parent of a teenager—the surge of emotion, part relief but also part rage, when the offspring you've imagined lying seriously injured, or even, God forbid, dead, in the middle of an intersection blithely reappears. I wanted to shake him and give him a good talking-to, but I didn't have time.

"Looking for the treasure like I wrote you. Come, you've gotta come with me right away," he said, pulling on my arm.

"Puma, I can't right now. I've seen your treasure. Now I've got to go and get help. Why didn't you come back to the commune or the hacienda?" I found myself asking.

He looked exasperated. "Because they're after me, like I told you. The Spanish. I came to get you again, but one of them was there. So I had to hide. "Come quickly," he insisted, pulling my arm roughly. "It's important. It's life or death!"

"Not the 'pocalypse again," I said, my irritation plain. I didn't want to shake him anymore: I was contemplating strangling him.

"No!" he exclaimed. "Real life. Now!"

This is ridiculous, I thought. But there was something in his voice, an edgy panic perhaps, that made me follow him across the sand toward a cluster of small houses not far away.

He gestured to me to be quiet and to crouch down as we drew near. Soon we were creeping across the front porch of the largest of the houses and up just beside the screen door. Inside, I heard the scraping of a chair against a wooden floor, a cough or two, and then a gruff voice said, "You are here to be tried for the murder of Rolando Guerra. How do you plead?"

God, no, I thought, leaning carefully over until I could just see into the room.

Steve Neal was standing there, his head in profile, hands tied behind his back. He did not reply to his accuser. On the far side of the room was a group of women and children. I could not see the speaker. "Go," I said to Puma, putting my mouth right up to his ear. "Go and get the police. Here, keys to the truck, by the highway," I said, pointing toward the clump of trees where I'd left the vehicle. Puma nodded and crept away. I hope they believe him, I thought, and I hope they hurry.

"How do you plead?" the voice inside said harshly. "Guilty or not guilty?"

Still Steve said nothing. I edged myself toward the door to see better. Steve, thinner already, with a stubble of beard, was surrounded by five men, all of whom I'd seen at Rolando Guerra's funeral, and none of them happy. The sixth, a forty-something man I recalled having seen in the nasty confrontation at the site, was sitting at the table, the judge of this kangaroo court. A little girl, Rolando's daughter, sat listlessly playing with a doll.

"In the absence of a plea, you have been found guilty," the man growled. "The sentence is death, by hanging. Is there anything you have to say?"

"Yes, there is," Steve said. The judge looked surprised, whether from Steve's perfect Spanish, or the fact that Steve was now intent upon being heard, I couldn't guess.

"Then say it!" the man ordered.

Steve took a deep breath and began. "It is not I who is on trial here, it is you." The men shuffled angrily in their seats.

"Quiet!" the judge ordered. "Let him speak."

Steve paused for a moment, then went on. "You are living in one of the most inhospitable places on the planet. This is a land of earthquakes, volcanic eruptions, floods, droughts, and disease. And yet," he paused, "and yet, on this tiny strip of sand, wedged between the mountains and the sea, a little over two thousand years ago, a great civilization was born.

"Somehow the people of this region gained control of the waterways, built canal systems to allow the desert to bloom, for a nation to flourish. They built cities that would reflect their power, huge ceremonial centers of towering pyramids, that must have struck other people dumb with amazement. These people are now called the Moche, after the river south of here, and the language, muchic, that was spoken in ancient times.

"Their cities held the largest adobe brick structures anywhere, anytime, expressions of their might, their temporal power. There were huge ceremonial courtyards lined with astounding works of art, frescoes that may have told their whole history in a single panel. These were cities where artists flourished, a civilization wealthy enough that the elite could support an artist class, some of the most singularly gifted artists of any age. The society of the Moche was one organized around rituals, some of them bloody indeed, and yet their art soared above the bloodshed, expressing their belief in the supernatural and in the sacredness of the everyday. They buried their dead with elaborate rituals and great care. You can tell a lot about people when you know how they treat their dead," he said, looking accusingly at every man in that room, one or two of whom squirmed visibly. "And the Moche buried even the lowliest among them with ceremony and respect.

"These people did what you do. They fished the waters off these coasts, they hunted deer, they engaged in athletic events, they had toothaches, they made war.

"How do we know these things? We know this because we are able to study the remarkable works of art they left behind. There are ceramic vessels that show us the faces of these people, portraits that we believe are uncannily accurate. There are other vessels that show us ancient fishermen using the same reed boats, the *caballitos*, that fishermen off these shores use today; we see scenes of the deer hunt, of ritual combat, of sacrifice. We look at their works, their craftsmanship, and we see a great people, the people who are your ancestors.

"Your children study the stories of the conquistadores, of Spain, Greece, and Rome. Should they not learn as much—no, should they not learn more, of the great civilizations from which they are descended? Of course they should.

"But every time you steal one of the objects the Moche created, and sell it to the *el Hombres* of this world, a little bit of your heritage is lost to you and to the rest of us. I know you are thinking that this is easy for me to say, that I live in a nice house in California, with two cars, and count as necessities things you can only dream of having, that I don't have to struggle to put food on the table. You're right, and I'm going to say it anyway. You are not just robbers of the dead. You rob your children of their heritage. You rob yourselves of your pride.'' He paused. ''That's all I have to say.''

Not one word was uttered when he'd finished. Some of the faces I could see showed confusion, others resistance. I felt it could go either way. Then an older woman, hair long and grey, a brown shawl wrapped around her shoulders, stood up. It was Rolando Guerra's mother, the woman who had walked dry-eyed behind his coffin. She began to speak quietly, so much so that I had to strain to hear. ''I have lost an uncle to this, I have lost a husband, and now,'' she said, her voice breaking, ''I have lost a son. Hear what this man says. We know why Rolando died. This man did not kill him. Rolando killed himself. This must stop. You say you do this, you rob the tombs, to make a better life for your families. But your children and your wives would rather have you with them.'' The other women nodded, the older children looked on solemnly, and the young ones, sensing perhaps that something very important was happening, fell silent.

''I would rather have my son alive than all the gold in Peru,'' she said, tears now in her eyes. ''We will survive without it. For God's sake, stop this now.''

Still no one said anything. I pulled the screen door open, stepped into the room, and said, ''*El Hombre* doesn't just smuggle antiquities. He also ships drugs. That is the kind of person you are dealing with. And tonight, he is flying cocaine and the contents of a tomb of a Moche warrior out of Peru from a dirt runway on the other side of the woods. What's it going to be?''

The Decapitator

18

T<small>HEY DIDN'T HEAR</small> us coming, the sound of the trucks muffled by the din of the incoming aircraft. Four trucks, each driven by one of the Guerras, dipped and dove around the woodland and across the desert sands, sometimes on a worn roadway, others overland. As we rushed forward on an interception course with the smugglers, the rains, long expected, began, the first drops forming tiny craters in the dry, dry earth. I sat with Steve in the first vehicle to point the way. Ahead of us, small fires flared up one at a time in two neat rows, and a plane, coming in low, hit the runway with a thump, and then whipped to a stop in front of the hut.

Four people were silhouetted against the light from the burning paint cans, their shadows dancing across the walls of the hut. Behind them loomed the Andes, implacable, immovable. One of them, catching sight of us in the distance, bolted to the aircraft. Within seconds, we heard the whine of the engines revving up, and the plane began to shudder as he readied it for takeoff. Another—Lucho, I was almost certain—disappeared inside the hut next to the runway.

"Cut him off!" Steve yelled, jumping out of the lead truck and waving his arms in the direction of the runway. "Don't let him take off!" The Guerras moved their battered old trucks into position. But the pilot, seeing them, swung the plane around and began to move down the runway in the direction from which he'd come. The wheels of our truck, driven by the youngest Guerra brother, Regulo, spun as he wrestled it across the sand in a futile attempt to catch the escaping plane.

The pilot let out the brakes and the aircraft began to hurtle away from us. Suddenly, just as the airplane seemed about to hit takeoff speed, the grey Nissan, Hilda at the wheel, bounced across the runway and careened to a stop right in the path of the airplane. I almost screamed in fear for Hilda as the door opened, and she tried to get out. Clearly in pain, she couldn't move fast enough. I thought she was almost certainly going to be killed.

At the last moment, the pilot swerved to avoid the truck, then lost control on the runway, already slick from the first of the rain. The plane plowed into the little hut, sweeping it right off its foundation, and then plunged into the woods, coming to rest in a thicket of thorn trees, one engine still shrieking at maximum power. Regulo Guerra pulled the truck off the runway and up to the plane, and Steve pulled a dazed pilot from the cockpit. Manco Capac made a feeble attempt to get away, but fell to his knees a few feet from the aircraft.

A shout went up from the Guerras. I turned and

saw Laforet's gold Mercedes wheel around, fishtailing in the sand, heading for the road. Carla Cervantes, now abandoned and left to her own devices, first tried to run after the departing car, and then headed into the woods, one of the Guerras in hot pursuit. Hilda had followed the Mercedes, I thought. She was here because she had followed Laforet from town. And now he was going to get away, as he always did.

The Nissan was still running when I climbed in. I pulled it into gear and started after Laforet. He had a good head start by now, but I kept going, thinking I would at least keep him in sight until help came along. He picked up the dirt road between the river and the irrigation canal, moving along at a good clip. Water sprayed from his wheels as he went. Water! I thought. Where is this coming from? But soon it was clear. The river, swollen from the rain in the mountains, was overflowing its banks. The water made the road treacherous, but Laforet barely slowed down. I knew if he made it to the highway, I'd never catch him.

We were almost there. I could see the lights of Paraiso off to the right. Laforet had a choice here. The shortest route to the highway would be a quick right across a stretch of sand a few yards wide, then on to the cleared area in front of Paraiso, then straight to the highway. The other choice was to stick with the road, turn left, cross the river on a little bridge, and pick up the highway to the south.

I found myself trying to second-guess Laforet. The shorter route was the obvious choice, but it was risky because he might get bogged down in the sand. Being in the truck, I had a better view ahead than he did, and I could see that the Paraiso route would not work for him. There was a flashing blue light in the parking area that signaled an official car of some sort. Perhaps Puma had brought the police.

I decided he'd have to go left, and although I was still well behind, I tried to make up some ground and head him off at the bridge. Laforet kept to the right, but seeing the flashing light, pulled the Mercedes into reverse, and then went for the bridge. I was right on his tail as he went over the hill and started down toward it. The bridge, once high and dry over a dusty riverbed, was covered with a film of water, and the road leading down to it was very slippery, the mud feeling like glare ice under the truck. I switched to four-wheel drive, but I could feel the tires loosing their traction as I crested the hill just a little too fast.

Ahead of me, Laforet's car began to slide. He made it onto the bridge, sliding sideways by now. The car made a wide arc, hitting the wooden bridge railing broadside. For a second or two, the car hovered there—I, and I imagined Laforet, holding our breath—then, with a sound more like a moan than a crack, the railing gave way, and the car plunged several feet into the raging current. I pumped the brakes, but it was too late. I too lost control and the truck slid down the embankment, but more slowly than Laforet had, missed the bridge entirely, and came to a stop heading straight down the riverbank, still upright, but with water rushing over the hood of the truck. Laforet, I could not see.

I tried to push open the door on the driver's side, but it wouldn't budge, the force of the water against it too great. The truck was now swaying and creaking as the water pushed against it, and it slowly started to tilt downstream. I knew if I stayed in the truck I was dead, that it would either flip or be swept away. I slid with difficulty across the front seat and pushed as hard as I could against the passenger door. It gave way, and I fell into the water. I'm a good swimmer, but the rush of the water was so strong, I could just barely keep my head above water. I fought the current but was tired within seconds. I finally just let myself go, gasping for air as I was swept along.

Many yards downstream I crashed against something and scrabbled for a handhold. It took me a few seconds to realize I'd been stopped by the Mercedes, caught against a tree branch that angled out from the riverbank. I saw—or thought I did, it was so dark—the lifeless face of Etienne Laforet, hair streaming upward, mangled hand pressed to the glass, eyes wide open, staring at me through the windshield. I grabbed the door handle and held on, screaming for help, knowing as I did so, that it was hopeless, that no one would hear. I knew that even though I was just a few feet from solid ground, I would never make it, that if I let go of the door handle to try to reach the embankment, I'd be swept away.

Just as I felt the last of my strength ebb from my fingers and arms, a dark figure loomed above me on the bank. It was Cesar Montero. He must have been at Paraiso and heard the crack of the bridge as it gave way. I'm dead, I thought. He'll just walk away and leave me, and the river will do the rest. No one will know. He disappeared, as I thought he would, but then reappeared a few seconds later with a long pole.

"Grab the pole," he yelled at me.

Was this a trick? Was he going to use the pole to push me off the car and into the raging stream? I felt the Mercedes shudder and start to slip into the current once more. Should I take my chances with Montero or the car?

In my fevered brain, I thought I saw Ines, dressed as she had been that first day I'd seen her, hovering in thin air, a few feet over the Mercedes. "What should I do?" I yelled at her.

She gestured toward the pole. "Take it," she said.

I let go of the door handle with my right hand and reached for the pole.

"Good," Montero yelled. "Now the other one."

The car started to slide. I had no choice. I let go of the door handle with my left hand and grabbed the pole tightly. The Mercedes flipped over and slid downstream once more. I felt Cesar pulling hand over hand on the pole. Then his arms grabbed me and pulled me to safety.

The worst of the rain held off until Manco Capac, shaken but alive and even relatively unhurt, had been led away in chains. The Guerras caught up to Carla, already badly scratched by thorns, only a few yards into the woods. Lucho took a little longer. He'd managed to make it into the tunnel before the airplane ripped through the hut, and was holed up in the chamber at the bottom of the spiral staircase. With the Guerras guarding the trapdoor at the runway end of the tunnel, and Campina Vieja's finest at the top of the staircase, it was only a matter of time before he surrendered.

There was no time for rest, to ponder what had happened and the terror of what might have been. By three in the morning, the rain was coming down in torrents. The Pan-American Highway was flooded, the irrigation canals, already full to overflowing from the water from the mountains, were now spewing their water in sheets across the land. The federal police were out going door to door, urging everyone to leave. A steady stream of cars, trucks, and motorcycles headed south for shelter.

There was no time to deal with the tomb of the Moche warrior, nor unfortunately with Montero, so the police moved the crates back underground to their original hiding place, sealed the trapdoor at the runway end of the tunnel, locked up the little house, and posted a policeman on the door.

"I'm not going. We've got to save the site," Steve said. "Anyone who wants to go can do so." None of us moved.

"All hands on deck, then!" he yelled, and we headed for Cerro de las Ruinas: Ralph, Tracey, Hilda, Pablo, the students, Puma, the Guerras, and any of the workers we could track down. Steve supervised from the top of the huaca, Hilda down below. It was back-breaking, bone-chilling work. I was so exhausted, physically and mentally, that I wasn't much help, but I did what I could. The Guerras brought large plastic sheeting to cover up the vigas as best we could. Slipping and sliding on the greasy surface, working in the dark, we all shoveled the back dirt, now mud, over the excavation. I had a niggling sense of unfinished business, something I should think about, but there was no time.

At the dark point just before dawn, I was sent back to the hacienda to find all the blankets and jackets I could. The road was pretty well gone. As I passed the commune, I watched one of the little huts slide several feet toward the sea on a pillow of mud. The commune residents, soaking wet, with their pathetic little bundles of worldly possessions, were moving out.

The hacienda was deserted when I got there, and, in the storm, the electricity, predictably, was out. I stood in the doorway, almost too frightened to enter for a moment or two. I could hear the waves crashing on the dunes not that far away, imagined ghostly whispers as the rain swept in sheets across the courtyard. Shutters banged intermittently against the walls.

Resolutely, I took a flashlight from the truck and made my way across the courtyard, now awash, and up the stairs. I could hear water dripping everywhere. As fast as I could, wanting only to get away from the place, I grabbed my sweater, waterproof jacket, and the blanket off my bed, then went into Tracey's room. She'd told me to take whatever I thought we could use, and, setting the flashlight on the dresser, I rifled through her closet, tossing jackets and sweaters on the bed as I did so. Grabbing them up, arms aching from all that had happened, I turned to go.

I wouldn't normally read someone else's mail, but something caught my eye.

Hello, Tracey, dear, the letter began. *It was wonderful as usual to hear from you yesterday. You seem to be making such nice new friends, and your work sounds absolutely fascinating. Hearing about your discovery of the huaca, and the possibility there might be a tomb there is so exciting. We feel as if we're right there with you every step of the way. And to think your stuffy old mother thought you should be a nurse. (Just kidding, dear. I never thought you'd be a nurse!)*

Buy yourself something nice with the money, and if you need anything, call right away.

Ted sends his love too. We miss you. Love, Mom

It was all very innocuous, endearing really, except for one thing: the words, embossed in silver across the top of the white linen paper. Mr. and Mrs. E. G. Edwards.

Of course it wasn't Dougall, I thought, Tracey's name. Ted was Tracey's stepfather. Ted Edwards, one of those names where the last name and first name are similar, like Ken Kennedy or Tom Thompson. Ted Edwards, Ed Edwards, or was it Edmund Edwards? In that split second, I knew I had made a deadly assumption or two. Tracey's stepfather, I suddenly knew with certainty, was Edmund Edwards of Ancient Ways in New York. Edmund Edwards was alive. He was not the old man in the gallery in New York, as I'd assumed. He was the proprietor, the recipient of stolen antiquities. He might even be the mastermind of the whole operation.

I'd left my business card at the gallery, and so he knew my name. But he'd known it before I ever got to New York. He would know me as the person who had bought his pre-Columbian antiquities at Molesworth & Cox, taken them right from under his nose, or more accurately, under the watchful eyes of his henchman, the Spider. He might not yet know me as Rebecca MacCrimmon, but he would. His stepdaughter would tell him, once they compared notes and she knew my real name. And he would not, could not, rest until I was dead.

I dashed out of the hacienda and back to the site. Leaping from the truck, engine still running, I yelled up at Steve, "Where's Tracey?"

Steve looked down at me. "Don't know. Don't care." He gave me a tired smile.

I cared. And there was only one place I could think she would be.

The policeman lay next to the door of the ruin, unconscious most certainly, and probably dead. The padlock was gone. I pushed the door open carefully and looked inside. A flicker of light came through the holes in the matting on top of the staircase.

As quietly as I could, I crept down the staircase. The treasures of the Moche warrior lay out on the table, glinting in the light. It must be pure gold, I thought, unalloyed, because it hadn't corroded at all. It was priceless, a fortune. Tracey was stuffing a large sack with the gold as fast as she could.

I stepped off into the water at the bottom of the step and she turned to face me.

"Rebecca!" she exclaimed. "I'm so glad you're here. I came over to make sure everything was all right, and the guard is dead! You've got to help me get the treasure out before someone steals it."

My, she was cunning, and very, very convincing. An hour ago, I'd have believed her. "I'll help," I said. "I'll hold the sack, and you put the stuff in it." Where guile is concerned, I like to think I'm a match for anyone.

She hesitated for a moment, but then handed me the sack, still grasping it with one hand all the time. I wondered what she'd do when the sack was full. I didn't have long to wait. As she crammed the last piece of gold into the sack, Tracey reached into her handbag, dropping her hold on the treasure sack for just a second. She's going for the gun, I thought, the missing gun. It was now or never. I grabbed for the handbag and knocked it out of her hand as hard as I could, then watched as the gun arced upward and splashed into the water.

We were holding the sack with both hands now,

pulling and tugging to get it, like two little kids fighting over a toy. Tracey gave a great pull on it, and I let go. She stumbled backward and, hitting her shoulder on the rock wall of the chamber, lost her grip. The sack opened, dumping its contents onto the floor of the chamber. Ear spools, necklaces, gold and silver peanuts, back flaps, gold pectorals, beads in the shape of spiders tumbled into the pool of water. The gilded bells jangled as they fell. The ripples blurred the edges of the gold, made it shimmer.

She shrieked, leaned over, and like some female Midas, started clawing at the gold. I grabbed her by the scruff of the neck and dragged her the few feet to the door into the tunnel. She struggled, but I was fighting for my life, and I knew it. I shoved her into the tunnel and slammed the door shut. As I closed the door, I heard her gasp, something I attributed to the sight of Carlos Montero. It gave me the moment I needed to push the table the couple of feet to the door. I piled the crates on top of the table, and one under, and watched as she tried desperately to push the door open. It would do her good, I thought, to be entombed with one of the victims of her little scheme. After a few seconds of effort, though, she stopped. I could hear her footsteps receding. She was going for the other end of the tunnel. There was a possibility that she had unlocked that end before going down the staircase. She might have been planning to leave that way, and gone first to unseal it.

I hauled myself up the spiral staircase and made for the other end of the tunnel to head her off. It was almost dawn, a wedge of light showing to the east. The shortest route to the trapdoor was through the *al-*

garrobal, and I plowed right in, never thinking about the danger.

The forest was still dark, the grey light of early morning not yet penetrating the branches of the trees. I kept my eye on the light at the far end of the woodland, and kept going, trying not to step in or brush through the thorns. It was deadly quiet in the woods, the only sound the hiss of the rain and the rasping of my breath, loud in my ears, as I struggled on.

I should have realized there was someone else there. Tracey's gasp as she saw the body of Carlos Montero should have told me she hadn't put him there. But I was too tired to think. I did not hear the quick footsteps until it was too late. I felt hands whip over my head, then a belt tighten around my neck. Gasping, I clutched at the belt, trying to pull it away from my throat. I felt a blackness around the edges of my consciousness, a high-pitched ringing in my ears. A sharp crack echoed in my head, but I could not tell if it came from within me or without.

Just as suddenly as it had tightened, the belt loosened, and the man I knew only as Spider crashed to the forest floor.

Jorge Cervantes, Lizard's brother, a dark, avenging angel, stood in the *algarrobal*, framed against the approaching light of dawn. Slowly he lowered his gun. "May you rest in peace, now, Ramon," he whispered. "May you rest with God."

Epilogue

I BELIEVE ABSOLUTELY in the right to a fair trial, in the presumption of innocence until guilt is proven. While I am aware that my actions have been known to belie my words, I do not believe that people should take the law into their own hands. I am convinced that to do so is to embark on a downhill slope that ends in the primeval swamp of anarchy. Having said that, I confess two things. One, I believe Etienne Laforet and the psychopath for hire, Spider—whose real name, in a stroke of irony of cosmic proportions, was Angel, Angel Fuentes—got exactly what they deserved. Two, I confess that the application of the system of justice that I so strongly believe in falls short of my expectations from time to time.

It would be the next day before the Mercedes would be found again. It had come to a stop way downstream, almost as far as the hacienda, Laforet dead, drowned, at the wheel. The man who always got away hadn't quite made it this time.

A few days later, police in several countries simultaneously raided Ancient Ways and all of Edmund Edwards's affiliate galleries, including Laforet's. They recovered over 500 antiquities that were illegally acquired. One of them was a *florero* with serpents snaking around the rim. The gallery owners, by and large, are pleading ignorance, and litigation to determine ownership of the artifacts will go on, no doubt, for years. Peru may someday, one hopes, get at least some of them back.

In China, I'm told, looters of antiquities are sometimes put to death. Not that I'm advocating that, of course, but I can't help thinking about it as I follow Edmund Edwards's journey through the courts.

Edwards and his stepdaughter are being defended by one of those flashy, expensive lawyers that lots of money can buy. Edwards has been charged with the only crime the police think will stick: not disclosing the true value of shipments to customs. The inadequacy of the laws that should prevent looting and illegally trafficking in artifacts leaves me speechless: The difficulty, I am told, is that the crime occurred in another country, not the U.S., and Edwards can only be charged under U.S. law for the crime committed there. If convicted, he will be fined and possibly jailed for a short period of time, nothing that will come close to justice, in my opinion. I gather, however, that in the social circles he travels in, his reputation is severely sullied. That may be the only penalty he'll care about.

Tracey continues to maintain that she was trying to save the artifacts, not steal them, an argument rather difficult to make when one's stepfather is on trial for his involvement in the matter. It remains to be seen whether her charmed life will continue.

So far the police have been unable to prove a link between Edwards and the murder of his employee at Ancient Ways, an old man by the name of Stanislaw Wozzeck. I'm sure it was Spider who actually did the deed, but in my personal system of justice, they're all guilty of his death. The murder of A. J. Smythson in Toronto is being reexamined in the light of what we now know.

Lucho, who is nowhere near as dumb as he appeared to be, has been charged with murdering his uncle. We think that Carlos Montero followed the electrical cord to the staircase, and discovered what his nephew was up to. For that he had to die.

I am not, apparently, the first to discover a relationship between the smuggling of drugs and the smuggling of artifacts. Both require stealth, lonely runways, and totally unscrupulous people from customs agents on down the line. Using the commune as a cover for his drug operation, Manco Capac made monthly drug runs at the new moon, when the night is darkest. He started buying antiquities as a hedge against slumps in the drug market, when various governments crack down on dealers and he'd have to lie low for a while. This eventually put him in contact with Laforet, whose operation was in temporary disarray because of the loss of three of his pre-Columbian objects, and later, a glitch in his preferred method of smuggling resulting from a change of heart of a customs agent named Ramon Cervantes. An unholy alliance was born.

Manco Capac's real name—and it has struck me many times since how so many of us were hiding be-

hind aliases—is James Harrington, and his various activities are going to put him in a Peruvian jail, the
conditions in which I can only imagine, for a long,
long time.

Jorge Cervantes has proven to be a gold mine of
information. He told the authorities that Carla convinced Ramon, in the name of providing a more secure
future for their children, to supply signed and stamped
but otherwise blank customs documents to Laforet,
used, of course, to expedite special shipments from
Fabrica des Artesanias Paraiso out of the country, and
to look the other way when the shipments came
through. Lucho added a crate or two to Paraiso's quite
legal shipments from time to time, and used the stolen
forms to accommodate the difference.

Jorge says that Ramon, whom I'll never call Lizard
again, somehow found out that drugs were also involved, and round about the time he found his wife
and his brother together, determined to set things right.
The police think it was Stanislaw Wozzeck, the old
man at Ancient Ways, who told him that three of the
Moche artifacts were up for auction in Toronto. Ramon took all the money he had and set out to try to
buy the artifacts back and return them to Peru. When
he couldn't buy them at auction, in desperation, he
tried to steal them from my store. Such disloyalty to
an employer is not brooked in this conspiracy, and the
Spider, who'd followed him to Toronto, killed him
there.

Jorge, consumed with guilt about what had happened to his brother, pulled himself out of his alco-
holic haze and began to follow first Carla, then Carla
and her companion, to Trujillo, where he lost them for
a while, then on to Campina Vieja. It was he I kept

catching glimpses of near Laforet's house and in the marketplace. He also saw Spider visit *el Hombre,* and later followed him to Paraiso. He saw Spider kill the police guard and reached some conclusions about what had happened to his brother. His timing, in my estimation, was perfect.

Carla Cervantes batted her eyelashes at every man she came across, maintaining she knew absolutely nothing of all this. No charges against her have been laid. Last I heard she was living in a nice little apartment facing the sea in Huanchaco, near Trujillo. Her rent is being paid by a wealthy Peruvian businessman, who visits when his wife isn't looking. Some women just have the knack. Ramon and Carla's three children remain with her sister, although I understand Jorge and his wife, now reconciled, are trying to gain custody.

On a brighter note, Wayne Colton—he'll always be Puma to me—decided he liked Peru, felt quite at home really, a state of affairs he credits to his former life as the friend of Atahualpa. He's put together a really fine magic act as Wayna Capac the Magnificent, which he does weekends at a hotel in Miraflores. He dresses up in an Inca costume that Steve and I helped fund, and the tourists just love him. He's off drugs, and has made a deal with his brother to gradually pay off the money he "borrowed." From his labored, handwritten letters, I gather he's getting along just fine. Pachamama, Megan Stockwell, has gone home.

Steve is already making plans for his next season at Cerro de las Ruinas. If he can get the funding, and he probably can, with the work he's been doing on the recovered Moche treasure, he's planning to hire the entire Guerra bunch to work with him at the site. They're guarding it for him until he returns. Tomas has signed on for the next season as shaman and worker, Ines as cook. No matter what it was I saw, or thought I saw, on the river that night, I'm happy to think of Tomas and Ines guarding Steve's work.

I think Steve's still a little embarrassed about his relationship with Tracey. It has not escaped his notice that she used him for her nefarious purposes. With his rumpled good looks and boyish grin, however, I'm sure when he's ready there will be women lined up to help him get over it. I'm thinking I might even be one of them.

Hilda will have to give up on fieldwork, but the events of the last little while have, for some reason, given her a kind of peace about her circumstances. She's accepted a position with a prestigious museum as executive director, and is planning, as soon as she can, to mount a splendid exhibit of Moche art. She's already telling Steve she'll never forgive him if the treasures of Cerro de las Ruinas are shown first somewhere else, and me that my presence at the opening is required. I think I just might go.

As for me, when it was all over, I called the people I needed most to talk to: Moira and Rob. Rob Luczka flew all the way to Lima to bring me home. It was really nice of him, all things considered, and he saved me a lot of time and trouble. It would have been a daunting prospect to get home without a passport or money. Having a Mountie for a friend has its advantages, it must be said. It was a long trip, and we had a lot to talk about, a lot of fences to mend, but for the first little while we stuck to small talk. Finally I tried to tell him how sorry I was about everything, about the guilt I felt regarding all that had happened, right from the start, and about how, trying to put it right,

I'd just gotten in deeper and deeper. He stopped me.

"I'm the guilty one," he said. "I know you left, tried to solve this yourself, because I wasn't there for you. I was a policeman, and a very rigid one at that, when you needed a friend. You were upset, understandably, over what had happened, and I should have known that. If it is any consolation to you, I have not slept a full night since you left, and my daughter is barely speaking to me. I wanted to follow you, but that fellow, that old friend of yours, Lucas, wouldn't tell me where you were. I figured Peru, of course, and I had the records of current entries to the country searched, but your name didn't turn up. Lucas kept telling me that if you wanted me to know where you were, you'd tell me."

He smiled suddenly. "Thanks for calling me, finally." He paused for a minute or two. "Are you still mad at me?"

"No," I replied. "Are you still mad at me?"

"No," he said. "Are you still in love with Clive?"

"Nope," I replied, and meant it.

"How about Lucas?"

"No," I said. "Over him too."

"Do you fancy that Steve fellow?"

"Maybe," I said.

He sighed. "Well, as the song goes, two out of three ain't bad, I guess."

"I don't know how I feel about Steve," I repeated. "But I called you." And that is where we've left it for now.

I do feel slightly guilty about it, though. Ms. Perfect, Rob's pal Barbara, has left him. She did not take kindly to his emptying out the joint bank account and heading off to Peru to get me. I'm not sure it was the money part of it that was really bothering her, either.

I have a feeling Sarah Greenhalgh is beginning to question whether she's cut out for retail. Needless to say, having someone murdered in your shop, then having the store trashed and burned, and your partner, suspected of insurance fraud, disappear for a few weeks hasn't helped much. I won't be surprised if she asks me to buy back her share of the business. If she does, the outcome will, I expect, be determined by the mood of my bank manager.

The best part is we're back in business. The insurance man, Rod McGarrigle, delivered the check personally, and I had the satisfaction of seeing him grovel. There is that to be thankful for, and, more than anything, the fact that Alex has recovered fully from his injuries. Sometimes I just stand in the store, looking about me, thinking how happy I am to be there, with Alex puttering about in the back, friends nearby, and my cat in the window.

Other than that, I can only report that, like so many objects stolen from Peru, the peanut has not been found. On the plus side, the 'pocalypse has yet to take place.

There is one other incident, I suppose, that I should relate. Shortly after I got home, I went over to Moira's, and sat at her kitchen table having a coffee. I had a sense of someone else in the house, I'm not sure why.

"We were terribly worried about you," Moira said, patting my hand, "and we're so glad you're home."

There was something in the way she said it, a faint emphasis, perhaps, on the "we." "Who's we?" I asked, but I knew, even as the words came out of my mouth, that this was going to be one of those moments in life.

She hesitated. "We," she said finally. "Clive. We is Clive and I."

So there it was. My best friend and my ex-husband. The choice was clear. Stay mad at Clive and lose a really good friend, or swallow my pride and keep one. For a few seconds you could have heard the proverbial pin drop.

"That's nice," I said at last. Some days, to borrow a phrase, you just have to go with the flow.

They are, when I think about it, perfect for each other, and for some reason I can't explain, it's taken a great weight off me. I feel my life is full of infinite possibilities now, in terms of love, yes, but also everything else.

There is one other bonus. It will be interesting to see whether Clive will have more staying power than Moira's former boyfriends, but I think he might. Should their relationship work out so well that they decide to get married, I won't have to go shopping for a wedding present. I have it already. A small jade snuff bottle. Something I picked up at an auction one time.